THE SPY IN THE
ORNA SANDLER

Production by eBookPro Publishing
www.ebook-pro.com

THE SPY IN THE SHADOWS
Orna Sandler Klein
Copyright © 2024 Orna Sandler Klein

All rights reserved; no parts of this book may be reproduced
or transmitted in any form or by any means, electronic
or mechanical, including photocopying, recording, taping,
or by any information retrieval system, without
the permission, in writing, of the author.

Translation from Hebrew: Matthew Berman
Editing: Nancy Alroy

Contact: orsakl2020@gmail.com

ISBN 9798343937220

THE SPY IN THE SHADOWS

A Gripping Espionage Novel

ORNA SANDLER KLEIN

Monday is the First Day of the Week

I'm in the avocado grove next to the house a few hours after it rained. The treetops sway in the breeze, and the scent of damp earth fills my nostrils. Leaves cover the muddy ground creating a safe path across. The air is clean. I take a deep breath and look at the sun's rays poking through the grey-blue sky.

"It's going to be nice today," I say to myself.

A loud buzzing sound shakes me out of my dream. Ugh. I open my eyes and the grove grows distant and, with it, the fresh air. I press the button on my alarm clock, fighting the urge to continue sleeping. If only I had known what was going to happen, I would have closed my eyes and gone back to the avocado grove.

Yes, it's 1997. I have been sent to Paris with my family by the Mossad. I roll out of bed and tip-toe to the tiny bathroom. I have to take a shower, otherwise I can't start my day. Luckily, the apartment is heated. If not, the temptation to stay wrapped up in the comforter would be even greater – it's difficult enough as it is. The water quickly washes away the sleep.

The clothes I organized the night before lay waiting for me in the guest bedroom. My work clothes – everything matches in order to make it easier to decide what to wear. Black pants and a black shirt with grey stripes that will never get wrinkled, even if it's been in a suitcase for a week. As I get dressed, I'm on hold with the taxi service. In the mornings, it takes them forever to answer. I'm always pressed for time and on a tight schedule, while they have all the time in the world.

I packed my suitcase quickly yesterday. I have a well-refined routine – I pack in the shortest time possible, and I don't forget a thing. I flip the bag over and empty the entirety of its contents, including any hidden pockets, so that I don't miss even the slightest scrap of paper. Only then do I begin packing.

Work and home are separate – they don't intermix. The clothes get packed in their typical order: underwear, bras, socks, undershirts, dress shirts, pants, toiletries. How many of each depends on how long I'll be gone, with options for any unforeseen turn of events. I take a small suitcase on the plane with me to reduce the time I have to wait. This flight was unplanned, but there are always last-minute changes.

I have guilders, Belgian francs and a few French francs in my wallet. I'm leaving Paris and will only be back on the weekend.

I'm still on hold. The phone is playing obnoxiously jovial music. I consider other options that never end up being relevant. There's no point heading down to the street with a suitcase at this hour – nobody is catching an "errant" cab around here.

Finally, the switchboard answers.

Silently, I go into the girls' room and gently kiss them goodbye. The older one raises up her hands, hugs me and murmurs, "I love you, Mommy, don't work too hard… oh, and call at night, okay?" She always remembers to tell me the words I so long to hear.

"I put a letter in your bag, but don't open it until you get on the train. Okay, Mommy?" says my younger daughter, Shir, with a half-smile, submerged in sleep.

I go back into our bedroom. My husband opens an observant eye. "Sleep, honey, sleep," I say. Somebody should at least enjoy the warm blanket. I drop a soft kiss onto his cheek and leave.

The French don't leave the house before nine. Until then, there's almost no traffic outside.

At exactly seven-o-five, the TGV high-speed train leaves Paris for Brussels. The taxi arrives twenty minutes late and we finally leave for Paris's northern train station, Gare du Nord. I still don't think I'll make it on time. The driver was Asian and drove with a confused expression on his face and a thin smile. I wonder every single time if they actually understand what I'm asking, if they know how to get me where I'm going without getting lost among the city streets.

The taxi meanders through streets devoid of people. The streetsweepers aren't up yet, the garbage from last night sprawls on the sides of the street and across the sidewalks. The contrast between the cold wind and flying garbage prevents me from beginning the week optimistically. We pass by the old houses of the city. It's just beautiful. Each home housed a treasure trove of history filled with love, war, wealth and poverty, success and disappointment. The faces, statues and accoutrements on the walls of the homes and sculpted wooden gates showcase the French appreciation for beauty and elegance. Somebody walked on these sidewalks hundreds of years ago, entered into the house we just passed, and had breakfast. It gives me a sense of eternity, power and energy.

A withered, tired old man is lying on the stoop, just up the three steps leading to the entrance of a building. Next to his head is an empty bottle of vodka. He is in a drunken slumber in a corner he managed to carve out for himself. The poverty next to the luxury, the splendor emphasizing the sense of injustice. In a little while, he will be driven off by one of the early risers, a man in an elegant striped suit holding an expensive briefcase. He will nudge him carefully with the edge of his shined shoe, and the decrepit man will wake up, startled, blinking his eyes, unable to focus in the morning light. He will get up, head bowed, and move himself to the stoop of the next building over. But perhaps the man who just now exited the building will show compassion to the destitute man, carefully step over his drunken body, and go about his way.

On the street corner, the *boulangerie* was already open, the breads neatly stacked on the shelves while crispy, fresh croissants lay on large trays at the counter. I can smell and almost taste them from the cab. On the other corner, the neighborhood cafe is in the same place it has been for ages. The smell of last night's cigarettes is still in the air, befouling the fresh fragrances streaming out of the of the bakery.

The cab glides over the streets in the 17th arrondissement, and I take in the sights and sounds. It's incredible how much a place, a home or scent can fill one with energy, memories and love. Leaving the city makes me sad every time.

It's six fifty-five. I burst into the train station. Statues adorn the ancient building from the outside, while inside is a giant, bustling terminal with long lines of people waiting to buy tickets. I won't make my train on time. I can buy a ticket on the train, but then I might not have a place to sit. It's illegal to stand on the trains, and I have to obey the law. There's a trick I learned after traveling a bit, a trick that only an Israeli would dare try. In the first-class car, where smoking is prohibited, is seat number 21, which is designated for passengers in a wheelchair. In most cases, that seat remains empty, especially early in the morning. I look at the passengers in line. I don't see any wheelchairs; it's all clear. I go sit in seat number 21, my blue Samsonite suitcase next to me like my bodyguard, my best friend. It's funny how one can become attached to an item, but this suitcase has been with me day and night for the last few years, following me around like a loyal dog. I neatly fold my long coat and place it on top of my suitcase. I made it. I calm my breathing and look around. Early in the morning, most of the passengers are men in grey suits with briefcases carrying cell phones and laptops. A civilian army all dressed the same. They aren't looking around, their heads are buried in their screens. The work day has begun.

As always, there is an aging American couple in the car, loud and confused, not sure if they're getting on the right train or whether they're sitting in the right seats. They will address everybody around them in order to calm themselves down. The locals will raise a haughty glance and derisively answer them in curt French with a bit of English. The train leaves the station slowly, passing dirty, painted walls of ancient buildings that have seen better days. After about ten minutes, we leave Paris behind and everything is green pastures, as far as the eye can see.

An elderly train attendant comes by with my favorite refreshment cart. I get a fruit salad on a tiny platter, a croissant and a roll, butter, jam, and cake for dessert. Perfect for me. "*Bon jour, Madame,*" he says, "what would you like to drink this morning?"

"*Thé au lait, s'il vous plaît, Monsieur,*" I reply with a French accent. He has no idea that this sentence is practically all I know how to say in French. "*Merci, Monsieur,*" I say, taking the tea and turning my head to look out the window so that he knows that our conversation has ended.

I don't talk to anybody. My body language and eyes always convey that to anyone who may strike up a conversation. I'm submerged in my own private journey on the train. A small door, hidden from strangers, opens to a place where the past mixes with the present and, sometimes, the future. Nostalgia and fantasy. There, I'm in complete control of the place, time and company around me. I traverse continents, change cities and places, choose which people I want to be with. This is my world for the duration of the trip, a world where I feel comfortable, safe. I smile inwardly and I feel my body sink into the seat. Where am I going today and who do I want to be with right now? What would I like to talk to myself about...?

Wait, Shir wrote me a letter. I quickly rifle through my bag. How could I forget? I find her envelope plastered with smiley stickers, hearts and drawings. I start reading, recognizing my daughter's round handwriting:

Dear Mom,

I didn't finish telling you everything. You came home very tired, grouchy and, as usual, with a headache. I have a recital on Wednesday at school, and I'm sure you won't be back in time. I'm tired of your work – it's always more important than anything else. Your bosses are mean, and what do you even do there anyway? I don't understand – why are they more important than we are? I miss you all the time and I'm sorry that I complain because I know that you don't feel so well, and it's no fun for you to be away from us, but that's your choice, not mine. All the parents always show up and Dad tries, but it's not the same. I need to talk to you about girl stuff, and Lior doesn't know everything. You promised me that we would go shopping, just the two of us and, as usual, we didn't. It's not fair, I'm sick of it – I can never do anything with you. It's impossible to plan anything. Even when you're home, you aren't really home. Don't think I don't love you anymore because I do, a lot, but...
I hope you come back soon this time and that the next visit will be better than the last one, and that this time you'll feel good and you'll be in a good mood and want to do things.
Kisses, don't work too hard, Mom, and don't let your bosses annoy you.

Love you... byyyyyyyyye
Shir

I feel a lump in my throat, hot and cold at the same time. If only I could smother her with kisses right now, hug her, protect her and draw strength from her. My family is more important to me than anything, so how did I end up in a situation where I abandon them every week, where I am away from them more often than not?

Shir was born on a rainy winter day. The expected delivery date came and went. For ten days I suffered, not only because of my gigantic stomach, but also because I had a baby who was less than a year-and-a-half old running around at home. The prolonged wait was indicative of a stubborn, opinionated baby.

It's my thirtieth birthday, and I wake up and get out of bed, each step heavy and awkward. The fetus is rolling around inside me, each movement turning my stomach around and around. Here is the head, there are the feet. The feeling of bringing another life into the world – there's no greater joy, yet here I am suffering.

"Enough already," I say to myself in frustration. "This was supposed to be behind me already."

Nathan, my husband, tries to calm me down. "Patience. Know that it will eventually come out," he said, stroking my protruding abdomen.

Wonderful – patience. I wonder what he would say if he had to walk around like this for a month, let alone nine. What do they know anyway? If we had to rely on men to give birth, the human race would have gone extinct long ago.

"Don't preach to me, my patience is up. It's hard for me to even breathe, let alone walk, and my back hurts so much, it's threatening to stick me in the ground."

At dawn, at exactly twenty minutes to five to be precise, I wake up with a sharp pain in my stomach. I try to walk to the bathroom and think to myself that I overdid it again with the birthday cake yesterday, and realize that the baby is finally ready. "Nathan, get up," I say, jabbing him in the side with my elbow. "It's time, we have to go."

Less than an hour later, Shir made her debut. The whole way, I experienced contractions – the little one who preferred to stay inside me until the last moment was now pushing with all her might to get out. I was doubled over in pain and barely able to get out of the car. Five minutes after entering the maternity ward, she was already screaming her lungs out. Pudgy and smooth, her cheeks bright red from the effort. Even then she knew how to scream.

I didn't have the energy to look at her. I had no will to talk or smile. The wait was over, yet I didn't feel any relief. Instead, I became increasingly despondent. I have two daughters, the older one not yet a year and a half. How can I distribute my love between them? Are we talking about a whole number that needs to be divided, or does each one get her own slice of love that isn't dependent on the other?

The nurse laid the little girl in my arms and I looked at her, hugged her, yet felt nothing. I was trying to figure out whether I wanted to cry or sleep. Lior, despite being older, was herself still a baby and the love of my life. From the moment she was born, I didn't think I could love anything else as much as I loved her. Two days after the birth, she arrived with Nathan to visit me, sat down on my bed, round and smiling, indulgently demanding the attention she was used to receiving from me. She crawled over to me; I was in agony. I felt overwhelming fatigue intertwined with pangs of guilt. What have I done? Am I allowed to admit to myself that the new little one just doesn't "do it" for me? I try picking her up in order to recreate that happy feeling I had after my first pregnancy, but I hit a cold front.

I nurse her, change her, talk to her, sing to her but, in my heart, I say, *Please don't let her feel it, don't let her read my thoughts.* I am doing everything I can to make up for the fact that I didn't fall in love with her at second sight, let alone first. Shir will breastfeed for eight long months. As if to infuriate me, she refused to drink from a bottle. At night, she would only fall asleep if I nursed her while holding her in my arms. Her total dependency on me made me bitter, tired, and depressed. I felt as if she was sucking the life out of me. Looking back, it seems to me as if Shir said to herself, "I'll teach her to love me like she's never loved anybody else."

Suddenly, without warning, I found myself looking and marveling with excitement at this sweet baby girl looking back at me. My heart beat like a raging river. I was able to look at both my girls with peace, and without a trace of frustration or guilt. So much love...

By the end, I understood that I was suffering from post-partum depression, which hit me during the last months of the pregnancy. A lack of energy, forlornness, no desire to communicate with the outside world, disconnecting from the things that were important to me before...

Hormones wrought havoc on my body and soul, but I eventually overcame them. I came out stronger. After months of struggle and understanding that it is easy to fall into the depths of despair, I looked despair in the eye and said, "No more." It's time to break free, to smile, to love, to enjoy – in short, to live.

"Would you like another tea, Madame?" asked the aging steward amicably, unaware that he jarred me back to reality from distant memories.

"*Oui, merci, Monsieur,*" I answered politely.

I hand him the plastic cup so he can fill it with more "tea" – the French don't quite understand this English beverage. However, the dull drink slides down my throat, warming it. I look out the window at the grassy plain. We fly at lightning speed past small lakes and rustic villages with old stone houses and ancient churches in their centers. The train glides along at over 180 miles per hour, the picturesque landscape constantly changing at a dizzying pace.

For the three years that we lived in the United States for my husband's work, I featured prominently, a feeling that was foreign to me. I greatly missed my place of work, friends, and the job. The pride of belonging to the security establishment and satisfaction from the job disappeared once the people around me had no idea where I worked – in those days, everything was top secret.

"What do you do?" was a question that everybody asked me.

"I work for the Ministry of Defense."

"Ah, like, top secret and stuff?"

"No, nothing like that. It's much more boring than you think." Constantly downplaying the significance of my position – to be considered grey, small and boring.

Most of us in the "Mossad" weren't looking for respect and fame. We were into ourselves and our work, and the satisfaction we derived from it. Except for a few glory seekers who were always dropping big fat clues about their work (and usually exaggerated), most simply did their jobs quietly and were content with that. Sometimes, a story would break that, for me, would be old news, but would become what everyone was talking about wherever I went. In my heart of hearts, I felt great pride and sometimes even had an uncontrollable urge to say: "It was us... I did that... my friends were there..." but never did.

"Mom, what do you do at your job? Why do you travel so much without coming home?" asked Lior during one of our conversations.

"I need to meet with all kinds of people all over the place, usually in their offices, and so I have to travel." I hoped I didn't have to get into the details of all my white lies that I've grown so accustomed to.

"But why do you have to tell them so much, and so many times?" Lior added.

"Each time it's a different subject, different things to different people. But I have to, sweetie, that's my job. I wish I could be at home more, I mean, you know how sad it makes me to be away, and how hard it is without you guys."

"Why do the other kids' parents come home every evening?"

"Everybody's job is different. The important thing is that you guys aren't alone. In Israel, most fathers work long hours. That's how it is, you have to try to look at things in the most positive light you can."

Lior stared at the television, pondering. I take hold of her little hand and she snatches it away from me without saying anything. We are sitting quietly in the small playroom, each in her own world. After a few minutes, her little hand inches its way over and strokes my palm. She lays her head on my shoulder and curls up in my lap.

The train crosses the invisible border into Belgium. The border isn't marked, but you can't miss it. The sky turned grey. In Belgium, the sun almost never shines, and the air is grey and dirty, especially in the cities. In less than a half hour, we will arrive at the south train station, where I'll need to change trains.

Two minutes before the train stops, everybody stands up in an orderly fashion, takes their meticulously folded coats and returns their computers back into their cases. The sound of phones disconnecting can be heard throughout the car. The phone goes in the coat pocket, the bag and umbrella in hand, and they walk toward the door.

The train comes to a screeching halt. I get off the train and walk along the platform towards the station's large hall, my suitcase rolling dutifully along behind me. I check out my surroundings, trying not to miss a thing. I recognize many of the people that I've seen here during my visits. I try to determine whether or not something is out of the ordinary, different, to get a feel for the place – is there something I should be paying attention to? There is a large crowd, so intuition and experience play a central part in analyzing what I'm observing. I go down the escalator to the counters and buy a first class ticket to The Hague, Netherlands.

We depart at exactly eight fifty. The train will stop five times before we arrive in The Hague. I sit in a single seat with one directly across from me. I place my trolley in the space between them and put my feet up on it. The car is divided into "smoking" and "non-smoking" sections, and the odor from the smoke permeates throughout the entire car. The smell of cigarettes gives me a headache.

The beginning of the trip is in a long tunnel. We will stop at three stations, and then the train will dive beneath the earth's surface. The journey is slow. I don't have the energy for these kinds of trips anymore. The next stop is Antwerp, next to the zoo. From the window, I spot the giraffes and a sad elephant. The train, which arrives traveling in a certain direction, began traveling in reverse, much to the surprise of the tourists, who were certain that the train was headed back to Paris. They jump up in a panic, running to the doors of the train, looking for somebody to ask what was going on. There will be somebody to calm them down; no, they didn't make a mistake. No, this isn't the last stop. And no, we aren't going back to Paris. Everything's just fine, it's just an engineering problem this station has and we are on our way to Amsterdam.

Raindrops slide down the window making strange shapes. The dismal greyness overcomes me, my eyes. I lay my head against the window, raindrops continue dancing uniformly across it. Two Belgians are engaged in a conversation in Flemish, a rather stiff language and even a little annoying. A young woman is dressed in the latest Dutch fashion trend – vivid colors with lots of red, green and orange accenting a slightly unrefined, old fashioned look. Next to her is a boy about four-years old with blonde hair and big blue eyes, babbling in a loud voice, not like the French children who sit quietly without uttering a sound. It's all about upbringing. The rest of the car is empty and I close my eyes. The slow and noisy rocking movement of the train calms me down. I don't fall asleep, but I go back to my inner place, in the staged reality of my current life. Where now? Where do I want to be?

Nathan. Last weekend at home was nice. I'm smiling. This time there wasn't any tension. I'm usually the one who ruins the atmosphere, primarily because I can't always leave work at the office. I returned home Thursday night, landing in Charles De Gaulle exhausted. Traveling takes energy out of me that I don't have. The girls jumped happily all over me, but it was late and they needed to get ready for bed. Nathan made me a cup of tea just the way I like it, along with a generous slice of his famous cheesecake. That perfect husband over there is mine.

A few generations ago in what is now Czechia, his family were bakers, a profession they continued when they reached Israel. When he was younger, Nathan worked in a bakery but chose not to pursue it. Here in France, he became the homemaker, and he gladly cooked and baked.

"How are you?" he asks tenderly, trying to gauge my mood. Should he tread carefully, maybe run for cover? Did they manage to piss me off and cause me to go into one of my prolonged silences? It's not easy being around me these days.

"All right," I said, trying to decide what mood I was in. I don't always know until I open the front door. Only at home do I allow myself the freedom to really be me, my true self.

"How was your week?"

I prefer to focus on my family right now. "It was fine. I don't really want to talk about it now. I'm more interested in the house, you, the girls... is everything all right?"

"Things are good. The girls didn't come home from school with any issues for a change."

"And you?"

"Dry... aside from all the regular things. You know your friend from work, my boss Eli, into himself. But never mind, it's not important. Okay, let's go to sleep. It's late. You must be exhausted."

"Finally, my own bed. I missed my pillow." If only I could take it with me when I travel. I have a hard time falling asleep if the pillow is too hard. Sometimes I'm like the princess and the pea.

Half an hour later, when I can still feel the warmth of the hot water from the shower, I fall asleep in Nathan's embrace, his arms relaxing me, giving me a sense of security, a sense of home. Paris isn't my home in the full sense of the word, despite my insistence on hanging all the pictures on the walls and the knick-knacks I scattered wherever there was room. The main thing is that this is my family. But, despite Nathan and the girls, I feel alienated. An inexplicable feeling of discomfort, despite all these years I've spent here and my great love of the city. I'm absent more often than present, and I'm unable to feel at home anywhere.

Sometimes, at night, I wake up and don't know where I am – where's the light switch? How do I get to the bathroom? I'm lying in bed, it's pitch dark, and I'm trying to identify something in order to figure out where I am. Am I home? In one of the many hotel rooms I stay in so frequently? One shouldn't have to try to find their bearings in their own home, and an unpleasant feeling washes over me. I look at the man beside me in the bed; the darkness is deceptive and his face isn't clear. *Who is this?* I ask myself. My eyes open and I try to detect a ray of light to help decipher this riddle. I'm a bit shocked, and feel like someone stricken with amnesia, unable to recognize even themselves or their surroundings.

I shut my eyes tightly and open them again. The eyes slowly adjust to the darkness and I calm down. It's Nathan. I'm so embarrassed. How could I wonder? What's the matter with me? Sleeping in different hotels causes me to become confused. I guess tonight I fell asleep without feeling the need to be "on guard." I smile to myself, relieved, and fall back asleep.

Shabbat afternoon. It's the last day of 1983. I get in my car and pick up my friend Donna and we go a New Year's Eve event that happened to be organized by Nathan's sister. That's where we met.

"He's exactly your type. You know I have the best intuition about these things. I'm telling you, he's going to be your husband one day."

"Oh knock it off, give me a break," I said.

"There is nobody more perfect for you than him," she said. At the time, I was involved with a married man. I thought that he was the love of my life and that he did too, but every attempt to sever the tie led to heartache. I thought that I wouldn't be able to live without him. A few days prior, we again decided to break it off. We knew that it was a complicated affair, and we wouldn't be able to live happy lives.

At the party, we danced, played stupid party games and, at midnight, he kissed me. At the end of the night, he walked me to my car, our arms around each other's waists. Donna got into the car with a massive smile on her face.

"I told you. He's perfect for you."

"Come on, nothing even happened, we just met."

"So how is he?"

"Nice. Very nice, in fact. You can tell he's a good person. I've never met a nice guy who was available before." I break into a smile; we both know why.

"He will never leave his family," Donna said. "He's told you as much. Yes, he loves you, that's clear. But you have to open your heart to somebody else and close this other chapter, once and for all."

"You're right." I know that she's right, at least in my mind.

"He's charming, but he's older than you, and he's married with a family. What's he thinking?"

"We fell in love. He's my soulmate. I know that it has to end, I mean, we just came to that decision at the beginning of the week. Let's see how it turns out, maybe today I'll begin a new chapter in my life," I said, smiling a sad smile.

The next day at the office, I met him, the married guy. He worked with me. I arrived early despite having barely slept, yet I went to bed excited, with a smile on my face.

"Good morning, we need to talk," I said.

"Good morning... how are you?" He looked at me with pained eyes. "Are you all right?"

"Yeah, I'm fine. Have you got ten minutes for me?" I was determined.

"What's with the toughness? Come here for a moment," he said, getting up from his chair. I'm certain that once he hugs me, everything will go back to the way it was.

I looked at him. Forty-something. A nice, good man – a very good man. A man who loves me, all of me, without wanting to change a thing. A real friend.

"No," I say. "Don't start this. I want to say something to you."

"Go ahead." He sinks back down into his chair.

Without hesitation I say, "I met somebody yesterday who, if I want, will be my husband."

"How can you know such a thing after one day?" he said angrily. "So that's it? You met somebody and in a moment, you forget everything?"

"I'm not forgetting anything. Listen. I didn't fall in love or anything like that. I'm telling you what my intuition is telling me. You need to decide right now: do I end this relationship, or more accurately, not start it. This is the moment that you need to decide and stop dealing with me theoretically. If you tell me not to start a relationship with this guy, then you need to take responsibility for our relationship. If not, then it's final. Signed and sealed."

He looks at me in complete disbelief. He was certain that I would always be his, and so he never had to choose. "I can't tell you something like that. Not now. Not yet." His family was more important to him than anything.

"Okay. So that's your decision. As far as I'm concerned, our relationship is finished, and this time for good." I can't believe that I was able to say those words and, more importantly, to actually feel them.

"If that's what you want. I suggest that you not make any rash decisions that you'll later regret."

"There's no point repeating everything we've said these last few months. We both know how much we love each other. We both know that you were never going to leave. Release me. Let me go. It's the right time." I'm smiling. The time has come to bid farewell to the man I loved so much. I kiss him softly on the cheek. "By the way, I'm taking a few sick days."

On Wednesday evening, there's a knock at the door. Nathan is standing there with a small, funny potted plant, dressed in an awful, bright-red sweatshirt. He enters, smiling, and shakes my hand. I feel his large, warm hand swallow mine.

"Come in," I say with a smile. "Something to drink?"

"Not right now, come sit."

He motions for me to sit next to him on the sofa. I sit down, excited. We sat and talked for hours. About him, about divorce, about his kids, his work, and about me, and a little bit about my workplace and lifestyle. It was warm inside the house, but I felt as if I was shivering. My excitement was palpable. I couldn't help myself. We made out all night with warm, caressing kisses. I had opened a new chapter in my adult life.

Nathan. I met him when he was thirty seven and worked for the military industry. Divorced with two kids, his older son was twelve, the younger son nine. He rented an old, unrenovated apartment near his kids – the apartment of a man who neither understands interior design nor cares.

For me, he was tall – about five-eleven to my five-three. He had broad shoulders and a circular belly that was slowly getting rounder, thinning black hair and a handsome face. When he smiled, I could see all of his teeth – that was one of the things I fell in love with. Something about him exuded abundant dependability and truthfulness, warmth and generosity, concern and responsibility. His big, beautiful hands infused me with a feeling of security. His whole being spoke to me without words.

Nathan was my best friend. I didn't need any friends other than him. We were both very busy with ourselves, our families. He is loyal by nature, homey, quiet and easy-going. At the end of the work day, all he wants is to come home. As far as he is concerned, work is secondary, the home is primary. The family. The wife and kids. I knew that he would love me forever and, if I asked him to pluck the moon out of the sky for me, he'd do it, or at least try. Despite just breaking up from a man that had been my whole life, things continued smoothly.

After ten months, we got married in the village's public garden. Everyone in my family had a role, starting with organizing tables and chairs, flower arrangements, cooking and baking, the wedding cake and music. I wore my cousin's wedding dress, but the veil I sewed by myself. I put on my own makeup and perfume and was embarrassed to go out. I felt like I was wearing a costume.

Contrary to the costumes I adorn for work, in my private life, I hate being the center of attention. But I was thrilled. The *chuppa* was set up amidst the broad pecan and fragrant guava trees. There – we have now been pronounced husband and wife.

The sound of screeching brakes startles me awake. We are approaching the outskirts of The Hague. I walk to the nearest taxi stand and get into a spacious Mercedes. I recognize the driver; I've made this drive with him before. The Hague isn't a big city. I give him the name of the hotel I'm staying in, and he looks at me through the rearview mirror. I ask myself whether he remembers that we've met before. The Dutch cab drivers always try to rope me into a conversation, and I do my best to ignore them.

"Pleasure or business?" the chubby cabbie asks with a grin.

"Both," I answer, looking out the window, hoping he will take the hint.

"It's not your first time here, is it?"

"Say," I quickly ask, changing subjects. "Is there a traditional market on the weekends here?"

"Yes, of course. Every Saturday they have something," he

says, breaking into a speech explaining everything he knew about the subject.

The hotel fancies itself as four-star, but it seems to have lost two of them. It's located in the center of town, about a ten-minute walk from the Israeli embassy, which is where I'm headed. I found this hotel by chance and, when I discovered that it is owned by a Jewish family, I made it my home base in The Hague. The hotel is managed by the owner's daughter, who is twenty seven, tall and attractive. I have a good cover story explaining why I come here every week for just one night. Changing hotels each time I come to The Hague will look suspicious if the Dutch authorities start poking around in my affairs.

I was greeted with a warm welcome by the receptionist, who is aware of my special relationship with the owners. I have never made a reservation.

"How are you today?" she asked in fluent English. "Today rooms 201 or 304 are available, which would you prefer?"

"Room 304 please. I always prefer the rooms in the back because they are quieter."

"As you wish, here are your keys, enjoy your stay," she said with a genuine smile. I particularly enjoy her English. Finally, English, so I don't need to stumble along in French.

I take the small, rickety elevator up to my room on the third floor, put my suitcase down and open the window to ventilate the musty air. The last time I was here, I had a hard time falling asleep. I was in a room toward the front, adjacent to the main road and above a local pub. The streets are narrow, and the road is made from cobblestones laid hundreds of years ago. The reverberation of passing vehicles resonates throughout every room in the front of the hotel, the clacking march of pedestrians echoing into the distance.

I go downstairs and exit to the street, trying not to slip on the wet cobblestones. I pass by the stores on the ancient streets: the colorful stationary store, a shop with antique watches, a photo gallery and a store with professional-grade kitchen appliances. There is a mix of Europe and America on the streets, the old with the new, greyscale with color. I recognize every store and every street in the small center. I hoped that maybe something would be renovated, but no.

I must be careful not to stand out. I walk as an unseen observer. Does that change my authentic identity? Have I become monochrome in essence? Can I take my mask off at will? Time will tell. I'm a woman of almost forty, short and round, as opposed to the Dutch women. They are tall, blonde, tanned, and they stand up straight. They are haphazardly dressed, despite displaying every color of the rainbow. I look like a simple, boring housewife going out to do her grocery shopping, which is exactly how I want to appear.

Here, I need to turn left toward the beautiful lake across from Huis ten Bosch Palace, the home of the Queen of the Netherlands. From there, I need to keep going in the direction of the McDonald's in the large plaza, and then turn right to the end of the street to an office building, which is where the Israeli embassy is. I push the intercom button, identify myself, and open the elevator door. I ignore the closed guard booth outside the embassy – inside are two Dutch police officers watching everybody who comes and goes from the building. I have no idea what they do with the information they gather, but I take them seriously. I'm out of the ordinary: an Israeli who arrives regularly, once a week. One could easily determine that I am part of the diplomatic staff of the Israeli embassy in Paris and, therefore, I have to start from the assumption that "they" know everything there is to know about me.

I push the button to go to the fourth floor and arrive at the security post of the embassy. The guard recognizes me and opens the door as he smiles. "How's it going?" he inquires. He has no idea who I am, just that I'm with those "other guys."

"Hey, how are you?" I greet Dalit, our secretary and the wife of an old friend. He and I started our careers at more or less the same time.

"Everything's fine. Listen, Yaron said that he won't be here until evening, perhaps even tomorrow morning."

"Okay," I say, and think to myself, *What else is new?* The guy has a very fluid concept of time. Why the hell didn't he tell me this earlier? Now I have to find something to pass the time with, which gets harder and harder to do in such a small town without much going on.

My team finished its last mission at the beginning of last week. Two colleagues flew to Syria to check on nuclear weapons that arrived from North Korea. Everything starts under the guise of business and team members must excel in both these fields: business and operations. Sometimes the business side of things takes precedence over the operational side, and the operational activities are carried out with extra caution. We cannot be discovered, especially when the mission involves a country that is not on friendly terms with the State of Israel. The staff in Israel received our team's first report and sought clarification. The guys already began putting together the full report. We prefer anything to sitting at a desk writing reports. But the purpose of our job is those reports, which ultimately end up in the hands of the relevant parties in Israel.

I go over the material that was prepared for me and put the things I need to take with me to the team meeting aside. I add a few notes that deal primarily with issues pertaining to manpower. Each team member has a family that resides in Europe. It's not a simple situation, mostly for couples with children. That lonely feeling has affected us all throughout the years. It's not easy to cope.

I have to wait for Yaron. I prefer to work with the team and not sit here doing nothing. I finish my office duties. It's already five o'clock, and I'm alone. Dalit already left, her kids are waiting for her. The rest of the people have gone home, each one to their domain outside The Netherlands. I shouldn't stay here any longer. It doesn't look good to the guards outside that I'm the last employee to leave, especially since I'm not part of the local staff.

It's already getting dark out, and I wrap myself in my coat and open my umbrella in anticipation of the rain that is undoubtedly on its way. I remember that I haven't eaten anything all day. I hate eating alone. That's one of the things I haven't managed to get used to – entering a restaurant as all the other diners lift their eyes and stare, only to eat by myself in total silence. Most of my colleagues have learned to take advantage of the opportunity to eat well, even without company.

I recall my time in Zurich. I was young, just after finishing my training. I had to stay in a hotel in the old city on top of the hill. During the day, it's busy, the houses and stores full of people coming to town. But when evening descends and the street lights come on, the area undergoes a change. The prostitutes venture out into the streets and begin their workday, each one in her regular spot.

I decided to go eat dinner. I saw the women on the street and felt the murmurs, which by then had become familiar and clear, of men looking for the right one, checking out "the goods." I went into the restaurant that was closest to the hotel. I knew the area. When arriving at a new location, we are trained to study the area and familiarize ourselves with the surroundings and learn how we can make use of them, as necessary. On the way to the restaurant, a few men stopped me with a word, wink, or even just an inviting glance.

As soon as I entered, the host asked me, "Do you have a reservation, Mademoiselle?" in a loud voice that caused some of the diners to look up.

"No," I said as quietly as possible. "I just came for dinner."

"Will Mademoiselle be dining alone?"

"Yes, thank you." Ugh. I regret leaving the hotel, and am even more sorry that it doesn't have room service. I'll have to learn to eat a good lunch so that I can skip dinner when it's just me.

He seated me in the middle of the restaurant, which was full of couples and groups of men who looked like they came to the city on business. I felt their stares. I ordered an entree without dessert. I ate as quickly as I could. When I finished and got up to leave, one of the men came up to me with a proposal. I politely refused and got out of there, back to my secure room. I had experienced the problematic unpleasantness of being a woman dining alone in a foreign city.

I walk through the Passage, an exclusive indoor shopping mall. I need to call home, something I try to do every day. A feeling of uncertainty accompanies me from the moment I leave until I get to the telephone and so forth, until the next phone call. Shir tells me, angrily, about the test that she "only" got a 95 on, and why she didn't get 100. She's a perfectionist, and it actually worries me quite a bit. It's a trait that is liable to cause her problems in the future.

After I talked with the girls, I walk down to the cinema and am reminded of Sergio. Sergio came to me to finish up his preparation before being sent abroad. He was approaching forty, had a family, smiled a lot and had a good heart. He had already received most of the relevant guidance needed to join a team performing special assignments around the world. His role was technical, but he had to be proficient in the operational aspects of the team.

After I ran him through all of the theoretical material, we went into the field. Everything seemed in order, clear. Sergio asked the right questions and gave the right answers. I was at ease. Another month and a half and he would relocate with his family abroad and play his role on the team.

The exercise began, and he left the predetermined meeting point. A surveillance team in the field, which included myself, followed him. To my surprise, he was acting strangely. I waited for him at the end point. He was late and arrived pale and sweaty with an unsettled look in his eye. A bad feeling came over me.

"Let's start at the beginning. Tell me what happened. When did you get to the exit point?"

"Uhhhh... I don't remember exactly."

"Did you leave when we said?"

"Yes, I think so. I went out. I walked according to the route I planned."

"What did you see?"

"A lot of people. I saw the girl who was looking at me from around the corner, she was wearing a short skirt. Also the guy pretending to work at the kiosk on the corner. He was also following me."

"Wait, let's stop here. Explain why you think the girl was following you? What was her role on the surveillance team?"

I was trying to get a sense of what he did and what he saw, and how he analyzed the information. Did he work methodically or was he spooked by every person on the street? After the debriefing, I was left with the sense that he had forgotten everything he'd been taught. We analyzed the drill, and he understood that his mental state caused him to behave strangely and to analyze things incorrectly. I sent him off to prepare for another drill and two days later, we returned to the field.

This time, Sergio was even worse. When we analyzed the event, I understood that he wasn't capable of recreating the way he had come, the places he stopped along the way, and who he saw and talked to. I was forced to bring the matter up during a meeting with the department sending him abroad. There, it was decided he would undergo a series of planned sessions with a psychologist. In the end, Sergio's trip was cancelled. He didn't understand his situation, and I was standing there in front of him feeling bad because he was a longtime colleague of mine.

It turns out that he's a perfectionist, and his need to be the best stressed him out to such an extent that he lost all sense.

"Good evening and good night," I say to the night clerk.

"You too," the young, dark-skinned man replies. The Netherlands isn't just blondes and redheads.

I open the door to a cool breeze coming in through the window. The musty smell has temporarily evaporated. From the window, I see the restaurant's courtyard adjacent to the hotel. Beside the restaurant are apartments. They don't have any curtains or shutters. Everything is out in the open. A Belgian friend from work told me that the openness of the Dutch comes from the principle of simplicity and modesty. Everything is open so that the neighbors can see everything and know that there is nothing to hide. Are the Dutch modest, or just cheap? I close the window. The television is on so I won't feel alone. The quiet nights never leave me feeling at ease.

A good shower and another hour has passed. I take a book from my bag, the last one remaining from a delivery from Israel. I love Israeli literature; it gives me a feeling of belonging. The book has an earthy, sea smell to it, sprinkled with a scent of orange blossoms. I manage to concentrate for a few pages and find myself reading the same page over and over again. I go back to flipping channels; perhaps I'll find a decent movie. The hours drag on and I'm restless. My thoughts wander, it's already three o'clock. It's so quiet outside.

Nathan is probably fast asleep, snoring on top of our pillows. How I miss his warm body to make me feel secure and at peace. The girls are curled up like little angels, so beautiful when they sleep. I think about hugging and kissing them.

Tuesday

I open my eyes at seven thirty. Out of habit and from years on the job, I start examining the room even before I'm completely awake. In the first few seconds, I don't remember which room I've woken up in, or what day it is. When I first started out, I would wake up in a dark room to my ringing phone. It would startle me. Where am I? Where's the light switch? What language am I supposed to be speaking when I answer? But after a few minutes of confusion and minor panic, I would manage to turn on the light only to discover that I was at home, and that it was Shabbat morning. That was one of the most important lessons I learned for my profession: never go to sleep in a pitch black room.

This time, light filtered in through the window. The greyness portends a cold, winter rain. On the way to the bathroom, I turn on the TV to hear voices, but also to see if anything happened that I should know about. I return to bed, but prop myself up on the pillows so that I won't fall back asleep. These are the best hours of the day as far as I'm concerned. I'm wrapped up in the comforter, a little more pleasant warmth.

The sky isn't as grey as I thought. A refreshing breeze pleasantly blows through my hair. I walk a little faster with a burst of energy. It's a new day; I smile to myself.

"Good morning," Dalit says, already busy with the morning telegrams, active and efficient as always.

I look at her and think to myself, *Way to go*. Two girls at home and a deadbeat husband who doesn't do a thing. At work, she is always smiling, seemingly content. Most other people in her position would be bitter, but not Dalit. She's satisfied with where she's at. A good-looking woman, takes care of herself, knows what she's worth, and doesn't need anything or anyone to prove it.

"You want a coffee?" I ask.

"No thanks, I had one already," she says, raising her eyes from her telegrams.

I make myself a cup of tea and join Dalit. I have barely spoken to anybody in two days. Many hours of silence. "Well, how was your week since the last time I was here?"

"Everything's fine. Avi didn't come back last night, so I guess he'll be back in a day or two. The weekend was actually pleasant. We went to the German border to look for antique furniture – it's ridiculously inexpensive there." She then asked, "How are the girls? They good?"

"Yeah, all right. The normal things. They fight a lot, but that's because they are just so different from one another. They are also very angry with me. It took them a long time to get used to this lifestyle and my working abroad." I sigh.

"I wish I could just do my job. I'm always caving to Avi. Every time I carve out a niche for myself in Israel, I find myself packing my bags for a multi-year trip. It's frustrating. The work here is boring. All of us stuck here, crammed up each other's ass, bored and frustrated women... it's a recipe for breakdowns and infighting."

"Yes. Thankfully, I'm out of that loop, both here and at home. Although I hear about all of it from Nathan."

The phone rang, and Yaron was on the line.

"You know I've been waiting for you since yesterday?"

But I know what his response will be: That's how it is, get used to it...

"I had to take care of something urgent. I'll be there in forty-five minutes. Wait for me."

I went down to buy Nathan a birthday present. Leading up to the trip to Paris, I made it clear to Nathan that this time, I was serious about antiques. Nava and Sami were even more into antiques than I was, so much so that their house was a venerable museum. I couldn't find better partners than those two. They had been in Paris longer than we had and knew every flea market and fair.

At first, Nathan wasn't willing to come along but, later on, he learned to love it and would arduously inspect every item. He began collecting clocks, which he taught himself to take apart, put back together and, primarily, to fix. Each time I came home, he would proudly show me a clock that he repaired. Later, he moved to weights and scales, and slowly became the owner of a unique and diversified collection.

I make my way back from the Passage with his present in my bag – an antique pocket watch on a chain for his jacket pocket. I came back to the office beaming, and Yaron came in ten minutes later.

"Hey, what's up?" He's the boss, and bosses are never late – they just get delayed. As for me, I am always five minutes early and the first to arrive. In our line of work, being punctual is an important quality. Being late can cause all kinds of problems.

I decided to keep my mouth shut. When working abroad, far from home, where every word matters, I decided to let this go – I have plenty of other things I can mention. "So then," I say to Yaron, "what's up? Anything new? I managed to go over the material. I worked on all the requests and questions about the report from the trip. I'm certain that we'll finish writing up the rest of it this week and we can get on with the next mission."

"Fine by me. What are you doing on Wednesday? Can you take a break from your team and lend a hand in Italy?"

"If necessary, yes." Great, there goes my weekend. The kids are going to be mad at me again. But that's the job.

"No choice, but it's short. You won't get stuck there for two weeks like last time. You'll be home by Friday evening, Shabbat at the latest."

"Fine."

"How's your team, everything good there?"

"They're good. Last week they were almost done with the reports. Now some questionnaires came so that will slow us down a bit."

"What about the Kid?"

"He's fine. I talked to his wife again and she sounds like she's recovered. It's not easy to be alone when there are complications with your pregnancy, especially with another little kid at home. I have to be in touch with her more often than usual in order to keep my finger on the pulse."

As a woman, I'm familiar with both worlds. Being alone at home when the husband has to leave for work, the feeling that everything is your responsibility, the solitude and the pressure. On the other hand, I'm gone a lot and know how hard it is to sleep in a different bed every night, to miss time with the kids that you'll never get back. The feeling of being disconnected.

"I trust you on this. If you need help or think of anything that I can do, just tell me."

There's nothing to say. Yaron wants to make sure that the families feel like we are taking care of them. He doesn't always notice the smaller details but, if alerted to them, he'll cooperate.

"And the Old Man? What about him?" he asked.

We call him the "Old Man" because he's been here longer than all of us. And he's only forty two. He has vast experience and, in his opinion, he has seen and heard everything. His family is organized and manages as if they don't need him at all. Last week I visited their home. Part of my job is to keep in contact with the family and help them. Sometimes families have to deal with things that are hard to figure out alone.

"The Old Man's good. He tried to argue with me about the number of reports and cast doubt on their importance. He likes to have the last word and doesn't like being tripped up. And our combat portfolio isn't always easy to manage. By the way," I continue, "the Old Man has to be at home this week for periodic medical exams. During my last visit with Dina, I felt something was off."

"What?" Yaron asked.

"Nothing happened, and maybe it's just my imagination, but something in her tone of voice changed, even though she's acting the way she always does. Strong. In control, doesn't need anyone. A feeling of deep sadness. Just my gut feeling." I always had strong instincts; I feel people. I learned to trust myself but, in this case, I hoped I was wrong.

"I'll talk to all three of them today, and we'll see how they can go home without impacting work."

"Dalit, please bring me the new file on Italy," I ask her and sit down to read over all the material. There isn't a lot to read; a new mission that deals with captives apparently being held in Lebanon, or transferred to Iran. Most of the people on the team were my students during my days as an instructor, which was before this current deployment. A good team.

My job with them is simple. They know the field, so all I have to do is receive their progress reports and advise about what comes next, as necessary. I am familiar with the area where the operation is taking place, it's just that the mission is new. I take out maps and go over the relevant information, jotting down what I need to memorize. Meeting places, names, phone numbers, places to sleep, addresses. Before I leave, I sit down with Yaron again to summarize the details and communications arrangements.

"I'm working directly with Israel but, if we are not able to communicate, we'll get a message across using them," I say.

"One hundred percent. Have a good trip. Keep me updated about your team's reports and I hope everything is fine with the families. Ciao."

The train departs and I think about Yaron, recalling when he started working with us in the early '80s. I was one of the instructors in his course. Fifteen students, all men. It was my job to cover the subject of how to act and operate in the field from a security and safety perspective. On the first day of the course, the instructor not only sizes up the students, but the students the instructor and, of course, each other. A diverse crowd, the common denominator among them being that they could speak a foreign language fluently, preferably as a mother tongue.

Yaron, a combat soldier who finished his tour with the rank of Sgt. Major; bachelor's in the social sciences, married, no kids, about thirty. European Jew, light-skinned, five-foot ten. Solid build, broad face, curly, brown satin hair, small eyes, brown and penetrating. His fingernails were completely chewed, betraying an otherwise calm outward demeanor. He seems to be concealing a perpetual sense of anxiety and restlessness.

I began as an instructor in the system at the age of twenty five – a little girl. Me, standing there in front of 40-year-old men with experience, some clout and self-confidence. We take regular people and put them in a world where the thought process is completely different, with distinctive concepts, the goals are not similar to any they have come to know until now, the level of loyalty required is absolute, and personal values sometimes conflict with the principles in the system. Yaron came highly motivated and came across as a little unusual. He wasn't able to express himself simply and concisely. He made no distinction between the main point and secondary issues, and insisted on things that were inconsequential. The people in the course weren't able to establish a common dialogue with him, and his evaluation of himself was higher than what the rest of the group thought.

He received merely a passing grade in the course. It was determined that he was unsuitable for most disciplines in the field, and was sent to the unit where most people who finished the course with mediocre marks ended up. Over the years, he was never considered a prodigy, but he was considered hardworking and highly motivated. His boss was promoted to some managerial position and made sure to promote him as well. Yaron succeeded in not failing, more than achieving actual success. The team that was with him became grumpy, tired, and turned off.

We're almost at the north train station under the bridge, next to the Moroccan district in Brussels. Here one can see women in display windows, displaying their bodies for rent, while men walk by alone or in pairs, checking out the goods. The girls are young, some of them practically naked, and I find myself feeling sorry for them, wondering how they ended up in this dirty, drug infested, violent place. Unfortunately, in my line of work, I have met many women who worked in the oldest profession in the world.

One time, I was on a mission in Milan sitting with Alex in the car, all night. This remote place was teeming with life by day but, at night, it was supposed to be very quiet. From our vantage point inside the car, we could see an old woman standing on the opposite street corner. Not three minutes had gone by before a car stopped beside her, opened the window and, after a few minutes she got into the car and drove off with him. While we were still talking, the car came back and dropped that same old woman off at exactly the same spot.

"I don't believe it. That old lady's a hooker!" Alex exclaimed.

"Who's looking for an old lady, let alone be willing to pay her?" I wondered.

Throughout the night, many cars stopped and picked up our old friend. We were amazed by her physical prowess.

In Paris, perversion had taken on the air of legitimacy. Every night in the Bois de Boulogne, a large public park just west of Paris, there's an area where men parade around in drag, most of whom are at least partially naked, showing off either their breasts, male genitalia, or both. Everything is handled discretely, and only rarely does the term "coming to blows" mean that an actual melee broke out between a couple of drag queens over a client.

If that wasn't enough, right next door to Nava and Sami is "masturbation road." That's where all the boys sit in the shadows with their hands in their pockets. As soon as a car stops at a red light, they all whip out their dicks and furiously (but joyfully) go at themselves, hoping to spray before the light turns green. Paris is full of sex, and they aren't ashamed of it, nor do they try to hide it.

The train was swallowed inside a tunnel but kept on going. I get off at the second stop, Central Station. I go up the escalators, stench and filth everywhere. I've never seen a sanitation worker in the underground area here. I exit to grey skies. In another moment, it will start to rain. On my right is an ancient church and I continue in the direction of the Grand Palace, the main square of the old city of Brussels. In the summer, at nine o'clock at night and again at eleven, there is a musical event in the square. Once a year, the largest carpet in the world made of fresh flowers, is rolled out in the square, creating a breathtaking spectacle. It has become one of the most visited tourist attractions in Europe.

I stop across from a gigantic bronze statue of the first mayor of Brussels. In the store across the street, I buy fresh rolls and some croissants, chocolate and plain, a treat for the guys who are sitting and writing. I walk past a statue of a kid pissing. The Belgians supplied him with his own personal attendant who dresses him in different outfits throughout the year, in accordance with whatever local or national holiday is taking place. It's nice.

I arrive at the apartment that serves as our meeting room. I sleep there if I'm in town. The apartment is comfortable and much more than just a room in a hotel. Here I can feel almost at home. Sometimes, an elderly couple that rents the apartment join me. He's a retired worker who comes to visit with his wife in order to assuage the curiosity of the neighbors. When they come for a visit, I am the recipient of home-cooked meals, a cup of tea with cake, and conversations that last into the night.

I open the windows; a little oxygen won't hurt, and the cold doesn't kill anything – it just makes things stronger. I put my suitcase in my room and go to the small but fully stocked kitchen and put water in the electric kettle. The gang will arrive soon.

In the afternoon, we are all writing reports. The Old Man and Handsome went to Syria after making a business contact at a computer trade show last year in Germany. The trip was successful from a business standpoint, but has yet to bear fruit on the intelligence front, a fact that doesn't deter us from continuing to try. We know of Syria's connection to North Korea, but we need to bridge some information gaps regarding the particulars of the equipment being sent to Syria.

It's difficult to sit in front of a stack of paper in a closed room. After a short while, the first volunteer offers to make coffee for everyone. In the background, the radio plays music whose purpose is to act as a buffer between us and the outside world. We always have to take into account the possibility that the wrong person might be listening in on our conversations, whether inadvertently or deliberately.

"Albert..." I call to the Old Man. Even 'Albert' isn't his real name – we all picked out pseudonyms so as not to unwittingly expose any operatives. "After you finish that report, let's talk a bit in the other room."

"I'll be right there," he says without lifting his head.

"Albert" is Joe, but "Joseph" is what's printed on his ID card. His mother named him Joseph when he was born, but the people around him called him José. He immigrated to Israel from Argentina with his parents when he was fourteen. His family owned factories that produced industrial machinery that were exported to Israel for assembly. José, which was Joseph's name when he immigrated to Israel, enlisted in the army where his name became "Joe" permanently.

Joe is the friendliest person I know. After he finished his regular army service, he refused to join the family business, opting instead to become a full-time soldier as he preferred a career in the army. A combat soldier in the 504th Infantry unit, an outstanding officer who was loaned to the Mossad, which became his second love and future.

His friends talk about his iniquities. A rascal who had a fondness for women and wine, fine restaurants and going out on the town – hedonistic and a bit of a glutton. He always had a gorgeous woman draped around his neck – his eyes never rested – always drawn to wherever the action was. Wherever he went, he was the main attraction; people loved listening to him. However, he had another side to him. He was basically modest, discreet, and loyal. There was an aura about him, mostly due to his enigmatic personality, lack of information about him, and the mystery he exuded. Those that knew him spoke of an extraordinary amount of courage, innovation and creativity.

Dina was the big change in his life. He met her under sad circumstances. His good friend, Yigal, was killed under unknown circumstances. At the funeral, he saw her standing next to the bereaved mother, hugging each other and crying silently. The little sister. Dina served as a personal affairs NCO in the Paratroopers Brigade.

He had the opportunity to speak with her at length during the *shiva* at their home, but left the house without getting her phone number since she was too young, as well as being Yigal's little sister. Later, he made up various excuses to meet up with her, and would show up at her base and take her to lunch. He drove her back to her base one cold Sunday morning, but refrained from making any commitment to her, fully aware of his flirtatious nature.

Dina didn't understand why he was hanging around her. Was he looking out for her as a promise to her brother? Was there a romantic interest? She liked him a lot, but she thought he was too old and too much of a playboy for her, so she preferred not to get involved with him. At her brother's memorial service a year after his death, his friends came, Joe in the lead. When he greeted her with a hug, she blushed and looked at him, embarrassed. He smiled, and stroked her hair without saying anything.

After she was discharged from the army, she worked as a waitress to save money for her big trip abroad. It was a quiet evening in the restaurant and two men entered and sat in a quiet corner. She came over to them to give them menus and, much to her surprise, Joe was there with another man much older than him. She waited on them and received a generous tip. At the end of her shift, the wait staff all went to get in a cab they had ordered, and she saw Joe standing by his car waiting for her.

"Need a ride home?" he asked.

"No thanks, I'm going to go with everybody in the cab."

"How many years do I have to wait in order to ask you for your phone number?"

The Old Man entered the room and took off his jacket, which happened to match his beautiful eyes. We sit across from each other on comfortable, padded chairs. Joe was meticulously dressed, everything ironed and coordinated, black leather Bally shoes made with soft, thin leather, and he wore a Breitling watch on his wrist. Joe was always crazy about watches.

"First of all, I bought Nathan an antique watch, the kind you hang from a suit pocket," I say and rush to produce the small package, opening it quickly. "Look at how beautiful it is. The watch is enclosed in a silver case, hand-made by a talented silversmith. Incredible. Did you see the inscription in the back? The mechanism? It's a 90 year-old watch and still keeps perfect time."

He checks the watch against his.

"Yep. I hope Nathan likes it, though it's a bit ostentatious for him. I imagine this watch might sit on his dresser forever."

"You know what to do if it turns out that he doesn't like it and wants to take it back…"

"Tell me, how are things at home? Is everything good there?"

"More or less. My oldest daughter and son both went on school trips this week. The youngest sat on my lap all weekend. My knee still hurts," he said, smiling.

"And Dina?"

"She's fine, you know her. Always organized and in control of everything."

"Yeah, she takes all that off your plate so you can have a clear head for work."

"Absolutely, but it also keeps me on the outside. I have zero say at home. Nobody asks me for anything anymore. My youngest daughter hugs me all the time but, when it comes to asking permission, she asks her mother," he said, smiling again, but this time sadly.

How familiar and how painful, I think to myself, and say, "It's just a phase, you know. Afterward they forget it all and everything returns to how it was."

"Don't be so sure. These rifts create crises that leave scars for life. Disconnecting like this from one's family confuses everybody," said the Old Man, deep in thought.

"You need to undergo some medical examinations and devote some time to your home. I'll talk with both of them and, afterward, I'll see what can be done. Now let's get down to business. We need to finish these reports by tonight, and we aren't stopping until we do. I have to travel tomorrow and I won't be back here until Monday it seems."

"That's pretty tight, I hope we'll make it," said Joe.

"Yeah, but the sooner we finish, the sooner we can solve everybody's issues about spending more time at home. By

Wednesday, you guys will come up with a plan whose main objective falls to Ludwig. He will get the initial assignments and that may allow Laurie and you to go home."

"The problem is that Ludwig still needs us, and it will be hard for him to operate independently," said the Old Man.

"It's time to let him loose and trust him to work independently."

While I was waiting for Laurie, I thought about myself in this male-dominated organization, a system in which a woman has to prove herself all the time, and go above and beyond at that. It's a man's world where men have decided that women aren't suitable and feel comfortable in a space where a woman need not tread. But the truth is, a woman can often succeed in a place where men fail. We are more creative, more sensitive to the environment and find it easier to improvise. The system is comprised of successful as well as average people, like every work environment. Over the years, we have become more average, because it's convenient to promote average people. We let the good ones go, the ones who were critical. We preferred not to listen to their criticisms in order to feel better about ourselves. We gave up on excellence.

Laurie sits in a worn-out armchair. He was born and on a kibbutz, his Levi's and t-shirts having disappeared after passing an accelerated course in the importance of external appearance. He purchased for himself some articles of clothing with the help of Albert, who was the ideal mentor for him. Before he came to us, Albert loved and understood the significance of quality clothing, who should be wearing it, when and for how long. He taught Laurie and, after a few months, Laurie was dressed to the nines in "work clothes" as he liked to call them.

They grew to love and appreciate one another; they completed each other. Each of them brought their own qualities and experience and, in this case, it was a big success. When organizing people into teams, there is always the concern that there won't be the right chemistry. Psychologists examine each person who is supposed to join the team. The discussions are long and exhausting and, in the end, only fate and luck determine whether it will work. Sometimes we have to make do with a team comprised of people who don't like or appreciate each other.

With this pair, they liked working together and it showed. The one that suffered due to the two hitting it off so well was the third team member, "Handsome." He always felt an acute sense of not belonging. "It's hard for me to hang around with the happy couple," he told me.

Laurie holds a cup that contains an herbal infusion – always busy with healthy living. He tried to get us to follow along in his footsteps, despite the fact that his speeches were always met with half-interest and an awkward smile. We knew he was right, yet were jealous of his ability to withstand temptation, so we ignored him.

"How's it going?" I asked.

"Great." He was always optimistic and smiling. "Celina and I rested and spent some time together, just the two of us. Bar was with friends part of the time, so we had some quality time together as a couple. This time she felt good."

"Good to hear. But since she's had problems mostly when you travel, you need to keep an eye on her."

"I agree. Celina is fairly sensitive and fragile. She cries a lot, is often on edge and loses her patience and gets angry with Bar. He has become a bit of a crybaby and clings to her."

"Did her test results come back?"

"The doctor said that at this point the situation is stable, but she has to take better care."

"Since you won't be able to be with her until the end of her pregnancy, we can send her to Israel until she's ready to give birth, or her mother can stay with her for a bit. We'll get her a plane ticket."

"Celina will need to decide, I'll let her know of your offer. If I can find a way back to Israel here and there, that would be fantastic," Laurie said, smiling at me.

It was decided to relocate Celina and Bar to London as Celina is originally from England and, therefore, there wasn't any problem getting a permit to live, work or study. As a combat soldier's wife, she had a lot of restrictions placed on her, mostly social, that made living in London an unattractive prospect. Celina intended to change her career direction when she got back to Israel. She began studying, but her problematic pregnancy screwed up her plans.

"Ok, that's settled – she'll check and we'll summarize everything later. Tomorrow, I have to travel." I don't share work with my people if it doesn't concern them. Compartmentalization is designed to maintain security. There's no way of knowing who might get captured and be forced to talk.

"We have to finish writing these reports today, and stay up all night if we have to. Will you be able to finish your part?"

"Yeah, no problem, we'll keep at it until it's done." Laurie never complains even if he has reason to.

"Albert and you might need to spend a few days at home, so Ludwig will be forced to work by himself in the office."

"Look," he said, "If Celina is in Israel, I can put in a lot more time at work than I normally do. In any event, we'll help Ludwig, we'll sit with him and go over all of the options. He can do it, he just lacks a bit of confidence, which causes him to work slowly. He needs to be pushed all the time, and the truth is, it's kind of our fault. We're isolating him."

About two or three years ago, Ludwig was just an insecure kid. He grew up in a kibbutz and lived in a greenhouse. But he had a brain that could come up with some pretty creative solutions. He radiated responsibility, work ethic, dependability, analytical ability and charisma. We all fell in love with him and knew he'd go far.

"I think you're right," I say to Laurie. "We need to see whether or not we may have dampened his confidence. He got here last and his position isn't on par with yours. You two go on missions together, and he stays behind like a member of your staff. We should probably open a door for him or, at least, a window. Ludwing is fine. Yes, he's slower than you two, but maybe your expectations of him are too high?"

"I don't think that's something that was maliciously intended, but with Albert, I found my better half. He's the big brother I never had. It may be that we are pushing other people away without realizing it."

"Look, we need him, and he needs us. Without him we can't do very much. Beyond that, he's a good guy and positive, and change will only be good for everyone.

"You're right, it'll be fine..." said Laurie.

"So then, let's get on with it."

"Yes, Sir," he said, saluting me with a smile. "Or, Ma'am?"

"Okay, okay, go write something instead of talking so much." I laughed fondly.

"Guys, what about lunch?" I call to them. "We need to eat something, don't we?"

"Yes, Mom," the Old Man said. "Good thing somebody remembered that we need to eat. With Laurie, it's possible to starve to death here."

"Hey, fat-ass, that's the only thing you ever think about. As soon as you finish eating, you're already planning your next meal. Who are you trying to kid?" retorted Laurie.

"Man's gotta live, no?" the Old Man said in his own defense. "Seriously, though, where shall we go?" He patted his belly contentedly.

"I suggest we go to that little restaurant next to the Central. They have fast service there. We can eat well and it's cheap – just the way you like it, Laurie. Just like on the kibbutz," I said, teasing him a bit. "Besides, it's one of the only places that has all-day service."

"Oh, I see how it is. Hold on, wait, now you're giving me a hard time? I remember every word said here and later I'll make sure to mention it at just the right time," said the Kid.

"I'm shaking in my boots. Start moving. Ludwig, will you be joining them?"

Handsome is still busy working and doesn't even look up. He rarely joined the conversation, and his presence in the room goes almost completely unnoticed.

"No. I don't feel like eating at all," he answered as he continued writing.

"Come on, let's go eat something. We've got a long night ahead of us, don't be a downer," Laurie said to him while looking at me out of the corner of his eye, smiling. "There isn't another normal place anyway, and later it will be too late and take too much time."

"Fine. But we need to be quick, all right?" Handsome said, agreeing.

I smile to myself.

They go outside. I don't go with them. They are working together on official business and I'm an Israeli diplomat. The less we are seen together in public, the better. I open up the refrigerator only to find it empty. In the cupboard, there are a few packages of cookies, pasta and rice. There's frozen bread in the freezer. How could I forget about the croissants from this morning? I decide that I'll have them for lunch today. I'm never going to lose weight this way...

After about an hour, the three of them returned and brought me a sandwich. I'll keep it for evening. I let them work quietly and without interruption. I have to go to my "office" in one of the phone booths far from the apartment anyway. I have to coordinate some things.

I head in the direction of the stock exchange, one of the oldest buildings in the city. There are many telephones all around the building. From one of the nearby kiosks, I buy a phone card, a means that serves us well. Phone cards are great for anonymity if they are correctly used and thrown away without anybody noticing.

"Good afternoon," Dalit says on the other end of the line. "How's it going?"

"I'm taking an afternoon nap," I say. "Listen, I can't make it tomorrow; ask Ami to call me if he can make it today by nine. I want to invite him to breakfast tomorrow at ten, at the coffee shop he so strongly recommended, the one with the special breakfast."

Dalit understands.

"He left for the afternoon and will call you soon. I hope that you are enjoying the city and that the food's good. Did you get to go to that museum you wanted to see?" Dalit is trying to weave a little small talk into the conversation. It sounds good.

"Yeah, I did, I really enjoyed it. By the way, I was in a fantastic restaurant. You have to try the mussels there, with the garlic and wine sauce, they are out of this world."

"I love mussels," Dalit sighs.

"I know, that's why I'm telling you. Over there it's all fries with mayo and ketchup in some oily paper on the street." I poke a little fund at the Dutch. What do they know about food?

On the next phone call, I book a flight to Rome, the tickets I'll pick up at the airport. And now, I just have to book a room. I have a list of about ten different hotels. It's not always easy to find a vacancy. On the fifth call I find a place that I have only seen from the outside. It's a good area, next to the Piazza di Spagna, the beautiful Spanish square. A good location in the center, and logical for a tourist my age arriving alone. I book a room for three nights.

The last phone call is to headquarters in Israel. My contact who helps me with everything. The middleman, the coordinator, the motivator and the consultant. It's the position of a man who sits behind a desk, on condition that he does his job faithfully. Like any job, only the one doing it determines the level of performance, success and effectiveness.

Yanke'le is an affable guy. Young and incredibly motivated, catches on fast, listens, asks pertinent questions, verifies facts and has vast knowledge. He should be arriving in Europe soon in order to "feel out the territory" for the first time. He's modest, knows his limitations and acts accordingly.

"Yankush, what's up?" I recognize his voice.

"Hey, I was hoping you'd call, I have a meeting soon and after that I need to run to another one," he said.

"Is there anything new that I need to know about?" I hope we won't be having anymore last minute changes.

"I understand you're flying out tomorrow morning, Menashe needs those guys' reports. In two days at around four in the afternoon, he needs to give a general review to the big boss."

"No problem, I'll send them with Ami in the morning. In the evening there's a mail pickup and you'll have them in two days, first thing in the morning. How about that?"

"Awesome as always." Yanke'le definitely knows that women enjoy complements.

"That's how I like you," I laughed. "You're pretty awesome too, you know."

"We could go on like this for hours..." Yanke'le says.

"Okay, fine. So, on to other things. I'm sending my flight and lodging details, meeting locations and other requests. I know that this isn't something you're handling, but please keep an eye out – I trust you. Besides, I have no intention of staying a minute longer than I have to, especially if something in the field that has nothing to do with us gets fucked up. If Danny doesn't answer me when I call, I'll call you immediately so that you'll have all the details. Okay?"

"No problem. Whatever you want, and don't worry, I'll talk to him. I'll wake him up." I can hear the joy in his voice. When they trust you, it's a good feeling.

I only met Yanke'le two or three times, during my visits to Israel this past year. He's been in his position for less than a year now. The familiarity between us is primarily built through good chemistry and on the phone. Not everybody likes working with women, and I don't get the impression that it bothers him, so for me, that's one less thing to deal with.

Yanke'le grew up in Tel Aviv. His father was sent to manage a bank in the United States for a period of five years when his son was in grade school, which resulted in him speaking excellent English. He served as an intelligence officer. A nice guy, intelligent and matter-of-fact, modest and shy. At the age of twenty-seven, he met Idit, his first girlfriend, and within a year-and-a-half, she became his wife. He studied accounting and afterward began working in a big firm to get experience before venturing out on his own, with his father's help.

He interned in international taxation, a highly sought after field that was very lucrative, but despite the money and promotions, it left him unfulfilled. Over the years, he couldn't stop thinking about his job in the army, about his familiarity with the Shin Bet and the Mossad, and about the ferocious passion he felt toward the field.

Yanke'le was afraid of leaving a sure thing, the career he had paved for himself so easily. He was married now, and it wasn't just him that needed to be taken into account. When he brought it up, his wife said, "You need to follow your heart. Otherwise, you're never going to be truly happy."

"But government agents don't make a lot, and we will never have the chance to be financially successful."

"I also work, but I'm not worried about money – there are more important things than that. You'll never forgive yourself if you don't try, and you can always come back to it later on."

The next day, he called a friend from the intelligence course who chose a career in the Mossad, and asked him straight up if he could recommend him for a position.

"Are you crazy?" his friend said. "You have an awesome job, what do you need this for?"

"I'm dying there, it's not for me."

"I'll recommend you but don't say I didn't warn you. Don't hold it against me, all right?"

"Thanks, don't worry, I can always go back to my career."

In his first interview, Yanke'le talked about his life sparsely. The recruiter was impressed by him as a positive guy who could be useful, (but working on the jobs nobody wants, seeing as it was on a spur of the moment referral) but not at a regular operational job, because he was too much of an introvert. So he was sent to be tested and recommended for something he could contribute to without field operatives who were born to do this trampling him underfoot – "the street cats" as we called them.

A full year passed until Yanke'le was accepted and began the course. He arrived ready and prepared not only to give, but to give one hundred percent, among the few who still believed in the values of Zionism. He told me all this during our first meeting. He was excited and proud to work in our department. He thought everybody was a hero, and me as a woman, a superhero. Since then, he managed to sober up a bit once he realized that Zionism wasn't the name of the game, and that Zionism alone doesn't pay the bills.

"All right, Yanke'le, before I hang up, try to find Danny. I need to have a word with him."

"Wait on the line, see you later and my best to everybody at home." Yanke'le goes to look for Danny, I can hear his voice down the hall.

"Hey, what's going on? I understand you're leaving tomorrow morning," says Danny in an authoritative and agitated voice. "I want you to write down for me exactly what you plan on doing before you leave."

"I can't right now. These are simple things that don't require special authorization or some out-of-the- ordinary directive. After the fact, you'll get all the details anyway," I say to him in a voice no less assertive than his. Kids these days, what do they understand? You'd think he was managing the world.

"Are you mad?" Danny asks, going on the defensive.

"I'm not mad. I'm just telling you so that you'll understand the correct layout of things."

"Do I detect a little female sensitivity?" If there is one thing that annoys me, it's that reaction right there.

"You moron," I shoot back in anger. "This isn't female sensitivity, it's human sensibility. Didn't anybody ever teach you manners? Learn to treat people who have been here longer than you have with respect, that's part of "reading comprehension" I believe. If you don't understand, then you're going to have problems after the summer's over." Danny had only finished level one of the basic course and still had two to go.

"Okay, okay. Don't take it so hard. I realize I didn't give it the proper attention like I should have."

"Listen here, bub, don't think that because you sit behind a desk that you automatically become the supreme commander. Here's a little advice for you – women in this business are just as good as men, so don't go there again. Rise up the ladder one step at a time, and don't be in such a hurry to race up the stairs. An important part of this job is interpersonal relations. Be aware of who you're talking to and how you ought to treat them."

I give myself a moment to pause and continue. "And now to the heart of the matter. Tomorrow you'll get all the details of my trip. Give me a way to communicate with you. I'm letting you know that if you aren't available, I'll do everything through Yanke'le. Look, I know the team in Rome, I'm aware of everything that needs to be done in order to get them through this upcoming chapter. I very much hope to be back home by Friday evening, worst case Shabbat morning. Do you have anything to add?"

"No. Thank you. Good luck," he says quietly.

These guys have to be taught how to behave in their infancy so that they'll become good team members. Confidence has to come with experience. "Bye." Now I feel bad that I went off on him. I'm not perfect either, and apparently frustrated, mainly as a woman in the system.

They are sitting in the apartment, focused on the reports, the three of them nodding to me without lifting their heads.

"Anybody want coffee?" I ask and make a round of coffee for everybody, including some Danish butter cookies and the rest of the croissants from this morning. Then I call to Ludwig with his cup of coffee. "And, last but not least," I say with a smile.

"Right? The part about not being the least I particularly enjoy." He arranges himself comfortably in his chair.

"What's going on with you? How was your vacation at home?"

"Oh, how wonderful that was. I got there on Friday and went straight to visit Roi." He looked pensive. "The next day, I picked him up for a visit to my parents in Tivon and, on Sunday, we flew to Eilat to Club Med. Roi blossomed. Activities, the sea, swimming pool, and three meals every day where you can hardly move afterward anyway."

"You're telling me? I swear, I won't go to another one of those places ever. I absolutely stuff myself with the amount of food there, and the cholesterol."

"Yeah, but you don't need to worry about a thing there. Plenty of food, things for adults and kids, and beautiful women. What more do you need?" he said smiling.

Ludwig got divorced about three years ago. His wife wasn't able to get past his lifestyle. He was self-centered and didn't devote enough time to her and their little boy. Today he is aware that he messed up with his son, the house and family, but back then, he didn't get what the problem was and why his wife was never satisfied. There were periods that she would enter a bitter funk and would leave him on a regular basis, going back to her parents' house in the center of the country. But then she would come back to him only to leave him again. One time, when he came to her parents' house to visit her, to get her to come back home, her mother opened the door.

"She isn't here," her mother said.

"When will she be back?"

"Later. I suggest you come back tomorrow. I'll let her know you came." Her mother was acting strangely, since she would always happily invite him in and always tried to appeal to him to understand the needs of a young and spoiled wife. "She went to a movie with a friend and will be back later today," she said quietly.

While he was driving toward the main road, he began to get suspicious and decided to park his car next to the small grocery in the middle of the village. Evening fell and night came, the hours went by. At eleven o'clock at night, he called her house, but her mother told him that she had already gone to sleep. At three in the morning, a car driving slowly passed by him and he recognized her profile inside.

The car stopped in front of her parents' house. After a few minutes, the door opened and in the driver's side was a man. Even before he was able to conceive of the idea, the man pulled his wife to him. For half an hour he watched them, during which his emotional state went from anger, to sadness, to self-pity.

"How could she do that to me?" he asked himself. "I mean, I never in my life looked at another woman."

In the morning, he went in to his lawyer's office and on his advice opened up a divorce proceeding in the rabbinical court system. He knew he could never forgive her, nor forget her cheating. He gave her the apartment with her half registered in his son's name, Roi, and every month parted with child support payments in the amount of a thousand dollars.

Ludwig felt alone. It was difficult coming to terms with the fact that he wasn't going to see his son every day. But the most difficult thing was getting past the affair. How could he ever trust anybody again? Even though he went out with women, all of the relationships were casual, temporary. Especially casual sex. However, everything changed for him one day when he found new meaning in his life. Purpose. Something principled with a lot of self-respect. Us. "The office."

Ludwig described every day of his vacation to me at length. Beyond the time he spent with Roi, he met Galia. Suddenly, I see a spark in his eye that I hadn't seen before. Did something inside him change because of Galia? He felt the need to tell me, but he also knew that he was supposed to mention things like this to the system. A serious relationship requires deep security background checks, which sometimes feels like they're snooping around in your underwear.

"Galia arrived at the Club with a girlfriend. I met her on Sunday when I was sitting with Roi on the beach at the hotel. We decided to play ball, and Galia asked if she could join us because she was cold. What can I tell you, Yemenite on both sides, small and compact frame, long, black curly hair, insane body, big tits, long legs, and that full-toothed smile that girls have, smiling eyes with laugh wrinkles in the corners and a dimple on the right side of her cheek. She didn't pay much attention to me at first, spending time with Roi. They ran with the ball and I was the goalkeeper."

"And..."

"It was the best vacation I've had in years," he continued. "Everything was natural. The whole vacation, we hung out with her and her friend. Roi was over the moon with her and kept trying to get us to be together; he's convinced that he's the one that orchestrated that deal. Maybe he did," he said smiling. "On the third night, Roi fell asleep and Galia's friend volunteered to take him to the room. We got a night off and made the most of it. Finally, for the first time since my divorce, I feel that my heart is opening up, that I want and am able to love again. We met up later in Tel Aviv. I spent another two days with her, without Roi. I don't know what that gorgeous woman sees in me, but there is nobody happier about it than I am."

"You're one of the more handsome men I know – smart, good hearted, and many more wonderful qualities. Why don't you believe in yourself?"

"I know, right? Maybe because when I felt good about myself I got a rather rude awakening?" he said, a pall falling over his eyes.

"Not everything was your fault. You need to stop going back there and look ahead."

"True, and I have. Despite the fact that I'm just starting a new relationship, I have a good feeling about it. For the first time, I feel like I've found a woman who isn't thinking only of herself and what I can give her. Even though it's still early, I've seen enough with how she treats Roi to know what kind of a mother and partner she'll be."

"That's great. It's just that this business isn't so easy. You're here and she's there. You can't let the work suffer, and you can't rush it. Wait, you haven't told me her age." I ask because I need the technical details.

"Ah… she lives in Tel Aviv on Marshall Street, next to the conservatory. She inherited her condo from her grandmother. She is twenty-nine years old, teaches special-ed in Ramat Gan. She has five older brothers and sisters – she's the spoiled baby of the bunch. Her parents live in Hadera and so does most of her family. She served in the IDF as a youth counselor. Did I miss anything?"

"Single? Divorced?"

"Good single girl from a good family. She had a boyfriend who was killed in a car accident. She only started dating again two years ago; they were going to get married."

Such difficulties people go through. Have to know how to appreciate every day of quiet and good news. It's what they call perspective.

"I'm dying to see her, now. But don't worry, I won't mess around. First, we'll build the connection and when I know that the relationship is stable, I'll consider the next step."

"Do you call her? What have you guys done about communications?"

"I told her that I'm in the middle of moving and that I don't have a phone number where she can reach me; I'll just call her in the meantime."

"Good, sometime later give her my cell number and introduce me as the department secretary or something. Tell her that I'll be your contact, that I'll always be able to get a message to you. You'll continue to keep in regular contact with her so that she won't worry or, God forbid, become suspicious."

I smell the makings of something deep and serious developing here, and I hope that it leads to a steady relationship.

"Good idea," says the handsome Ludwig.

"Okay, on to our business at hand," I say. "How are you feeling?"

"You know that I still feel like the outsider, but I think that I'm also starting to fit in," he said.

"Good, I agree. You need to try to connect with them. Even though they have a strong bond between them, it's not like they've rejected you, and they also feel that it wasn't handled correctly. Your job is different from theirs, a job you see as less exclusive but, without you, nothing can happen. There's a reason that each person does the job they're best suited for."

"I know that in theory if I think about it logically, but I feel less successful, less brave and less sophisticated."

"First, that's not an accurate conclusion. Second, you are strong in areas they are weak in: organization, management, business savvy, etc. Third, you're still new at this, you have a lot to learn and a lot of room to grow. You need to be more independent, enterprising, a little quicker. In any event, you're on the right track." I'm smiling wholeheartedly.

"I know that I haven't acted ideally, but it'll be fine, you'll see."

"I'm going to insist that you make good on that promise soon. They need some 'home time'. You'll be on your own. We'll all prepare a plan of action together. But the main operational effort is going to have to come from you."

"I'm happy for the opportunity and I'm ready to take the plunge. I also think it's about time."

"Good. After you finish writing those reports, we'll all sit and summarize everything."

"Excellent." He turns to go.

"Just don't forget the send me Galia's details, for the security check. ID number, private phone number, residential address and where she works. If everything is managed right, in three weeks you'll be heading back home on Thursday, or a few days after. Don't promise anything until it's all set."

I hope Galia will be able to hang on. Not everybody is ready for a "boot camp" style romance at this age. It's amazing how things work out suddenly. I was overcome with an outpouring of joy and hopefulness. The only thing left is to say a few prayers to ward off the evil eye and to sacrifice a cat during a full moon. How fate can take a dramatic turn, how optimism can change in a moment.

I want to call home. I don't have much time, the conversation needs to be short. I tell them that I have to travel again and I'll only be back on Friday evening or Shabbat morning. I can hear the disappointment in their voices. "I wish I could finish earlier, but of course it's not up to me."

"Okay," he says in a despondent voice. "We'll be all right."

The phone in my bag starts ringing; it's Ami. I was expecting him to call me hours ago. "Where are you? I've been waiting to hear from you forever."

"Don't even get me started on the day I've had, I'm falling asleep standing up."

"Okay. Tell me about it tomorrow. We're meeting..." I'm certain he's going to try to get out of it.

"Are you sure you can't come to me? I'm really swamped," he says, exhausted. "look, you know that I'm always ready to help, especially you."

"I need you, and no, I can't come to you," I say, trying my best to remain calm. The man whose job description is logistical support for field agents is busy with everything except logistics. For some reason, Yaron is convinced that Ami is the right man for the operations but according to system guidelines, he shouldn't have been allowed anywhere near them. His English sounds so Israeli.

"Are you going to make it?" I ask.

"Fine. If there's no choice. Next time give me more notice; don't ask at the last moment."

My patience just expired. "Listen here, you jackass, I was only told about this today, and you know that I also have to finish all the paperwork from last week that's been waiting. I realize that you're the only person working hard here, but that's just how it is." Sometimes I really don't know how to keep my mouth shut. "Are we good with ten-thirty at the big, pretty plaza?"

"Yes. One hundred percent. It's nice there."

All in all, Ami is a good guy. Young, ambitious and motivated. He offered to be the logistics support in order to live abroad with his family and make more money, something that foreign service can help with. Yaron's support for the guy is exaggerated, though. Especially since it has become too dangerous for my taste. The guy is dealing with things in which he simply has no experience. His suitability to the task was never checked out.

Every so often he would arrive enthused with action stories that terrified me. That's not how we work. We adapted to amateurism instead of professionalism. Israelis act too often using the "trust me" method. Gambling on luck and not understanding that, in the end, it eventually runs out, relying on adaptation and improvisation instead of focusing on a well-organized plan. *Don't get annoyed*, I tell myself, *just focus on your business.*

I get back to the apartment, flip through the reports to make sure that they didn't forget anything. "Okay. The final summary of the trip will be done next week when I get back. Do you guys have anything to add to the reports?"

"I hope that we've finished the matter," Laurie says.

"I was able to go over part of it while it was being written and it looks good. I'll go over everything when you guys leave," I say.

"Let's go over it next week. I'm traveling tomorrow for a few days. We need to prepare the work plan as we agreed by Thursday. Most of the work will anyway fall to you, Ludwig." I look at Laurie and Albert. "On Friday, you guys are going home. On Tuesday, we all meet back here. This leaves you two days to prepare the plan. I'll try to call the office around five in the evening every day. Any questions to this point?" When people are this tired, there aren't usually any questions, rather general agreement. "Albert, don't forget your medical exams, and Laurie, you owe us an answer."

They both nod.

"Okay, is there anything anybody wants to say before we disperse?"

"We didn't get any feedback about our trip," says Laurie.

"Yeah, I know, we'll get a response only after a summary at headquarters. Don't worry, they never forget to mention things," I laugh.

"That's what I'm worried about," Laurie says.

"Don't worry, the citations are on the way, on an El-Al flight," says the Old Man.

"That never arrives on time…" Ludwig says with a smile.

Okay. Go home already. It's impossible to get rid of you guys, like glue. To the bathroom and to bed." I signal to them towards the exit.

"We got it. My lady is sick of us. We can take a hint." They all get up in unison. "Have a good trip, and don't get too connected to those guys. You need to come back to us," Albert says, smiling.

"It was a Catholic wedding, no?" I respond. "You guys are mine and I'm yours, forever and ever."

"Enough with the sweet talk," says Laurie, "good night, everybody."

"We'll be in touch," I say, closing the door behind them, locking both locks and turning off the lights in most of the apartment. I take the dishes to the kitchen, wash them and tidy up. Usually they clean up after themselves in rotation. This time there wasn't time. I take out my toiletries and go to wash the day's tribulations off of me. After a hot shower, I feel better. I get into bed with the reports. I have to go over everything before sending everything back to Ami and I put them in the safe. Now it's time to go to bed. I hope I'll be able to fall asleep better than last night.

While falling asleep, I'm reminded of my previous boss. The one that caused my big crisis on my detail to Paris. The man who I won't mention by name, a man my age, a *yekke*.[1] An arrogant and evasive man. Very creative, but not somebody who instills trust. He arrived for his mission two years before me, without any serious operational background. He didn't come for managerial purposes, but became the commander when his commander returned to Israel. From day one he tried to humiliate

---

1   Term for German Jews, who are known for their rigorous exactitude.

me, to disparage me and my professionalism, presenting me as having no value.

"Everything you have done until now is worthless. I'm treating you like a rookie who needs to prove herself," he told me during our first conversation on the job in Paris.

"What does that mean?"

"As far as I'm concerned, you need to justify your position here. Mine is the only opinion that matters; now I'm in command."

Who is this guy? That's how you welcome your colleagues to work? I have a lot of operational experience, certainly compared to him. Who is he to talk like this? I hoped I'd be able to make it work, since we aren't talking only about me, but also my entire family that is with me. His desire to prove that I'm not suitable, a man determined to complete his missions. He was afraid of competition and was afraid that I would do to him what he did to his predecessor. A friend from work called in order to warn me. "Listen up, he's going to cause you damage."

"Forget it, I know the type. It will be fine."

"He isn't like everyone else. He's sick. I'm telling you. He does things that make no sense. Just watch out."

"I'll keep an eye out. The problem is that it's just me and him in our department. Everything that happens, happens between us, and I'm not running to headquarters with every problem I have – how would that look?"

"I just hope that your division will notice that he is neither logical nor normal." I thought my friend was exaggerating, but I found out I was wrong.

In the coming months, I understood that the guy had a mental problem. I hoped I would be able to deal with him, but the situation developed in ways that were simply unbelievable. Everybody in the system who heard about what went on didn't believe that such a thing could happen to us. To my delight, he got into trouble for stealing money. It was decided to cancel his appointment as commander, and he got another job.

Ten years later, he was indicted on charges of sexual assault on young women under his command. He was convicted and will never set foot in "the office" again. We also have our share of weeds.

Wednesday

I have a travel-packed day before me.
Before I set out for my meeting with Ami, I add my telegrams to the bottom, including my arrival details into Rome and personal matters that I felt I should share with headquarters about the team, such as the details of Ludwig's new girlfriend. I prepare all the paperwork that Ami is supposed to take with him as per the regulations and guidelines. That's it. Everything is ready.

I head to the meeting.

The Irish pub is located behind the stock exchange. It's a chain of pubs throughout Europe and some other locations around the world. Rooms designed as if we were smack dab in the middle of Dublin, giving a sense of privacy. Irish music plays in the background. It's a comfortable place for couples in love to sit and enjoy some intimacy. When I learned how to choose a suitable meeting location, the instructor told me that any place where a married man would bring his girlfriend on a date is the right place for meetings like ours. There we can transfer packages without anybody diverting their gaze toward us out of curiosity; there, we can sit and talk comfortably.

Along the way, I check to see if anybody is following me. If somebody is watching what I do, a figure that doesn't look right, out of place. If I have to give or receive material, it's my job to make sure I arrive "clean." Everything looks good, and I enter the pub, sit in the corner of one of the side rooms and order a cup of tea.

Ten minutes later, Ami enters smiling.

"How are you?" he says in thickly accented English, trying, unsuccessfully, to sound European for the waitress.

"Thank you," I answer quietly in English, mostly so as not to draw attention to his massive Israeli accent.

"Coffee, please," he says, turning to the waitress while still standing, as if he were in Tel Aviv. "And bring me a cake, please."

"How are you?" he says to me in Hebrew as he sits down. "I have a very stressful day, they dropped a few more things on me that that they don't have anybody else to do."

"Nice," I say and think that pretty soon he'll start to preen since there's nobody else to do it for him.

"I brought you the money and the file you wanted. I'm telling you straight up, though, I didn't have time to check the money or the file; Dalit arranged it.

What a moron. Didn't they teach you never to trust anybody and to check each thing you take with you? Maybe Dalit made a mistake and gave you somebody else's file? How irresponsible can you be?

"No problem," I say. It's not my job to audit his performance, and I already learned that he will just get all flustered and not even try to understand anything anyway. "I'll check. I'm giving you the package with all the reports that the guys wrote up and some things from me. You need to send them so that they go out in tonight's mail. They are eagerly awaiting them at home."

"I'm not sure that I'll be able to get back on time today."

"Ami," I say assertively, "you're going to send them out today. As far as I'm concerned, go back now to The Hague, or check if we can send it from here, on condition that they have outgoing mail this evening. Under no circumstances can this wait until tomorrow." I get up to go to the bathroom in order to check the paperwork he brought me and to count the dollars and lire.

"I don't have time to chat with you. I have a flight to Rome soon," I say and leave him to pay the bill.

"What are you doing going to Rome now? When are you coming back?" he asks, surprised. The guy is spacing out.

"Friday evening or Shabbat."

"Your poor husband. I would never let my wife..."

I cut him off. "Ciao. I know that the woman's place is in the kitchen. I've heard that before." Under my breath I added, "Looks like your place is in a barn."

"I'm kidding," Ami said, trying to apologize.

I didn't even hear the end of the sentence. I had already split. Why do I let insignificant words irritate me? Where did the nice, modest guy who was sent on this mission disappear to? I'm in a cab, this time to the airport far from the center of Brussels, about a forty-minute drive. The driver is Moroccan. There is a large Moroccan community in the city. Slowly and methodically they took over many neighborhoods. A few Moroccans move into each neighborhood, and as the Belgians move out of entire communities, they soon become primarily Arabic: neglected and dirty, noisy, overrun with crime and drugs. They devised a method whereby a family member arrives in Belgium, and as soon as they receive a visa and access to the national insurance program, they invite their families from abroad to join them. That's how the whole family arrives, and they get to live off the state.

The cab driver read the Koran at every stop sign and traffic light. I sit quietly in the back seat. I'm not worried since the Moroccans are not friendly like the Dutch, who always want to chat. They don't try to form a connection or look you in the eye. I'm not recognizable as an Israeli and certainly not as an employee of the Israeli security establishment – being recognized could be problematic.

I smile inwardly and think... I could write a book on all the cab drivers in all the different cities I've been to. I arrive at the airport and at the counter, pay for the tickets I booked and head for the exit, passing by the stores without looking at them, having weaned myself of the habit long ago. Maybe this needs to be the way to treat people addicted to duty free shopping – give them an overdose.

The flight is over ninety minutes long. As luck would have it, the flight was empty, middle of the day. The morning and evening flights are full. I can stretch out in my seat and put the armrests up. I sit comfortably and savor the time I have to be alone with my thoughts.

The pilot announced our descent. Rome, here I come...

We land at Fiumicino, a huge airport. My carry-on is with me, so no need to wait further. I'm equipped with a few Italian phone cards. When I exit the airport, the cab drivers descend upon me and call after me, "Taxi... taxi..." These guys aren't licensed cabs, and they'll take you on the scenic route and overcharge you for the privilege. I learned that lesson a long time ago, and I keep on walking to the regulated taxi stand.

"How much to Piazza di Spagna?" You need to verify how much you're paying in advance.

"Seventy-thousand lira, Madam," one of them says. Sounds reasonable, that's basically what all the licensed cabs will say. I put my small suitcase on the back seat and sit down. The route takes us through farmland outside of the city.

While still passing by the green fields, I recall a previous trip to Rome. Two years ago, still at the beginning of this mission. It was a cold, rainy winter Shabbat and I have a lot of cash on me, as well as very important documents. On the advice of my previous boss, "The Maniac," I travel by train from the airport to the city. I soon discover that he led me astray once more. In contrast to his description of the train being spacious and a pleasant ride with few passengers, I found myself on a packed train with nowhere to sit. With my old suitcase and a bag with all that money and paperwork on me, I had the sense that it wouldn't be too difficult to rob me. I never should have gotten myself into that situation, given all the money I had on me.

Since I'd already boarded the train and the doors had already closed, it wasn't like I could change my mind. Finally we arrived at the city center in Rome. I had to get to my hotel immediately, but since it was a Sunday afternoon, there wasn't a single cab at the stand. I decided to cross over to the other side of the main road. It was a hot and humid day, and here I am embalmed in a suit and all this gear, walking, and in my head, having an imaginary conversation with my boss. Suddenly, I feel something damp drip down my back. I turn around and see a young man walking after me pointing to the big tree above us, one of the trees tangled along the avenue, and says to me in broken English, "The birds." I understood that he was talking about the pigeons taking their afternoon nap in the treetops. I let a particularly vulgar curse slip out from under my breath. What am I going to do now? I don't have another suit, neither do I have the time nor energy to deal with this now, but at least this nice guy comes up to me and hands me a paper napkin as he walks past. I take the napkin, thank him, and try to wipe off my back, but unsuccessfully.

To my surprise, he turns back around. "Come, I'll help you. There is water faucet in back."

In a matter of seconds I pick up on what was really happening. The stories and warnings of the Italian thieves set off an alarm in my head. I smacked his hand away, checked to make sure all my stuff was with me, and yelled, "Get out of here! Fuck off!"

The "friendly" fellow took off running and disappeared.

"Are you all right? Do you need help?" asked an older gentleman who was sitting on a nearby bench next to us, and I answered in the negative. Perhaps the guy has a clandestine partner? Another person who, as it were, wants to "help" me. Yeah, well, I'm done with that.

I kept walking until I got to the road and saw a woman getting out of a cab on the corner. I hailed it and got inside, sweaty and tired. At the hotel, I discovered that it wasn't bird poop on my jacket, but rather ice cream the guy threw at me on purpose. "Fuck those Italian thieves," I muttered to myself and added with a sigh of relief that perhaps I was pretty lucky. I mean, he could have hit me a few times and I wouldn't have been able to handle that. Since I had some time, I went down to reception and asked for an iron. After an exhaustive ironing, the jacket forgot the trauma that we experienced.

I sail back through older memories to my first trip abroad for work. It was part of our apprenticeship. We split into pairs, with everybody but me being a guy. We got to Rome and had to find a hotel to stay in on our own. We walked around for hours but found nothing, not even a tiny room. Our budget for food and lodging was low as it was, and we didn't have an extra penny for anything. When it was finally late and we were all exhausted, we found a room with a wide bed and an in-room bathroom with a shower, so we compromised. It made me feel uncomfortable to sleep with him in the same room and in the same bed, but we didn't have a choice. When I entered the room, I couldn't believe what a dump it was. A shabby little room, a shower with folding walls, dry-rot and mold raising quite a stench. The bed was not particularly comfortable, especially with Ron in the room with me. Ron was a self-proclaimed slob, but from a professional standpoint, he was quite talented. He used to be a pilot in the air force. Coarse, unrefined and disheveled – after fifteen minutes, his suit looks like it's been through an arduous day's work. In my mind's eye, I can still remember his suit, orange and brown in color when he got off the plane, wrinkled and hanging off him awkwardly.

That night, I barely slept. The disgusting shower, the towels and the sheets that were made of the same fabric, t-shirts that I wore as pajamas that weren't meant to be seen by anybody else, and my close proximity to a man that, despite getting to know over the past year, wasn't a close friend. Ron, on the other hand, felt completely at ease in his underwear and fell asleep immediately. His snoring quickly turned into an irritating background noise, together with car horns honking all through the night. That night I came to a lot of conclusions on the subject:

Need to make reservations, and I have final say on our accommodations if there's a choice. Need a decent pair of pajamas and for trips to Italy and need to pack a towel. Some conclusions were sometimes only good in theory, like having a room with no window, where I lived for a week in a room where the only source of fresh air was the door, was difficult...

The room in Rome was very small. A narrow bathroom with a mini-window high up on the wall near the ceiling. A feeling of claustrophobia comes over me. The bed is small, and the pillow is too hard. They say that a sailor has a girl in every port. I, on the other hand, have an empty bed in every city. I flash a crooked smile, each person with their own situation. Once it was said about airline stewardesses that they had a glamorous job, but today it's understood that they are basically waitresses who work hard.

I have almost an hour before my first meeting. It's an ideal time for making phone calls, but I need to distance myself a bit from the hotel, to walk around, to feel the place out. A mixture of languages and excitement. Loud mopeds flying around me left and right. Men walking in pairs, winking at the girls. The winks are accompanied by cat-calls. Happy. Welcome home to the Levant. I recognize the phone booths from past visits. I call headquarters, report that I have arrived and give them my hotel information.

I continue walking around and look at all the display windows, gushing over the various designs. The Italians are good at this. Usually, the Italian design is rather minimalist and very colorful. On the way to the cafe, I pass by an ice cream stand. The Italians are the world champions of gelato, soft and rich ice cream with an actual fruit taste.

I arrive at the Tea House, with its tiny display window that wouldn't attract anybody who doesn't know the place. Inside is a gigantic room full of antique furniture – charming. I'm looking for the pair I'm supposed to meet, trying to adjust my eyes to the darkness. They haven't arrived yet, so I grab a spot where I can see who comes in, with my back to the wall. This way, nobody can surprise me from behind, and I'm in complete control.

The two come in and sit down beside me. The conversation takes place exclusively in English. "So, how are you guys? Long time no see," I ask with a smile.

"Fine, thank you. Nice to see you, too," Erik says to me.

Before we do anything, we get straight what it is the three of us are supposedly doing here together. Who am I to them, and they to me, if anybody happens to ask. As far as I'm concerned, they're tourists who got turned around and need help, and I invited them to sit and have something to drink, because it's nice to have a friend in a foreign place.

We ordered hot drinks and got down to business. Erik explained to me the chain of events and Sheila added various things that he forgot to mention. Erik smiles a lot, but is on point, whereas Sheila looks tired and introverted. The object the group is interested in lives in a neighborhood that's located in a district a bit outside the city center. Each of the team members received tasks that, together, will paint an overall picture. The purpose, of course, is to get to know the object and his environment, the people around him, and to identify weaknesses in order to get an idea of how to operate. And each stage where information is gathered, we have to analyze it, determine what's missing, how we operated in the field, whether any mistakes were made that could lead our object or the authorities to us, and whether to change operating methods or the operating team. Sometimes a neighbor, or old person sitting out on his porch can notice something, without us noticing him, and call the police. In some cases our people were brought in for questioning, and in the worst cases, arrested. In Switzerland, this is a common occurrence. We have started saying that there, every citizen is a cop. Every infraction, even jaywalking, could lead to a cross-examination. We've been in this situation more than a few times.

Erik describes everything to me so that I can transfer the information to headquarters, as if I was there, but also so that I can decide on their next moves this evening and throughout the following day. "The object lives on a street that's behind the neighborhood's main road. Relatively speaking, it's very quiet. There aren't a lot of options as far as watching the building, but lucky us, there's a coffee shop close enough that we can watch the entrance to the building. We still don't know exactly which apartment, so at the moment, I don't know where we can watch from, and whether there's a line of sight to the apartment from the street, or more precisely, to the windows of the apartment."

"I got you. What else is on the street that could help us?"

"Just a vegetable store and that's it. But at the nearest intersection, there are a number of shops, another coffee shop, a post office, a public phone and a restaurant that looks to be pretty fancy."

"What about street parking? Is it allowed? Problematic?"

"It's possible. Each building has parking. It's possible that the object drives straight into the parking garage rendering watching the entrance irrelevant. It's possible to stand on the other side of the street across from the object's building. That's the quietest place and you can check to see whether he left or came back in his car. We don't currently have any information about the object's car that can help us. We also need a cover story for why we're sitting in our car on the street."

"Of course," I answer. "We can't enter a quiet street and park a car there without a compelling reason. A car is like an ID card. Once you have a car's details, you can check who's in it, where they're from, the name or names of whoever is renting it. It's better not to arouse suspicion by sitting in a car. "What about a larger radius? Is there any reason to be in the area? Maybe we could wait for him farther away?"

"There's a movie theater two streets from the object, but the movies are in Italian. There's a street with a few galleries that aren't too bad, and there's a street with a lot of stores where we can find a good reason to walk around. That's it, beyond that, there's not much else."

On the surface, it doesn't look like there are any particular problems with their operation, and we decide that at this stage, late morning tomorrow when people have already left to go to work, we would figure out which apartment belongs to the object, something that will help verify his daily and nightly routines. The names of his neighbors – maybe there's somebody there who might pose a problem. Or the opposite – somebody who could help us. During the same operation, we can verify the apartment number and find his car, or his parking spot. The type of lock on the door to the building as well as the apartment is information that will be useful to completing our goals later on.

We agree that the first step will be for Sheila to enter the building alone and that Erik will enter only if there's a need. Women tend to arouse less suspicion, so might as well take advantage. Sheila will arrive with pastries and a slip of paper with an address similar to the object's. If anybody asks, she can show them the slip, and realize that she's got the wrong address.

After she enters and gets as much information as possible, she'll leave and meet Erik at the coffee shop in the city center. There they will decide if there's any reason to go back in and fill in any holes. Everything is done carefully, so as not to expose ourselves or the object.

Erik asks me for more money. I send him to the bathroom with the money so he can count it and sign on the receipt, and

I have some time with Sheila. "How are you doing? You don't need any money yet?" I ask.

"Not right now. Maybe before you leave," she answers quietly.

"Is everything all right?"

"Yes and no. Dean and I broke up before I went on this trip. We didn't have a chance to really talk, and I left. It's so frustrating."

"I understand, that really sucks."

"I wish I understood exactly what happened. Dean and Sherry's last trip created tension. I'm certain that something is going on between them and it's killing me. Why did it have to be with my friend?"

"Are you sure? Did he say something to you?" I try to say something that will lift her spirits. It's not good working in this condition. Her head won't stop thinking about her problems instead of being free to concentrate on the mission.

"No," she answers. "He didn't say anything, but things were more restrained, different than usual. It bothered me so much that I couldn't let it go, and the longer I went on, the more he simply refused to talk about things, until I finally just told him to go to hell."

"Perhaps you were too quick to come to conclusions? Perhaps there's something else going on that has nothing to do with you or her?"

"Maybe, but my intuition says otherwise."

"You know that I always say to go with your intuition, but it isn't a hundred percent – it's not an exact science. What if you're completely off? Wouldn't that be a bummer? Have you tried talking to him since?"

"No, why would I talk to him? He needs to talk to me, especially since he knows I have a trip coming up and it's better to say something beforehand so that I don't leave in this state."

"You're young and stubborn. Take it from somebody a little older who's been there and still remembers a thing or two," I said, smiling. "Men don't think like we do, and if you are blaming him for something he doesn't feel guilty about, then he expects you to come apologize to him. Take into consideration that you may have made a mistake, and that you may have been the one to damage your relationship."

"Yeah, maybe... I really don't know."

Erik came back to the table, and we agree that they will call me for approval before going in. I let Erik go and we set a time to communicate this evening. I ask Sheila to stay with me for a few more minutes. He sends her a worried glance and tells her he'll meet her at the ice cream place in an hour.

"Sheila, honey, life isn't black and white – let a little grey in. Maybe your intuition is justified, but maybe you're completely off, and then what?" I say, returning to the subject.

"What are you saying? Are you saying I made a mistake?"

"I have no idea, kid, but take everything into account, just like at work. There's a saying in the instructor's course that goes like this – the facts aren't determined by our conjectures. It's basic, but that's what you did. I suggest you call him first chance you get. You know where you can catch him?"

"Yeah, but he won't be available until evening."

"Until then, just think about what I said and smile, be optimistic. Positive thinking creates positive energy. If your love is strong, it will withstand this fight, as well as the next one. Make him communicate immediately, and don't let things get out of proportion."

Advice that is easier said than done. I'm a master at being so stubborn at times that I go into a silence that lasts for days, and until they finally come crawling on all fours, I don't budge. Why doesn't anybody tell me at the time to change direction?

"You're right. It's nice talking with a woman for a change." She finally smiles.

"It's one of the things I missed so much while hanging around for weeks with guys and only guys. Back then, in the time of Methuselah, there weren't more than one or two women."

"You know that Erik and I get along great together. Even though he is much more experienced than I am, he doesn't feel the need to prove it. He always listens and asks my opinion."

"Yes, true. He was always like that. I believe that it comes from having real self-confidence. He's professional, but also a friend. Learn as much as you can from him; he is one of the best role models there is. His operational analysis is impressive. I think that he is somebody who isn't locked into a line of thinking like most of us."

"Maybe I need to start up with him instead and forget about Dean," she said, laughing.

"That's a whole other story."

The less feelings get mixed up with work, the better.

Erik is twenty eight. Every woman's dream. Tall with a body toned from years of sports, mostly running. He loves running cross-country, among the trees and fields, over rocks and puddles that form in the winter. The feeling of freedom and being free gives him the energy he needs at work – the flights, the long hours when he's forced to stay in hotels, on the streets and in cars. Erik has the smile of an arrogant little kid, like one who knows he did something wrong and has no intention of apologizing for it.

After his military service as a combat medic, he decided to study medicine, since that's where he saw his life heading. It was impossible for him to get accepted into medical school in Israel, so he decided to get his degree abroad, which meant he could save the money he was earning in a job he could do while also studying. That's how he found us. His dreams were put on hold because he caught the bug that virtually everybody in our profession comes down with. He loved the work, despite the fact that it went completely against his basic desire to be free and independent.

From the beginning, he was exceptional as a member of the team. He proved to be a charismatic leader who creates consensus effortlessly, modestly and humbly. He had the respect of his friends and superiors. Everybody foresaw a bright future. At the end of every trip, he would return home to his solitary existence. That's how he preferred it. When everybody else went to the pub at the end of a drill, Erik would go so as not to be anti-social, but he usually left early. He never developed deep friendships. A mysterious lone wolf. Management also was surprised by him. Various people tried to determine why this man, despite his abilities, was disinclined to form friendships and, he would dismiss the inquisitors by saying, "Everything's fine." Erik was someone who would always lend support when needed, who you could always count on, and who had no reason to prove his leadership. One could never know what he was really thinking, feeling, or who he really was, but it didn't bother anybody or cause an uncomfortable situation. Weird.

"All right, young lady," I say to Sheila. "So we're agreed?"

"I don't feel like my mood is impacting my work."

"Make sure that doesn't happen," I say. "We all have these kinds of problems. I'm happy we had this talk. See you later."

Lately, I find myself functioning as a counselor and social worker, mother, and two-bit psychologist. But in order for things to get done properly, we have to manage people in every facet of life. I'm happy that they trust me and confide in me. In my opinion, returning a smile to somebody's face and removing a little worry off their mind is worth all the energy spent, and the work benefits as well.

The story with Sheila and Dean began in a course about three years ago. At the beginning of every course, they emphasize to the new students that "they must separate work from their private lives." This prohibits romantic relationships, which make it harder for the couple to function, and by extension the team, but it isn't always preventable. Sometimes, when the heart speaks, the brain shuts up. They were part of the same team on the first operation in the course and there were quickly fireworks, resistance, and anger on both sides.

"I can't work with him, he's completely self-absorbed, and he isn't willing to listen or compromise."

"She's impossible," said Dean to the same instructor. "She's always going against what I do, and disputing every word that comes out of my mouth." They couldn't stand each other, so the instructors decided to separated them with the goal of hooking them back up together later on. Tenuous relationships between two people can interfere with their ability to function on the job. Later on, they realized that this wasn't the way to do well in the course, so they decided on a relationship that was more or less amicable. The arguments became fewer until they disappeared completely. Near the end of the course, the instructor caught them making out. It isn't clear who was more surprised, the couple or the instructor. Who would have thought?

They were called in for a clarification session with the course management and were reprimanded for not disclosing their affair. The question of whether to throw them out of the course or just punish them came up, whether they would be required to call off their romance, or just moderate it. Establishing rules requires consequences when they are broken, but it's also clear that you can't just keep people from seeing each other. After all, plenty of couples were formed at work. In the end, despite the concern that their relationship might disrupt the stability of the team (and romantic relationships always create tension and stress), it was decided that they would only be reprimanded, but also discouraged from those actions for the remainder of the operation. The risk of losing two good field operatives drove the decision to punish them lightly.

Their love blossomed. They became a stable couple. They still had professional disagreements, but they performed well at work. They worked with other couples and would rarely travel together as part of the same team, except for times when a large team was needed. The two of them never complained about the disconnect and were grateful to the system for giving them a chance to prove themselves.

I go back out to the street. It's time for a little sightseeing. I need to be an anonymous, grey tourist. I'm tired of going to the Vatican, or to piazzas, or museums. I decide to go window shopping. That's what a lot of tourists do. I decide to go into a shop that sells handbags. One of my known fetishes – I'm addicted to leather handbags. I enter the store Mandarina Duck and buy a beautiful grey bag on sale, and two incredible white bags.

It's six thirty and I call Albert.

"Everything's fine, dear," he says. "I miss you." This flirtatious style of speaking is in case anybody is listening in.

"Me, too, honey," I say, imitating his flattering tone. "Everything's good with me, what are you up to?"

"Quietly suffering missing you. When are you coming already?"

Maybe he can't talk right now. Maybe somebody is with him? I think to myself.

"Soon, soon, I promise. Where are you? Is somebody with you?"

"Just some people around me. I feel great, and my friends all send their best regards and kisses."

"Send them my best as well, and kisses too, see you soon."

No need to say more. Everything is fine and there is nothing new I need to know.

Nir is my dinner date. He is picking up the relevant intelligence on the object's office for the mission while Erik and Sheila check out his home. I chose the Trastevere on the other side of the river, a touristy area with excellent restaurants. I sit next to Nir, who arrived before I did. Everything is quiet, calm and pleasant.

Groups of Asians are occupying almost every table. They all order the same things. The head waiter tells us that this happens here every night. A popular tour guide from Japan gave a good review of the restaurant and recommended the dishes people *have* to try. Japanese discipline at its finest. They seem to prefer to be told what and how to do things. We Israelis do the opposite of what's recommended. We're the nation that feels the need to be contrary.

Nir. A man in his thirties, married to Amelia for some five years, and they have two kids. Amelia was a stewardess for El-Al, and gorgeous. Nir was a guy you wouldn't look twice at if he crossed the street. We call him "the Chameleon" because he blends into any situation and any place. He can look like the CEO of a European bank when he needs to be put up in a fancy hotel, or like a bum living in some dusty old, flea infested motel. On the street he could look like a common fool, grocer or businessman. Whatever is necessary. Open minded, not set in his ways, diversified and unique.

Many people who met Amelia thought, "What the hell does she see in him? How does such a beautiful woman fall in love with somebody who looks like that?" Nir is short, has thinning hair, and has the beginnings of a nice beer-belly. No knight in shining armor, no white horse. But Amelia still looks at him with towering admiration, six years and counting.

On the flight where they met, he sat in business class, tired, barely noticing who was around him. Business class was practically empty and the stewardess had free time. She offered him something to drink and sat next to him to rest, perhaps because he seemed like the harmless type, like somebody who wouldn't read too much into her sitting next to him, somebody who wouldn't ask for her number or try to get her to sleep with him. They idly chatted about life in general, spending about an hour together until she got up to continue working. Before landing, she gave him her phone number without him asking for it.

They had their first date the next day. She couldn't explain what happened to her, what she saw in him that she didn't see in any other suitor. Amelia was fed up with romances that ended badly, fed up with dates that didn't lead to anything, and the more time passed, the more closed off, reserved and indifferent she became, sealing herself off from forming new relationships. She preferred to go out with her girlfriends or be with friends from her past that with whom she had platonic relationships (especially gay flight attendants).

After dinner in a small, intimate restaurant in Tel Aviv, he took her back home, kissed her on the cheek next to the door of her apartment, and left.

"Wait, don't you want to come in for a cup of coffee?" she asked.

"Sorry, not tonight."

She looked at him, astounded. It even annoyed her a bit, but she also kind of liked it. When a few days past and he didn't call her, she was frustrated and angry. A week passed and on a return flight from Greece, she saw him whispering in the ear of a cute girl that he certainly knew from before. *He must be married, or something like that,* she thought. At night, while sitting and resting in her living room, she heard a knock at the door. Nir stood there with a large bouquet of flowers.

"Good evening," he said.

"Good evening, and good night," Amelia answered him and closed the door.

"Wait, wait," he said, and slid the edge of his shoe into the doorway to stop the door from shutting.

"Listen, Nir, forget it, we went out, it was nice, it's over. Bye." She shot him a look that couldn't be misinterpreted.

"Let me explain. Ten minutes. If you don't accept my explanation, I'll leave and I won't come back. Okay?"

She looked into his eyes and again felt the excitement she felt on their first date. She let him in and sat across from him in an armchair.

"I'm part of the security establishment. I traveled on an

urgent matter early in the morning after we parted. I didn't have time to call, and I couldn't from abroad. It was obvious to me that I left things open, just as it was clear to me that when I returned, we would continue where we left off. I haven't been with anybody for over six months. You're the first girl I've been interested in in a long time – very interested in. It's impossible not to notice that you're one of the most beautiful women anybody anywhere has ever seen, and seriously, it's not clear to me why a gorgeous girl like you wants anything to do with a guy like me. But that's your problem. I see beyond your outer appearance. You're a woman with inner beauty and a good heart, smart and interesting. I've thought about you every day since we parted, and I've waited for the moment where I could just sit and look at you. The girl that I was with was "my spouse" for the trip," Nir said, finishing his explanation and looking into my eyes, waiting for her reaction.

"I have been angry for the last week. I was mostly mad at myself that I was tempted to contact a passenger against my better judgement. You didn't call after an incredible night, what was I supposed to think?"

"You're right," he answered her. "It won't happen again."

"I hate liars, just so you know. I've had enough of men that make empty promises. I've had enough of the wrong type of men who are attracted to me. I prefer to be alone," Amelia said.

"Me and lies don't go together, I promise. I'm straight as an arrow, shamelessly so sometimes, you'll see," he said, caressing her with his eyes.

She lifted up her gaze, tears in her eyes, and said, "I don't want to be hurt again."

He came closer to her, stroked her hair and face and said, "You're so beautiful," while smiling at her. "I won't hurt you, Amelia. I'll never hurt you, I promise."

Electricity was in the air, like that portending new beginnings, a great love, a new family. Since then, six more months had passed, then another six months, and then another five years. They got married and had two kids. She still looks at him like the knight of her dreams, and at night, her stomach turns over in anticipation of his return. He checks every morning to make sure she's still there, still not believing that he found her, that she wanted him. This couple was the envy of all other couples. The hope for a happy relationship.

"I recommend the seafood pasta," I say to Nir, knowing his culinary tastes. Though I have never eaten here, reviews get passed around the office, and we have all become amateur restauranteurs.

"I actually feel like something simple. I'll go with the garlic pasta, olive oil and mozzarella. I had a steak this afternoon."

I haven't been eating regularly for a few days now, and finally, I have a date for dinner. The waiter places a large, hot plate in front of me and I savor every bite. The pasta is perfect, and the pink shrimp are basted with a wine and garlic sauce. It was worth the wait.

"You want a bite, Mickey Mouse?" I ask, smiling. "You're missing out, it tastes like heaven."

We trade bites and Nir agrees that I won. There's nothing like Italian food, especially pasta. We can't talk business on account of the waiters constantly hovering. "How's the family?" I ask.

"Great. Our youngest has me wrapped around her finger even more than our oldest."

"How's he doing? Making trouble like the other kids his age?"

"He's a little criminal. He's always pulling one over on me, so cute." He stares into the distance as he recalls his son.

"And what about Amelia? How's she?"

"She's looking for a job. Now that the little one is big enough. She wants to open a business. She'll succeed at whatever she chooses to do."

"She's lucky she has a husband like you who is supportive of her."

"I'm the lucky one, you mean," he says. "I mean, you know her. Can I really ask for more? And don't forget, it's me we're talking about."

"You guys are a real danger to other families, you set such a high bar, that mutual respect... knock on wood..." I respond.

"Don't exaggerate," Nir answers back, smiling. "But seriously, there isn't a day that I don't thank God for setting me up with Amelia. Enough. Next subject. What about you?"

"Fine. Difficult. The girls are mad at me, Nathan is also mad at me. Even I'm mad at me sometimes," I answer with a crooked grin.

"Are you sure this whole business is worth it?" he asks, meaning taking the family abroad for a few years at this particular time.

"I'm sure it's not worth it. I was promised one thing, and it's become another. I'm not home often enough, much less than what was promised me before I set out. It's like buying something at the store and once you pay, there's nobody to talk to."

"There's something to that. But we old timers already know how it works. The question is, have you gotten tired of the work yet?"

"From the work itself, no, from the people I work with, no, but the rest, yes. Not always, but in general. The banality is killing me. The feeling that you're theirs 24/7 doesn't always sit well with me."

"What about the chauvinists? Do they bother you?" He knows why he's asking.

"You know them just as well as I do. They don't scare me, I know what I'm worth. But I get tired of the wisecracks."

Finally the noise around us has died down. I order a tea and Nir is sipping brandy, a beverage with a high alcohol content that is supposed to cleanse the digestive tract after a meal. To me it seems like a punishment.

"This morning I went into the object's offices that are

connected to Hezbollah; it actually constitutes their unofficial representation regarding acquisitions from Europe to Lebanon. The office is officially listed in Arab countries as a real estate agency. I represented large construction companies interested in Kuwait, Saudi Arabia and Lebanon and other countries interested in building modern skyscrapers. The meeting was arranged weeks ago over the phone and email."

"The beginning of the meeting was good. I didn't meet the object, and later my gut told me that wasn't good. The number of questions, the looks, the qualifying language, something didn't add up. Nothing was definitively stated, on the contrary; we scheduled another meeting. The object came into the office a few minutes before I left, but his behavior was extraordinarily aloof.

"I managed to check out the office, the alarms, the locks, the windows, the layout of the rooms, who has what job. We didn't finalize what was to come, and because of my gut feeling, I said to them that I might have to return to the US immediately because of a problem with a different project. That way I can continue on with them or not, whatever we decide."

"Try to be more specific, so that we can determine objectively, beyond your gut feeling," I say.

"Mahmoud, the man I met with, was anxious. He got up and left the room and came back a number of times. He went to consult with somebody. He returned with another man who asked the same questions. They photocopied my paperwork. That's not rare or critical. I had already copied it for them as well as sent it by email."

"You're right. There is nothing definitive here one way or the other, despite the fact that you can't ignore your intuition. For now, don't go near their offices. I'll transfer the information to headquarters and see what they say. They have additional ways to check what was going on with the other side at the time of the meeting. Wait for me at the hotel. I'll call in the morning. If we need to meet, we can meet at the McDonald's at Piazza Republica. Okay?"

Setting a meeting place in advance avoids headaches. McDonald's at the piazza. A large public place with nooks and rooms where we can sit without arousing suspicion.

"Okay, sweetie," Nir says to me. "I hope it works out and that there's nothing happening beneath the surface."

"I hope so, too. But knowing when to stop is also the mark of a true professional."

"Yeah, but who wants to be professional? We want to knock these missions out, no?" Nir said, laughing. The man who was the symbol of perfectionism and professionalism…

We paid and left. Nir, like a true gentleman, waited until I left in my cab before getting out of there.

The cab ride takes about ten minutes. I get out of the cab, walk a bit, check to see that I'm not being tailed, and then take another cab to the center of town in order to speak to headquarters. I know that we have help from an agent that is close to one of the office managers, so maybe I can talk to him to find out if anything unexpected happened. Did anything raise their suspicions in the last few days?

In bed at the hotel, I think about Nir and the guys, and about the feeling that bothers every one of us. Sometimes something isn't right, but you can't prove it definitively. I say that we have to listen to our gut feelings – they are usually right.

I'm reminded of one time in Israel, even before I traveled, I had an uneasy feeling. I couldn't explain, even to myself, what it was or why I didn't want to go on the mission. I lay in bed at night, bag packed and my alarm clock set. In the end, I fell asleep knowing that I couldn't cancel the trip based solely on my inexplicable feelings. *What's the worst that could happen?* I thought to myself. Until then, everything had been fine. Even though we had to get out of Dodge a few times, and sometimes had to cancel things at the last minute, we never got caught. At least, not me.

The telephone woke me up. It was still dark out.

"Hey... sorry about the hour, but I called to tell you that the trip tomorrow has been cancelled," the person on duty said to me.

"Cancelled, why?" I said, trying to sit up in bed. "Did something happen?"

"No. No. We'll talk tomorrow, but there's no need to get up early."

"Okay. Thanks. Good night."

I place the telephone back on the receiver and set my alarm for seven. I'm not travelling tomorrow. I feel relieved, and in one big breath, the evil air rushes out of me and I put my head on the pillow and fall asleep.

The next morning I arrive at the office.

"Good morning, everyone. Well, I'm here, as you all can see. Would somebody kindly tell me what I'm doing here?" I ask with a smile.

"Come in. They'll explain," the department chief says.

"Good morning... from our source, who we call "Flowerbed," we received a tip that shows definitively that they knew in advance that you guys are about to arrive. Their intent was to arrest you upon landing. So the whole thing was called off and looks like it won't happen at all."

"You don't say." Huh. I had to wonder how was I able to feel something like that? Why did l have a feeling of unease about the trip?

"Super lucky," the commander said to me. "What can I say? Lucky we have additional sources who keep us in check so we can put the brakes on."

I'm again reminded of the mantra that all the students in all the various courses over the generations have been told: "We don't come to conclusions based on our suppositions, but on facts alone." We, who try to ensure that our way of thinking and analysis is based on irrefutable proof, find ourselves feeling things intuitively and sometimes acting accordingly.

Thursday

In the morning, my cell phone rings right while I am in the shower. I go out in a towel, dripping wet. My wet footsteps run the length of the floor, and I'm being careful not to slip – it's so annoying when that happens.

"Hello," I hear Alex say. "You're not going to believe what happened. I'm so excited. Can you come over for a visit?"

"Now? It's a bit early, no? I'm in the middle of showering."

"That's funny. Don't go catching a cold on me, now. I'd be happy to meet as soon as you finish your vacation, I have a nice surprise for you."

There's news, I say to myself. Something that can't wait. Alex asked me to call him back immediately, because he didn't want to talk to me on my personal cell phone. I have to call him from a public phone. I dry off, put on some sweatpants and sneakers and head out. My dry mouth and sleepy brain is stunned by the cold morning wind. I have a bad feeling. I break into an easy run that becomes a fast, athletic walk. A morning workout. What we won't do for a cover story. A little fitness. A brisk walk in the fresh air on a fine Roman morning, before the mopeds pollute the small, narrow streets with their noisy stench.

"Thanks for calling," says Alex. "Listen, about last night. We received echoes regarding the screw ups of the band that has been playing these last few days. The musicians didn't play well enough together and it showed. The band manager decided to cancel the tour and return the musicians back home to sharpen up their chops."

"You don't say. I was looking forward to seeing them perform. Too bad."

"It's not because of the lead performer or the wrong notes we talked about last night. It's because of other musicians you don't know. We received reports from various people who brought it to the band manager's attention that he should probably rethink employing them, we can't besmirch the good name of the band."

"Of course not."

According to what Alex tells me, Nir's report from last night isn't the reason for the change. Something happened that doesn't have anything to do with our guys that might impact them in the field. Something that requires a new discussion on how to handle the object.

"I understand. I understand that the decision to send them home immediately has been made," I say. "Do they have to return on the next flight out or can they hang out a bit and do some shopping?" That is, do they have to clear out of the field as fast as they possibly can, or can they wind things up without any pressure.

"They can shop in Israel. We have everything here, and we aren't getting paid for the cancelled shows, so they should come back. Can you organize that?"

The decision was made after a discussion and the approval of all relevant bodies. I have to make sure that they check out of their hotels as fast as possible and go straight to the airport. Each one will fly out in a different direction, and from there fly back to Israel. Alex inserted a code familiar to all into the conversation: get out now. The code also assured me that nobody was in immediate danger.

Shit. Another something that was delayed or canceled before it began. Maybe the information reached us too late. If we'd known, we wouldn't have sent the team in the first place. But better late than never. Now we'll have to come up with a new plan that explains Nir's absence or the delay for the job with the object's office – we need to leave the field clean.

The conversation with Erik was short. I activate the code, and as far as he's concerned, this means he needs to let his spouse know and check out of the hotel and to make sure to book the earliest flight to Zurich, Switzerland, and from there home.

"I'll wait to hear from you…" I say, meaning: after checking out and booking the flights, let me know the details so I can set up a meeting in Zurich with his contact.

Nir answers on the first ring. He had a feeling. The senses are working. I hear disappointment in his voice.

"Keep smiling, honey," I say in English. "There are plenty of fish in the sea. Every setback is for the best." He'll fly back from a different city and will get a detailed explanation in a private meeting. I'd rather he be depressed for another hour. He'll smile afterward.

Last phone call, this time to headquarters. I report that the team is aware of the end of the mission. I have to wait until the last team member leaves Italian soil before I can leave. I go to the closest coffee shop, small and picturesque. I have to have a cup of tea and something to eat while sitting, not standing like the Italians or French. I don't understand standing in a coffee shop all morning, as if that's the greatest thing in the world. I sit in a corner, looking at the tourists sitting beside me, a mixture of languages and excitement. For some reason, the tourists in Italy are always excited.

We all need to get used to the fact that things don't always go smoothly, and sometimes that's a good thing, because it forces us to be prepared, to take care of the details and follow precautionary guidelines. I'm sorry that we have to leave. I also think about Nir who is grilling himself over where he went wrong, how he could have done better. These tribulations are known to every person who works in the business. It's like an old friend of mine used to say: "You'll never make a mistake if you don't do anything." Tomorrow there will be some other mission that will succeed.

After all the administrative work, I turn to my own affairs. Despite the fact that it's Thursday, I can still pop over to my team before the weekend. As I land in Brussels, I call Albert.

"Good that you called. We need to talk," the Old Man says, and I hear stress in his voice.

"In private or collective?" I ask.

"Completely private. Family."

"Tell your friends to come at four. I'll be home in forty-five minutes, see you then."

Albert entered the apartment, closed the door behind him, and with him came a heavy feeling of sadness. "Hi," he says completely despondent.

"What happened?" I give him a half-hug.

"Breast cancer. That's what Dina has. Cancer." He vomits the news out of him. "This whole time she kept it from me, her concerns, and me like an idiot just kept on as usual."

"Oh, man," I say.

"It's been two weeks since she found a lump. She didn't tell me anything. A week ago she went to get checked out, yesterday she received the results. I called to tell her that we need to talk and she burst out crying. Why didn't she say anything? I have to come home immediately." He stood there helpless. I take him by the hand, sit him down in the armchair and sit next to him.

"Joe, I am so sorry, but today, medicine is able to successfully treat a majority of the cases. It's rough, but you'll get through it."

"Yeah, I know. But it's supposed to happen to other people, not Dina. She doesn't deserve this." He leaned back and gripped his head, his eyes becoming damp.

I try to hold back my tears. I hug him gently, trying to think about something smart and comforting to say. "You have to be strong for her, you know," I say quietly. Maybe it was a stupid and annoying thing to say. He's allowed to be weak right here, right now. "Up until now she's been so strong for you."

We called Dina "basalt." She never broke, and nothing was difficult for her. Even though it will be hard for her now, as well as for the whole family, it's only temporary. Women have the strength to take the pain, and Dina is as strong a woman as they come. I believe that. There are people that you know in advance how they're going to act. "What's your plan?"

"I'm catching the train at four. Is that all right?"

"Of course it's all right. I'll be in touch. I also want to come to visit you guys, we need to figure out how, where and what to do. I'll call you when I get home."

"Okay." He stood and gathered himself.

"It'll be fine. We've got our fingers crossed for you," I say. "Have you told the guys?"

"I wasn't able to."

"To tell them?" I ask. It was clear to me that he was afraid of breaking down in front of everybody, so he preferred to remain quiet.

"No," he answered quietly.

"Okay. I also have to report home."

He nodded. We hugged and he left without saying another word.

What a cruel, shitty world, I think to myself and unwittingly clutch at my breast, and then the other, to check if there isn't something I wasn't aware of earlier. That affliction penetrates every part of the body and kills us with excruciating suffering. I'm part of the pessimistic part of the population for whom it isn't a question of "if," but "when." As if it were clear to me that this disease is coming, and every unexplained ache or swelling brings thoughts of death and suffering. They tell me that positive thinking brings good energy and optimism brings success, good health, joy and happiness. I accept that. But how can one stop being full of negative feelings when one isn't feeling well?

The years have turned me into a hypochondriac of the type who doesn't go to the doctor, rather avoids it. It's better not knowing.

Shai, a good friend, contracted a fatal tumor, the largest part of which was inside his brain. It started with throbbing headaches. When we sat in the car one morning, he described his headache to me, and as an expert in migraines, I didn't like what I heard. It didn't sound like anything regular or normal.

"Go get checked out immediately, Shai. That doesn't sound good to me."

"What could it possibly be? It'll pass, probably just a virus." Shai never suffered from headaches, never went to the doctor, wasn't sick and never took pills. After three days, the nightmare still not having passed, he went in for a CT. A "small" tumor, they said at first. He started chemotherapy, had surgery, and more chemo.

The picture of health, athletic, tanned skin and blue eyes. Charming and always smiling. Wonderful husband, father of two girls. At work, he was glued to cell phones the moment they hit the stores. The radiation from these devices, and I have no doubt about this, was the cause of Shai's tumor, which was at the exact angle at which a telephone is held to the ear.

A week after it was discovered, he called me. "Are you going to Roberto's funeral?"

"Yeah, I think so." Roberto was a friend from work who lost his battle with cancer after a few years.

"Can you pick me up? I'm not allowed to drive."

"Yeah, of course."

We got to the cemetery. Many of our friends from work were already there.

"Hey," Shai said to the first one we met. "I've got cancer in my head, have you heard?"

I stood behind him, shocked. Throughout the entire funeral, he informed everybody while smiling with an ease that was difficult to fathom. I had never seen anybody who felt the need to declare his illness like he was doing. Most of our friends didn't say anything, they just looked at him. What was there to say?

My admiration for him grew. Masking the torture he endured, he insisted on coming back to manage a department in the system. Though not an operational department, still, it required a special effort on his part, and I never heard him complain. I guess that things were a little different in his own home. A person can't wear a mask all the time. In a place he feels safe, he can release the pressure, frustration and pain. His wife, daughters and brother stood by his side. Shai's family had a lot of love.

After a few years, still suffering from terrible headaches, Shai passed away, tired from the struggle. I think about him frequently, recall his blue-eyed gaze and smile. Each time his voice echoes the sentence he said to me on the way back from the cemetery: "The only thing that worries me is that I won't get to see my girls grow up and get married."

Unfortunately, we tend to forget tragedies and disasters as part of our defense mechanism. We have to remember that we are here on borrowed time, and the days and weeks pass quickly, and soon after, we move on.

I report the bad news to Yaron. We have to arrange the best care for her, and the team will get a little smaller. There's a knock at the door. Handsome comes in, followed by the Kid. "Hello," they both say, surprised to see me.

"I came back early. We finished there. What about you guys?"

"We're good," says Laurie. "Say, where's Albert? I thought he'd be here, he left the office early without a word."

"No, he's not here. Albert had to go back home. Unfortunately, I have to tell you that we are entering what will be a difficult period. They discovered his wife has breast cancer. Sorry that I'm dropping this on you like this, but I don't know of a good way to deliver bad news."

Laurie sat down in an armchair as if all the air had been taken out of him, and then Ludwig sat down. They looked at each other, then at me. "Since when?"

"Since today. Albert spoke to his wife this morning. We met here two hours ago and then he left."

"He was quiet today. I didn't want to ask, I waited for him to say something," Laurie said, pained. He felt bad for his good friend, his partner.

"Look, I don't know how bad the diagnosis is just yet. In any event, we'll see to it that she gets the best possible care. Let's stay optimistic. Modern medicine has the solutions."

"Of course, we'll do everything we can," says Ludwig.

"You'll have to work a little harder, and Laurie also needs some time at home. We might need some temporary help. We also are taking that into consideration." It's not easy to bring in somebody who fits in, but if we don't have a choice, then that's what we'll do.

"I hope that Albert comes back as soon as possible, and more importantly, that his wife gets better," Laurie says. "I prefer to be optimistic, it's easier that way. I hope we'll figure it out without taking on somebody new," he looks at Ludwig for confirmation.

"Yeah, I agree. Sometimes it's harder to start with somebody new as opposed to making do alone," says Ludwig. Suddenly he feels part of the team and not an outsider.

"We'll prepare a number of alternatives so we can get help on short notice. What about the plan for next week, have you finished it?"

"Almost done. There are a few things to complete."

"In any event, Laurie, you go home tomorrow morning until Monday. We'll meet back here as usual. You, Ludwig, are staying to tend to the fire."

The time is five-o-seven in the evening, and the conductor's whistle signals that the doors are about to close, and we start to move toward Paris. On Thursday afternoon, everything is crowded and slow. Each train has hundreds of passengers, and many of them will return home by cab after. The long line snakes around the stand, everybody waiting silently, albeit impatiently. The steward stops beside me with his cart. This time, afternoon coffee or tea awaits with a fruit salad, small sandwich and piece of cake.

I remember that I haven't eaten in a few hours and my stomach growls in anticipation. After about five minutes, the tray and cup are empty. I lay my head on the headrest. Last night I ate pasta with Nir, and here I am in Brussels, and this evening I'll be in Paris. Time has a different meaning when I analyze the events. I look out the window at the blue sky. The fields are resting after the day's work, and the stalks sway slowly and gently.

Suddenly I notice a couple sitting one row ahead of me. I see them in the long mirror on the ceiling of the car. The angle requires that I lean back in the chair and look up. It's an old habit of mine to always be in control and to observe from the widest possible angles; most people don't notice that there's even a mirror.

The man is hefty with a belly and slicked back hair. On his finger is a big diamond ring and he's wearing a grey suit with a white button-down shirt underneath. An important, serious person. She is in a short, thin dress, her jacket on a small hanger next to the window. She has red hair and fair skin, almost transparent, long arms, and bright red nail polish adorns her fingernails. She takes her shoes off and stretches out her legs, resting her knees on her boyfriend's long legs. What got my attention was her giggling. Giggling is frowned upon in this car. They aren't aware that it's possible to watch them from behind. They feel comfortable because the people next to them are asleep.

I'm spying on them. I feel uncomfortable. I'm too close to the intimacy between two strangers. I can almost touch them, smell them. It turns me on. She takes a package of pralines out of her bag and puts one in her mouth while batting her eyes and smiling. Another praline she places in his mouth with the tips of her fingers. She's giggling and he seems to be enjoying himself.

The next praline she gives him wrapped in a kiss, which causes him to sigh, and she laughs with her mouth full. He puts his hand under her skirt, which lifted up revealing a pair of long, shapely legs. His hand strolls along her thigh, while looking to the sides to make sure they don't have an audience. She cleans the remnants of chocolate off him with her tongue before moving to his neck and ears. I feel uncomfortable for them. Hey, I'm right here...

Her hand is resting on his pants, between his legs. She gently rubs him with short motions, up and down, his head tilted back, his eyes closed. "*Arret... arret...* stop..." he whispers, trying to stop her hand from movi ng.

"Come on," she smiles. "*Encore*. No... more..."

The buttons on his pants are open and she reaches her hand under his underwear. Her other hand reaches for her jacket and she takes it off the hanger and places it over her hand. His face reddens, his breathing becomes heavy. Her face is concentrated, excited and proud that she is getting him off like this. She has him, literally, in the palm of her hand.

Then suddenly, the rest of him stiffens and in an aggressive whisper says, "*Arret!* That's final... stop. That's enough."

She takes her hand out from under the jacket and looks at the people next to them, checking to see if they were caught. "*Porquoi?*" she asks, insulted.

Why? I ask myself. *What, it's not obvious?*

"*Venez ici...* come here," she says, pouting like a little girl.

He looks at her with anger that quickly turns to a smile. He sees her devious eyes and her blushing cheeks and places his hand on her neck. She rests her head on his shoulder and licks his neck, biting him softly. He reaches under her dress and panties and the jacket again censors them. Her head leans back and she starts to moan, grips his arm strongly with her accented red fingers.

I close my eyes. I can't any more, it's already too much as it is. Nobody will believe this story. Another travel experience with pornographic overtones in the train cars of Europe.

One evening, I entered the Thalys train that was the Parisian TGV on the Dutch side. From The Hague to Brussels. I was again in the first class car on orders from headquarters because of criminal activity that took place and it was better not to get mixed up in it. Train stations the world over are a magnet for all kinds of strange activities.

A young man got on the train behind me and sat a few seats away from me. I followed him with my eyes, mostly because he didn't fit the description of somebody who travelled in first class. It didn't look like he had enough money on him for a fare that cost double the regular price. He sat in his seat, his head and hands fidgeting restlessly. These are things that should alert my attention. Surprisingly, I saw the nervous guy pull a sack out of his bag. He looks right and left, and then suspiciously and quickly, he hands the sack to the guy sitting next to him, who is wearing a grey suit. I immediately avert my glance to the window. I didn't see a thing. Didn't hear anything. Didn't smell anything. I didn't say anything.

The guy in the suit put the sack in his bag, pulled out an envelope and handed it to the unkempt guy, and both of them sat back without acknowledging one another. Fifteen minutes later, the train pulls into Rotterdam station. The sloppy guy is first to jump up to the exit. The guy in the suit lets an older woman exit before him. The train stops, and suddenly the disheveled guy goes back to his place and signals to the guy in the suit to sit down.

The doors open and three police officers get on the car. The police check each one of us. They stop next to a young American touring around Europe, whose accent betrays his origin.

An innocent kid making his way on the train, jeans and a heavy coat, high shoes for mountain climbing, and a heavily packed backpack.

"Passport, please," the officer says.

"Please," the fellow answers. He looks like he just awoke from a deep sleep.

"From Amsterdam?"

"Yes, great city," answers the fellow in a friendly tone.

"Come with me to the other carriage," says the officer politely.

I'm dying to stand up and say something. I'm a law abiding citizen, but I remain quietly seated, looking on with the look of a tourist who doesn't understand what's happening. Curious, but not really interested. After about ten minutes, the kid comes back. Half of the contents of his bag in his arms. His clothes are a mess.

"Thank you, and sorry," the officer says politely and backs away.

The kid sits in his chair in shock. In the meantime, two youths pretend to be asleep. Hiding behind their closed eyes. The officers look at them and continue on without saying a word. I discern the furtive glances the two shoot at each other and feel them breathe sighs of relief. There are events that don't end well. Some of my friends were robbed and beaten at train stations in other places. I have luckily never been accosted. In the case with the ice cream in Italy, they made sure to send me a letter of commendation and warned my colleagues to be aware of thieves in Rome. Their flattering words weren't justified. If he would have used force, I wouldn't have been able to withstand him – I can't stand up to a man who is bigger and stronger than I am. Therefore, I always try to appear like somebody who has nothing worth stealing.

The train pulls into its final stop in Paris. I walk quickly past the crowd. I have to talk to Albert. His team members aren't allowed to contact him, only I as the contact person can set up a meeting if necessary. The phone rings for a while. Maybe they went out? Maybe they can't answer? Should I hang up? Try again later?

"Hello?" I hear the young voice of his son.

"Hi, how are you?" I ask softly.

"Good," he answers without worry. It doesn't seem like they told him. "Do you want to speak to my dad?"

"Yes, please, bye-bye." He doesn't have time for idle talk with adults and runs off to play on the computer or watch television.

"Hi," Albert says on the other side of the line.

"Hi, yourself," I answer. "What's up?"

"Not much," he tries to stay calm. In the background I hear him say to his son, "Go out for a moment, it's work. Dina is fine. Everything is out in the open, and she gives me the impression that she has managed to get herself together and muster some strength. You know what a lioness she is," he says proudly and hopefully.

"Yeah, I know. That's good. What do the doctors say?"

"The lump isn't large and there are treatment options. She needs to take a few more tests."

"I talked with everybody at home. You guys can catch the first plane home and finish all the tests there if you want to, or send them the tests and get a second opinion from experts in Israel."

"Dina says that she trusts the doctors here. I'm not so sure."

"Look, in France there are excellent centers for cancer treatment and research. Patients from all over the world come here, so there really isn't anything to worry about. The only difference is that in Israel, they speak Hebrew and it's your home. Apart from that, the office has connections and a lot of help in this area. What do you think, should I come visit tomorrow for an hour or two? Only if it works for you, though. Ask Dina and don't be embarrassed to say 'no.'"

"Wait," he answers and puts down the phone. "Dinush... come here for a sec."

"Hi," I hear Dina's voice. "What do you say about all the trouble I'm causing? Am I keeping you guys from managing your wars undisturbed?"

"Don't be silly," I answer seriously. "Now is the time for your war." A real war. "You're a hero," I say, and mean it.

"You didn't see me before. Scared crybaby," she tells me.

"A hero is not somebody who isn't afraid, rather one who overcomes her fear."

"I heard that you want to come over tomorrow, we'd be delighted. But don't you have a home?"

"I'll go home right after our talk. Tomorrow morning the kids are in school. I'll be home on time. Besides, I really want to come."

"So we'll see you tomorrow morning."

In the meantime, the Thalys (which would become the Eurostar) train from London has arrived, and the station fills up with Brits who came to hang out in the City of Lights for the weekend. They are colorful and raucous, and I'm annoyed about the line and wait time for a cab. A half hour passes before I find myself seated in a cab.

It's seven thirty in the evening and I ring the intercom. I'm too lazy to get my key out.

"Mommmmmmy!" my girls shout out happily.

I am excited to see them, to touch them. A nice warm and relaxing hug. I go up the elevator and when it opens, they jump on me. Lior rolls my suitcase inside, and Shir takes my small bag and coat. How nice it is to be home. Nathan is in the kitchen among the pans. The aroma arouses my senses. My body is hungry... I give him a kiss and rest my head on him, trying not to disturb the chef at work.

"Hi," he says. "We waited for you for dinner."

"I'm starving," I say, happy.

"When did you last eat?"

"I ate something in Rome, and a bit on the train."

"If you ate in Rome, then how did you comeback by train?" Even after so many years, he still finds it difficult to understand how so much travel is possible. Nathan needs rest and a break between things. An organized plan in advance is the name of the game for him.

"Yeah, crazy day. I also have a bit of a headache."

Now *that* he's used to. He hands me a pill and a glass of water. "Drink all of it. You don't drink enough."

"Don't ask," I say in a half-whisper while taking a sip. "Joe's wife Dina has a tumor in her breast."

He knows the people I work with, despite never having met them.

"You don't say. Poor thing. Since when?"

"I only found out today. Tomorrow morning I'm going over to see them and I'll be back around three."

"That's fine, that takes priority."

"I'll prepare letters that you'll send on to Israel, yeah? I won't have enough time to make it to the embassy."

I lean on him. I need the warmth of his body. His hands hug me and give me peace and calm.

"Careful, my hands are dirty," he warns.

"I don't care." I close my eyes and give myself over to the warm feeling enveloping me.

The girls burst into the kitchen and pull me outside with a shout, competing for my attention. I expect an argument or at least a vocal tiff developing.

"Wait, wait. I have something for you guys. Please don't shout, I just took an aspirin for my headache."

They quiet down – they know the drill. They aren't allowed to argue or fight for the first hour of my arrival, until I get used to my surroundings, until my headache passes. I open my suitcase and hand out presents, knowing their responses will be in their eyes. This time I got it right.

"What a pretty bag!" Shir cries out in excitement. "Wow,

home run, Mom. Nobody has anything like this at school!" Her need to be different and unique, familiar to us from day one.

"Cool, Mom, cool! Awesome bag," Lior says. Lucky.

Sometimes I see disappointment in their eyes and I'm sorry I missed. They never complain, but I know. I take out some Chianti that I brought with me from Rome. Nathan is a veritable sommelier, and he always enjoys a good wine. I send Lior with the bottle. I take off my work clothes and put on some old frocks that smell like home. I wash my hands and face.

That's it. I'm home.

"Take a shower," Nathan shouts from the kitchen. "You'll feel better."

"I don't feel like it now. Who has the energy?"

I feel like sitting and listening to the sounds of the house. But quietly. Shir is all over me. Her head resting on me, hands embracing me. Sometimes I feel uncomfortable. I'm supposed to want them around me all the time. It's hard for me to feel like a part of the house each time anew. When I come home, the first thing I do is turn off the radio that Nathan turns on when he comes in. I turn down the television or put it on mute. Quiet. That's what I want and need.

"You don't give us enough hugs and kisses!" the girls complain.

I agree with them. I'm restrained, much more than I used to be. I always had a bit of a cold streak in me. In my parents' home, I was rarely hugged and kissed. I never doubted my parents' love, but also wasn't aware that other people hug and kiss as much as they do. At a good friend's home as a teenager, I discovered how nice it is to hug, the warmth and security. I thought that I would be different with my family, but when the girls got a bit older, I stopped hugging them without noticing. Now, since they started complaining, I try to give them what they, and probably I, also need. I have to learn to hug and be warmer. The job has turned me into a lone wolf.

"Dinner's ready," Nathan calls from the small, French kitchen. There's barely a centimeter between the small table we bought at IKEA and the refrigerator, with the fourth chair being brought in from the living room for when I'm home, and sits up against the garbage cabinet and sink. Everything is compact. Shir shakes me. I fell asleep without noticing, a light sleep. My headache is gone, and I get up and trek to the kitchen to find a festive meal. *My God, how great is this man?* I say to myself.

"Wow," I say. "What is this? Is there some event I forgot about?"

"No. This is how I make dinner every night. Right girls?" Nathan asks with a smile.

"Of course, for sure," they answer merrily. "Usually, it's actually even better."

"After you get to know us, you'll see that it's fun to eat dinner together, and maybe you'll want to stay and not leave all the time," Nathan says with a smile.

The girls giggle. Although that stung, I remain quiet. Why stick it to me? As if I want to disappear from the home all the time. I know I'm almost never around. I know that he didn't mean anything by it, but I can't ignore how I'm feeling. I sit down. Nathan keeps on doing his thing. He looks like a waiter with that dish towel stuck in his pants. He dishes out the food, explains what everything is and how it was prepared, and feels proud. Lior likes her father's cooking. She likes the taste and texture. Shir is stuck on certain tastes. We both like simple food – kids' food.

"Who's going to clear the table," Nathan asks.

"I cleared yesterday," says Shir.

"That's a lie, you weren't even here last night for dinner!" Lior yells.

"Enough, enough," I plead. "Don't give me back my headache. Look, you guys have a schedule for whose turn it is, don't you?"

"We had one but it got lost. Shir is so lazy, I'm tired of it already. In the end, I always have to do everything," Lior complains.

"You don't do very much, so just calm down," Nathan says, getting mad at her. "Don't exaggerate, and let me parent Shir. Okay?"

"Lior in fact does do more. Shir, you need to be a little more considerate," I say.

"You aren't even here, so how would you know?"

"I've known you for a few years now, young lady, if you don't mind," I answer aggressively.

"Let me handle it, please," Nathan says, angry.

"Sure. Okay. I get it." I get up, take my plate and put it in the sink. I leave the room and enter the bedroom where I lie down on the bed. Tears well up in my eyes and I try not to cry. The room is dark. Only the light from the street lights shine through the tree branches and into the window. I'm not even part of my family anymore. Alone.

After fifteen minutes, Lior quietly enters the room and checks to see if I'm sleeping. "Mom, are you okay? Do you have a headache? Can I bring you something?"

"No, sweetie. I'm just a little tired. Let me rest a bit, okay?" I say to her quietly.

"Okay, Mommy," she says and kisses me gently on my cheek, tiptoes out of the room and closes the door so that I won't hear the voices from the next room.

I feel shitty. This feeling that I don't belong is killing me. I know that Nathan didn't say what he said in order to hurt me, but deep down, he's mad that I'm interfering. He's angry at the system that brought us to the point where we have become disconnected, and he's angry that there isn't even anybody to be angry at, or anywhere to discharge that pent up anger.

The girls take a bath. Tomorrow is a school day, so they have to get organized. The wall behind me is quiet. Nathan finished doing the dishes and cleaning up the kitchen, thank God. The walls in the house are all made of drywall and there's no way to hide anything.

Shir enters the room in her pajamas that I bought for her in London. She smells like flowers and looks like a little angel.

"Mom, are you asleep?"

"Hmm..." I don't have any desire to talk. I can say whatever I need to with grunts and groans.

"Can I get into bed with you?"

"Mmm..." I answer. She gets under the covers quickly, before "good mood" mom changes her mind. She cuddles with me and I end up hugging her with both hands. She doesn't give an inch.

"Are you mad at me?" she asks, obsequiously.

"No," I answer her softly. "I just have a bit of a headache." I know that it's wrong of me to take my mood swings out on them. So stupid. I'm ashamed and hide behind headaches that have become excuses to act childishly.

Lior bursts in having just brushed her teeth. "Move over a little," she says to Shir.

"Come to the other side, I want to be in the middle," I say. "Just without fighting, okay? Otherwise I'll throw you both out," I threaten.

Shir falls asleep and Lior drifts off. I look at them, relaxed and peaceful. I stroke their soft hair. Nathan comes into the room and says, "All right, everybody into their own beds. I'm not planning on carrying anybody. There's school tomorrow!"

That works immediately. The girls jump up, hair strewn about, eyes shut. They each give me a hug and a kiss and go to bed. Nathan changes clothes and puts on a pair of sweatpants. He must have come straight from the embassy and not had time to change clothes. *You're disgusting*, I think to myself. *Go over to him, smile, enough already with the tension and being offended. He didn't even mean anything by it.* But I just keep lying in bed without moving a muscle or saying a word.

Nathan leaves the room and I hear him sitting in the living room, playing with the remote control. He's probably looking for a basketball or soccer game to watch. *You have to put an end to this. It's hard on everybody, not just you,* I think to myself again. But I work so hard, there's a very good reason that I'm never home. I'm sick of my not belonging being thrown back in my face every time I have something to say. *So then tell him that's what you feel, don't just stick yourself in bed. It would be a shame to screw up the whole weekend, but that's what's going to happen, and all because of your stubbornness and passive aggressiveness.* It's tough with me. That's how I summarize it between me and myself.

I grudgingly get out of bed, put on my worn-out slippers, which I love, like the rest of my tattered old clothes, clothes that symbolize to me home and security. I sit on the sofa opposite him and he continues watching the damn game like it's the most important thing in the world right now.

So, I came. I got out of bed and came over to him. So what? I continue my conversation with myself. *Go ahead, do something, do it like you mean it and not like somebody's forcing you. You've missed him when you weren't at home, and he hasn't done anything wrong.* I try convincing myself. *At least have him give me a sign that he's interested*, I say to myself again. *What gives, are you in high school?* I ask myself mockingly.

"So," I turn to Nathan," is this what we're going to watch this evening? Soccer?"

"It's what I'm watching," he answers, angry. "Do you want to watch something else?" he turns to me, his eyes hard.

"It's all in fucking French anyway," I answer quietly.

"Yeah, true. Fuck. I forgot that in Holland it's in English. More fun."

"What are you trying to tell me? That we should go back there? That's it's better for me there?" There I go making things worse.

"If that's what you want, it just seems like there is better for you than here." His gaze is rooted to the screen.

"Much..." I say, and fall silent.

The game continues and the ball bounces from player to player, foot to foot, forward and backward. Nobody scores a goal and nothing changes. *Stupid game. Life is aggravating*, I say to myself again. This isn't working, he won't budge, better to just go to bed. I get up slowly, hoping he'll say something. A small word that will bring order and happiness to our home.

I fall asleep quickly despite being rather worried. My soft pillow. I'm in bed under the comforter with Nathan's smell. I'm home. I wake up when Nathan comes into the room. He climbs into bed wearing an undershirt and underwear, and turns his back to me. I'm at home with his back to me.

"That's it?" I ask him and wait for his answer. "No response?"

"What do you want?"

"Nothing," I go back to being an iceberg.

"So, good night?" he says quietly.

"Are you mad at me?" I ask, when what I really mean is that I'm angry. I have the right, he doesn't.

"Are you joking? Seriously, have you no shame?"

"Me? What should I be ashamed of? Is this how you treat guests in your home?"

"You're mad that I mentioned that you aren't here often enough to be judging anything, and you think you're a guest? I don't understand you."

"You make me feel like I don't belong with how you react sometimes," I try to explain.

"The feelings are yours, don't try to put them on me. You act like a guest. Everybody needs to walk on eggshells when you come home. I suggest you check yourself."

"You're trying to hurt me because you're mad at me," I say quietly.

"I'm trying to hurt you? That's why I came home and made a nice dinner in your honor? I didn't even have time to take a piss, and what do you do? Get all upset about a single reaction that might have been a bit out of place."

"You don't understand that that small snub hit me right in my conscience?"

"Fine, but an extreme response that blows things out of proportion? Every time you come back you bring a bomb with you. We just want to have a good time when you come home."

"You're right about that. But even so, you have this anger that jumps out without you noticing and it hurts."

"You annoy me, so I get angry. Tell me, you want me to greet you with the face you put on after not being here for a week? A face that's tired and estranged?" His tongue was a whip.

"Very tired. That's right, I had a tough week."

"I understand that. I understand that all the time. But I have gotten to understand it so well that I'm beginning to think that it's making me stupid. I want you to also understand." This time he didn't let it go.

"Nathan," I say in a voice that trembles a bit, "think a bit about what you're saying, about how you're saying it." I try not to let his words get to me so much.

"I'm sick of it. I'm alone all week. Take care of things, take them to school, clean up, work, go grocery shopping, talk with the girls about what's going on with them, and what comes from all of it? Even when I'm not alone, I'm alone. Even then I clean up after everyone, and end up sitting in front of the television alone."

"You're right, and I'm right, too. But you're a little more right." I relent. This is my pathetic way to admit that I was wrong. "So how does it help to sleep back to back?" I try to suck up to him.

"At least get a good night's sleep, you're tired, aren't you?" He won't back down.

"Who can fall asleep feeling like this?" What about our rule we made when we first got together that we wouldn't go to bed mad?

"I don't want to argue with you. You always drag me to places I don't want to go. Don't you understand that?"

"So then why don't you lead the discussion and drag me along behind you."

"I don't have the energy for that either." Stubborn.

"Fine. So let's just be at odds and be done with it," I answer.

A childish argument stuffed with lots of frustration and complications that a couple who leads a strange life encounters. We are lying in bed. Each one looking at the ceiling with thunderous silence. We wordlessly trade blows. He turns to face me suddenly. Hug, no-hug.

"Stop. Enough with the nonsense already," he says, now sucking up to me.

"You always – beyond being as cooperative and supportive as anybody can expect, and I mean that truthfully – try to slip in some comment that brings my guilty conscience to the surface. As if you're constantly trying to tell me over and over that I'm not okay."

"Maybe you're right. I don't know. I know that you not being here isn't your fault. On the other hand, being alone all the time is very hard on me."

"We both know that we're stuck with this thing, and that we can't do anything about it. If we break, what good will that do? I need you to have my back, to give me the strength to continue. My conscience is killing me as it is, and it's not easy missing you and the girls so much. But that wasn't my intention when I entered the service. My career, as far as I'm concerned, doesn't come first. Everybody who really knows me knows that."

Friday

The alarm wakes me up too early. Without opening my eyes, I can smell the familiar scent of my pillow, soft and pleasant, and I curl up in the fetal position. I'm happy. Nathan is caressing my body, hugging and pulling me against him, and I relish the contact, the warmth and the feeling of belonging.

"You're traveling today, aren't you? The earlier you head out, the earlier you can come back." He smiles at me. That's how it goes after making up. Everything is nice and pleasant. A rekindled love.

"Y...eah. You're right, but I don't feel like getting up. This is nice. Warm and soft," I indulge myself a bit.

"Not for long. If you stay here in bed, then you'll have to face the consequences of your actions." Nathan began applying them immediately. His hands wandered the length of my body. I feel my body start to come alive long before my head even knows that it's morning.

"I wish," I say, "but that will take too much time, and time is not something we have at the moment," I say as I sit up.

"Too much time?" Nathan asks, feigning shock. "Can I prove that it doesn't have to take long?"

"If it's quick, then I'm not interested. Save your strength for when I get back, and then we can take as long as we need," I say and jump out of bed.

"That's what I do when you aren't here. I save it for later," Nathan says and twists up his face.

"That's what you tell me. But I wonder what you really do," I say, and giggle.

"Me? I'm a monk who has taken a vow of silence," he says, seriously.

"That the monks don't speak in the monastery, I know, but beyond that, it's anybody's guess." I lie down on top of him. "Let's see you not say anything now."

"I love you," Nathan mouthed to me silently.

I kiss him lovingly. Words are cheap anyway. I think of my mother who never knew how to express affection. An inexplicable handicap. It is clear to me that I inherited that defect. Otherwise, there's no real explanation for my inability to express my love.

I take a hot shower. I wash my hair and rub lotion on my body. I take my time and enjoy the moment without rushing. In the hotels, the shower is a place where you wash up and go without delay. In the background I hear the girls waking up. I have to hurry because this small shower is the only one in the apartment, and everybody has to use it.

Nathan is packing sandwiches and we are drinking our morning coffee and tea quickly. The girls run to the neighbors who drive them to school, Nathan heads to the subway on his way to the embassy, and I catch a cab to the train station on my way to Lyon. At the station in Lyon, I find a small grocery store and buy some cheese, smoked salmon and olives, and at the bakery next door, I buy whole grain *baguettes*. In my bag is some Leonides chocolate – it was the least that I could do. I get on a bus and on the way enjoy the blue skies and special vitality of France, a gentle breeze against my face.

I arrive at Joe's building. I take the elevator up to the third floor and ring the bell.

"Hey." A kiss on the cheek. The French kiss twice, once on each side, and we elected to go with half of that, which is a stretch even for us.

"Are you good?" I ask Joe.

"I will be. At the moment, I'm trying to get past the first stages of shock," he whispers. "The kids are at school, it's just the three of us here."

"Okay. We have two options. One, go grab breakfast, or two, we eat what I brought."

"Dina will decide," Joe says and calls, "Din... shall we go out for breakfast or stay in with the pile of groceries we just received?"

Dina comes into the room. Calm, peaceful. She's dressed in white, made up as if it was just an ordinary day. I hug her gently. What can you say to somebody who you just want to be all right?

"I'd actually rather stay in. I'm hungry and I don't feel like grabbing a coffee and a croissant." She's right. Here, there is no Israeli breakfast; the most one can get is a *croque monsieur* or *croque madame,* a grilled sandwich with pork salami and cheddar cheese, the only difference being that the monsieur is more like French toast and the madame has a fried egg on top.

"Great," I say. "Sit, I'll make it." I want to spoil them a little bit.

"No, you're not making breakfast. You are our guest, I'll make breakfast," Dina says, making her way to the kitchen.

"I have a solution. The three of us will make breakfast, and chat while we do it," I say, following after her. "I hope there's room for all three of us in your kitchen – I know there isn't in mine."

"No. Sit in the living room, and I'll make you two something to drink. Let a man humble himself," he said and smiled his smile that drove all the girls crazy at various times during his life.

"Dina, first of all, you have warm regards and the best of wishes for your continued health from everybody, management and friends. We'll do whatever we can to help out." Even though

I hadn't actually talked to anybody at headquarters about it yet, but in this respect, our system is solid. Picking it up when we need to.

"Thanks, I know," Dina said with a small smile.

"The department that handles medical matters makes inquiries about the best hospitals here and in Israel. At the end of the day, it's your decision. Any choice is a good one, it just depends on your personal preferences and any family issues that may factor in."

"I wasn't sure when talking with Joe yesterday. I think that the right thing at this point is to finish all the tests here. We started here, so it's better to finish here. And the kids, we'd prefer to keep them here with their friends. We haven't told them anything yet. I want to know what the procedure is first, how long treatment will last and its effectiveness. The tests will be finished on Monday, and the results will arrive up to ten days after. Of course, I want to get a second opinion from doctors in Israel, especially regarding which hospital to be treated in."

Dina sounds on point, calculated and even a bit aloof, as if she were talking about somebody else.

"It's not a problem. Joe will stay at home as long as necessary and until you decide what you're doing. Don't worry about work, just do what is best for you. And anything you need, you just ask."

"Thanks. For now, we're fine. Maybe it's even better for Joe to go back to work. I think it's hard for him to be here. He's worried and stressed out."

"Joe wants and needs to be a part of everything you're going through. At work, he would just worry more. Don't push him away. I know you've gotten used to being independent, but now isn't the time. You both need to be there for each other." I am giving my opinion, one woman to another. I hope she doesn't think that I'm being intrusive.

"Yeah, maybe, but he'll go crazy with nothing to do here. You know him, he can't sit still." She continues thinking about him instead of thinking about herself. Or maybe not?

"We aren't talking about months, just the next week or two. Get past this stage and then decide. Don't waste your energy worrying about him, save it for you."

"I just want to know what I'm up against, to make whatever decisions and get on with fighting this battle. I'm strong, you know."

She sounds strong, and that was great. Even if it is just an act, it helps. She can't break. I believe that. If you get up bummed out but keep smiling, it will put you in a better mood. Autosuggestion. It's a great way to solve problems, and also to cause them.

"Dina, you're the strongest woman I know. Everyone admires you. The truth is, I'm thinking about Joe now. He's also in this business, almost as much as you are. You guys are family. He needs this time with you and the kids. He wants to feel like you need him. At the office, he isn't the same." I want her to understand that just because she agrees to let him stay home, it's not an admission of weakness or neediness on her part. It's important for her to continue to project strength and independence.

"It's hard for me. He's always talking about what's going to be, and I prefer to keep quiet. I don't want to analyze it too much; I just want to wait for the results and then come to a conclusion."

"I understand, but maybe he's still in shock. Give him a chance. Explain to him how you want things to be handled. Tell him that you need quiet. He'll understand. I'm certain."

They have already forgotten how to communicate with each other. It happens to everyone. Last night was a good example of this. How much easier it is to see other people's problems as opposed to our own.

"Yeah, talking's not my thing," she said quietly with a smile that was somewhat sad. "So this is what happens when the husband or wife is on the road, eh? We've all been there. At first, it's the alone that kills you, the quiet, and then you learn to enjoy it, until the quiet becomes a part of you and you can't do without it. Dime-store psychology, but that seems to be our reality, at least, as far as I can tell."

"Something like that. After many years of being alone, I need my quiet, for independence, like air to breathe. Where was Joe when the kids were born? When they cried and got sick? He wasn't by my side when I grieved for my mother, or when my nephew was killed in a military mishap. He doesn't know how I deal with things because he's never been around." Dina leaned her head back as her fingers fidgeted with the tissue in her hands. "Even he says that. When he was young, it was extremely convenient to run away to work. Today, he feels like he missed out on life, the feeling of being part of a family, experiencing things together. He actually talked to me about that just recently. That's his most painful regret, that feeling of missing out."

I'm supposed to keep these conversations about Joe between us, but Joe would approve of me telling her in this case. He needs to reconnect with his wife, whom he loves with all his heart. He needs to feel that he is part of a family, including the day to day aspect of it.

"Too bad these insights come later. Joe caused us to create a world of our own, a world where he's just a guest."

"Better late than never," I say, and immediately chide myself for saying it. That sentence always sounds like a pathetic excuse. Something that somebody says when they don't have anything better to say.

"I'm not so sure. If he didn't suddenly feel like that, I'd find myself alone in this fight, doing it my way, quietly, just me and myself," she says somewhat coldly, her thoughts wandering.

I don't have an easy answer. I understand both of them and the difficulties that our work causes. "A psychologist once told me that people in our line of work, who are away from home so much, learn to live just fine with themselves as long as they spend time in different circles. The difficulty starts when they return to everyday life and come home every evening. Their wives, over the years, get used to living alone, caring for the kids, taking care of the bills and all matters of the home. The men enjoy their license to be free from all responsibility. It's when either side's independence is threatened that the problems begin. The balance has been upended, and most people aren't able to deal with the change."

"We know a fair number of couples like that," Dina says with half a smile.

"But both of our families are still here. I was once an emissary's wife, and now I'm an emissary. I'm one of the few who can see both points of view of this issue, and I can tell you that both sides suffer the same amount, despite the fact that each side thinks that they are the injured party." I feel stupid when I think about the drama I caused Nathan yesterday. What a waste of time.

"You know what?" I ask Dina. "I need to get rid of this feeling of being alone and start acknowledging his way of doing things. I mean, I am going to need his help, he's the love of my life and my best friend."

She smiles and sits down in a chair. "I have tremendous love for my man. Let's go eat something. I'm hungry." Dina gets up and puts her hand in mind. "Hey, chef, is the food ready? We're starving in here." Dina hugs Joe from behind as he sets the table. He extends his hands toward hers and looks at her with a smile. "What did you make us?" Dina asks, "It smells great, I can only imagine."

"I hope you can do more than just imagine," Joe says, giving her a look that seems to have a double meaning.

"Shall I go for a walk and come back later?" I chuckle.

"I meant her appetite. You and your dirty mind. Dina needs to eat healthy," Joe says to me with a rebuking grin.

We sit down to eat. The atmosphere is relaxed and pleasant.

The fresh baguettes are still a bit warm and the crust crackles as we tear into them. The dough is still soft, melting in our mouths. A huge, seasoned omelet and a finely chopped salad with tomatoes, cucumbers, bell peppers and onions, on which Joe sprinkled feta cheese. He set out a plate of French cheeses, including a runny camembert, and those little round garlic cheeses with their red wrappers. Pink salmon strips and canned pickles from Israel, seasoned black and green olives and a carafe of freshly squeezed orange juice, tea brewed with mint and lemongrass leaves, and cups of strong, black coffee.

"Bon appetit, girls."

"Bon appetit," we answer together with big smiles on our faces.

We eat, talk, laugh, and the food is quickly devoured. At the end of the meal, each one of us holds a warm drink.

"I can't move," I complain.

"Who asked you to move?" Joe asks. "Rest, drink. Take a load off."

"Joe, you've been appointed to make all our meals," I say.

"Looks to me like you guys are having a lot of fun hanging out and working a little..."

"Hanging out? Fun? Us?" says Joe and turns to me. "You tell her."

"Hanging out is not what we do, Dina," I say with a smile.

"Oh, that's a relief." She's smiling at us. Of course.

"Well, guys, the food I have eaten, the tea I drank. I won't end up getting a nap in today, and I still have things to do. I guess I should go," I say and get up reluctantly. I don't want to leave.

"Thanks for coming," Dina says to me and gives me a warm hug and a kiss on each cheek.

"Thank you for having me, be brave and strong. We'll be in touch, of course," I say and give her a hug and walk to the door, where Joe is waiting for me. "We'll talk on Monday. If there is something, anything, you'll know where to find me, right?"

"Of course, and thanks. Best regards to our friends. I hope to see them soon."

I board the train and ride from Lyon back to Paris. The food made me tired. I'm not used to eating such a heavy breakfast and try to stay away from them.

When I was discharged from the army, I began studying at the Hebrew University. In a conversation with my brother, I complained, "This isn't for me right now. I don't have the patience. It doesn't interest me." My matriculation scores were so average that they didn't give me much of a choice. I went to study because that's what everybody did.

"There is something for you, if you'd like," my brother said. "I won't explain, just know that it's hard to get accepted."

"I trust you." My brother was part of the Ministry of Defense, and that was enough for me. I wanted to run away from the university, and it seemed like a good solution.

I got to the first interview, the second, the third, I was checked out by a psychologist, various tests and more interviews. After a month and a half, I sat in the company of twelve recruits at a festive start to the course, where all I knew was that the course would last more than a year. Adventures and surprises I like, they are the essence of life. Let's go...

"Welcome to the Mossad Institute for Special Positions," said the man presenting himself as the head of the instructional department. What did he say? The Mossad? Where am I? What am I doing here? My brother brought me here? Is he here too?

"I congratulate you, men and woman," he said turning to me, the only woman sitting at the table, "on reaching this day. I'm sorry about the long process, some of you have been waiting almost two years for this course." I look at the other members, trying to spot the suckers who waited around.

The man continued. "But it was hard to find you guys, the best among those we met. As proof, we strove to have two women join, but only managed to find one." He looked at me and smiled. Me? I'm just a regular person. Lousy matriculation scores, not a genius, and not particularly brave...

"To be a part of the Mossad is an honor, but it's also a responsibility and requires dedication and hard work. You have a long year of studying ahead of you. We're not talking about a nine-to-five job here. You may start every day at nine a.m., but it's anybody's guess what time you'll finish, sometimes at nine in the morning the next day."

I look around me. The room is full, but there are only two women besides me. One of them interviewed me on the first day and the second I don't recognize. It's a refreshing change from my time in the army where I was in a predominantly female environment.

"Right now, I don't intend to tell you what you're going to learn in the course. That you'll discover every day in class. The process is not just to teach and mentor, but also to select. Not everybody will reach the finish line, some of you won't work out, or won't want to stay. It's a two-way test."

I won't be here long, I think, *because I don't have all these wonderful characteristics. What do I possibly have to offer?*

The man described the system and its function as part of the greater security establishment: the division of labor between the Shin Bet and the Mossad, the various departments of the Mossad, especially the operations division. *Who can remember all this?* I think to myself, still stunned that I'm actually sitting here.

He concluded by introducing us to the course commander and his right-hand man: two people about thirty-five years old, maybe forty. The course commander had an operational background that began in the Shin Bet, and after that, when he transitioned to the Mossad, he accumulated a record of successful operations abroad. A cool fellow with an easy gaze. His assistant was a bit younger, pudgy with smiling blue eyes.

"I won't drag this out," said the course commander. "You guys are a bit stunned by the status. Just allow me to present to you the names and positions of those you'll be getting to know better over the next year." He turned our attention to the various attendees who nodded as he pointed them out: department heads, deputies, and professional instructors.

"You'll meet these people over the duration of the course, and obviously on the job in another year. I wish all of us an enjoyable learning experience, hard work and a high level of motivation. Good luck!" said the commander. "Oh... I almost forgot the most important thing. We are headed downstairs, where there are refreshments waiting for us at the entrance. Each morning at ten and also at four in the afternoon, the course coffee cart – which has our famous sandwiches – will be available for us in the kitchen. Drinks, *halva* and chocolate. So let's go, bon appetit."

We stood there somewhat awkwardly. The people who were introduced to us came to shake our hands, give us a clap on the shoulder, and a special gesture just for me – they stroked my cheek and hair. A tall wagon was waiting for all of us downstairs, like in a kibbutz or in the army, and it had tea and coffee urns, and in addition to the usual daily fare, there was also sponge cake.

For the first few days, everything was new and different. Long, exhausting lectures on intelligence units in Israel and abroad, the status of Israel and its enemies and allies, assignments that have been placed on the Mossad's shoulders. Already during the first week, we went into "the field." We were split up into pairs, and each pair had its own defined assignments. My partner was the oldest in the course, a thirty-four year old guy who was very tall with curly hair, smiled often and, as it turned out, a really good guy. He came from the north, and me from a small town – basically, two trainees who were unfamiliar with the big city, Tel Aviv.

"Where's north?" he kept asking every time we turned onto a new street. "Where's north?"

"Remember everything according to the list that I gave you," said the instructor. "Tomorrow, first thing in the morning, there's going to be a test that will check what you picked up on and what you didn't."

That's a lot of pressure. How do you remember every payphone, park, public structure, coffee shop, one-way street, bus number, exact location of streets and their names? At home, late at night, I sketched a map of the area, recreating every detail according to the list. I discovered that I had a good visual memory, but what will happen by tomorrow morning? I'll probably forget everything by tomorrow.

Course members bonded during breaks. During breakfast, lunch, and especially at the ping-pong table. I started playing ping-pong when my head barely reached the top of the table. My ability at ping-pong improved my standing, which wasn't high to begin with seeing as how not everyone was thrilled with the idea of a young girl joining the exclusive course.

In the second week of the course, we were split into three groups. The purpose of the exercise was to determine our ability to think operationally, how well we assimilate into the field, self-confidence, ability to improvise, to keep one's cool and to learn from mistakes and fix them. One by one, the commander took each of us aside and gave us our assignments.

"You have to go into this men's shoe store and stay there until you get a signal from me. You have five minutes to decide what you're doing there."

Why think about it and plan? I thought to myself. *I'll just go in and figure it out.* After a few minutes, the commander came back and said, "Well, Miss, what's your plan?"

"I'll just figure something out. What's the big deal?"

"No, improvisation is good only when you don't have a choice. You have to be in control, and leave as little as possible for the other side. A plan of action is the basis for everything we do in this line of work."

I entered the store and explained that I'm waiting for a friend.

I looked around and realized there wasn't much to look at. I started feeling a bit uncomfortable, but stuck to the mission. He left me hanging out to dry there for a reason, I suppose.

"How was it?" he asked after letting me out.

I told him exactly what I saw, every single detail.

"Very good," he said, and that made me feel good about myself.

I discovered that I was pretty good at field assignments. I also understood that women are allowed to do almost anything without arousing suspicion or antagonism. The guys had a hard time, some of them did not find the assignments easy at all.

Life in the course wasn't easy. I felt singular. I found myself grouped with the folks who were less popular. The elite group was made up of two pilots, two naval officers and an engineer who also had a black belt in karate, and they arrogantly looked down on everybody else. Over time, we understood that it was the guy who knew four languages, had lived in Europe as a child, and was generally open-minded who had better skills for this job. I learned that people can be excellent on paper, but completely different in reality.

Only ten of us finished the course. The naïve girl from the small town was gone. I was smarter, had more confidence, and was more mature and assertive. I traded my sandals for heels and my jeans for fashionable skirts and jackets. I felt like the work gave me more than any academic institute could have. At twenty four, I was a woman out in the world. I moved to Tel Aviv and even managed to buy myself a car. But when I would come back from trips abroad to an empty refrigerator and a locked door, there was nobody to greet me. I was on the move all the time, tired from being on the road and lonely. A girl from a small town who just wanted warmth and love.

That's it. I'm home, the weekend has begun. The door opens and the girls scamper happily into the house, throwing their bags and coats in the hall. The wood floor creaks with every step. Mom's home. Nathan got home in the afternoon and brought with him the weekend edition of the Israeli newspaper. Friday afternoon with an Israeli fragrance.

This evening, we are all invited over to Hani's. The day we moved into the apartment and unloaded our things, Hani went over to Nathan and introduced herself. Hani arrived with her husband Joel and their two kids to work for El Al in Paris. They became like family and the kids got along great. Nathan and Hani became drivers that chauffeured the kids back and forth from the Israeli school. We shared Friday night dinners, holidays, weekend excursions, and even went on vacations together.

We arrive in our Shabbat clothes with a bottle of wine and a cheesecake. *Kiddush*[2] is more exciting abroad. Joel makes the blessing, all of us stand. Friday night kiddush in the Diaspora connects us with our roots, to our heritage and our essence. I don't believe in God, but I like the tradition. The traditional Friday nights take me back to my childhood, to my family and I feel an inexplicable pinch in my heart each time.

Dinner ends, the kids are playing in their rooms, and the four of us decide to go out. We head into the streets of Paris, the city of lights. There's nothing more fun than simply walking around and opening one's eyes. At this time of night, I love going to the eastern side of the city on the banks of the Seine. We pass by the Louvre, illuminated in all its glory, and arrive at San Michel. The lights on the old, sculpted bridges are breathtaking. The old buildings look out at the river, which is flowing in the opposite direction than we're heading. Our bar is on the second bank; we managed to find a parking spot that opened up close by – a rare occurrence indeed.

We go into the tiny bar and sit in a dark corner. Next to the piano is a singer with a phenomenal voice. The men order beers, Hani orders coffee, and I have a vodka with orange juice, the only

---

2   Blessing made over wine to sanctify the Shabbat.

alcoholic beverage I like because I feel it's warmth as it slides down my throat, and afterward, I am relaxed and smiley. A pencil thin girl joins the singer and a monstrous voice erupts out of her. I like *chansons*. The melody, the language and the accent. I learned this musically guttural language and it penetrated my soul. I lean my head against Nathan and close my eyes, letting the music and the warm drink to help me relax and feel good. Serenity.

The French simply understand the secret of the good life, and we Israelis have to take a page out of their book. They know how to eat well, to appreciate a good wine, to rest and not just work incessantly. The go on vacation five times a year, primarily to resort towns or neighboring countries. It's so different from the lifestyle Israelis have, both in our daily life as well as on vacation: work ourselves to death and then visit five countries on a vacation that is basically one long shopping spree. The French discovered the delicate balance of work and leisure. My thoughts are interrupted by a gentle nudge... turns out I fell asleep.

"Hey, lady, you fell asleep," Nathan says to me.

"Huh..." I stretch with an indulgent smile on my face.

"Let's go home, it's late," he says and helps me up.

We head out into the freezing cold outside. Good thing the car is close by. We get in the car and immediately turn on the heat. Despite the exhaustion that seems to have overtaken me, I look out at the streets, buildings and lights. The city of magic. There's something about this city I can't explain that causes me to miss it even while I'm still here. At home, the kids are asleep in Lior's room on the bed and on the floor. They enjoy each other's company, and I smile to myself. I take a shower to get the stench of cigarette smoke off of me. I have to wash my hair and air my clothes outside on the balcony in order to feel clean. I get into the cold bed and try to use my still-warm body from the hot shower to thaw it out The window is open because I need fresh air, which is obviously just an illusion in Paris, proven by the grimy filth stuck to the wallpaper.

    I'm drifting off but trying to wait for Nathan who, even in the shower, is incapable of being quick. Everything with him is chill. He comes out with a damp towel, the steam enwrapping his body like an aura. He's warm and smells like soap as he sprawls under the covers. He's content. We're content. Peaceful. A feeling of being together, safe. Leg on leg, holding hands. Connection. Every corner of us is familiar, every feeling. That scent, this specific temperature. The sensation of legs enwrapped, the arousal, the desires are obvious. The ability to go full out, not hiding, out in the open. We fall asleep together silently into the sweet world of dreams. I love you, us. Who would have thought that this would be the last night before everything changes...

Shabbat

"**Mom, get up, Dad, get up!**" Lior is standing in the doorway. "It's eight-thirty, Dad, you have to make schnitzel for the trip."

I open my eyes. I'm home. It's Shabbat. Trip. Schnitzel. Get up. In a minute. I close my eyes.

"Lior, five minutes," Nathan says. "Five more minutes and then come back to make sure we're up."

"Five minutes are up, it's eight thirty-eight." Lior lies down between us. Shir gets into bed. Shabbat. Kids.

"Let us wake up quietly," Nathan said from under his pillow, annoyed. He's not a morning person.

"Dad, get up, get up, get up," Shir says, pounding his back with her feet.

"That's enough, Shir, sweetie. Let Dad wake up, go get dressed. We're getting up."

An hour passed before we headed downstairs, the other families waiting for us. The men decide on the first meeting point, Lior and her friends get into our car while Shir rides with her friends in their car. My work phone rings. It's a call from Israel. Something happened.

"Hello..."

"Shabbat shalom, can we talk?" I don't recognize the voice.

"One second," I say and move to the side. "I'm with you."

"Something happened that isn't related to your immediate job. We need help. You have to get to the red telephone in the embassy as fast as you can."

"Okay," I answer. "Who do I ask for?"

"Let the attendant on duty know that you've arrived and they'll contact you."

"I'll ride with the girls," Nathan says. "We're used to it, no?" His smile is one of solidarity.

I go up to the apartment and change clothes and I'm on my way.

"What's up?" The embassy security guard has been in Paris for two years and remembers me from the days when I used to come here more often. "It's Shabbat, what happened, did a war break out?" he asks.

"Haha... right..."

"All right, have a good day," he says.

I go up. There is always one of us on site. He opens the door to my office for me and I enter and pick up the red telephone. "Hello? I was told to call," I say to whoever is on duty. "Can you transfer me to whoever I need to speak to?"

"Yes, they're waiting for you. Hold the line."

"Hello?" says a voice from the other side. "N speaking." The deputy chief of the Mossad is calling me directly. What the fuck???

"The daughter of the head of the Mossad is on a class trip to Poland. Last night she went missing." *What does this have to do with me?* I ask myself. "There are a few directions this investigation can take. I'm sending you all the material we have, for your eyes only. One option is that she arrives in France or Belgium, and you consolidate the matter in Paris. Please go over the paperwork and get back to me. We can continue from there."

"Understood," I say. "I'll read it and call you back."

I go back to the person on duty to see if there is anything for me in the hall.

"Yes, it just arrived. I'm sending it to you now."

I go up to my office and open the file. What's the connection between Poland and France? Who is this girl? I feel for both the head of the Mossad and his wife. I think about Lior and Shir. The first letter contains the schedule for when the class was to visit the concentration camps. The second one had the names of the kids, teachers and accompanying adults. The third one contains personal information on Noa, the Mossad chief's daughter. I read everything twice. After about an hour I call N back.

"I read it..."

"The most relevant option as far as we're concerned is that the identity of the girl was obvious to whoever took her, and that we'll hear from them soon. But we have to try to look at every possibility. Paris is extremely relevant in her case, because maybe she chose to run away and meet her boyfriend."

"Are you sending me a team?"

"They're already en-route. What I'm asking is that you begin making some inquiries and then later meet with the head of the team. The meeting details and names are already waiting for you. Beyond that, you have to be in touch with David, who will be the coordinator at headquarters. He will report on the developments in real time. Saul will be the coordinator in Poland and is already there with his team. They will go over the material, investigate whoever they can together with the local police. One thing is clear. Not a word. The media can't know. We are even weighing delaying the group's return. Not a word, not even to our forces."

"Understood."

"Take one of the phones that hasn't been used before and give us the number. We'll be in touch. Good luck to all of us," he said and hung up.

I don't like this mission. Since when do we deal with kids? I look at Noa's picture. From the picture, one can see that Noa isn't an obedient little girl. Ripped jeans, ripped black shirt, and untied black high-top Allstars. She had black makeup around her eyes and purple lipstick. Her hair was dyed charcoal black, multiple ear piercings and one in her right eyebrow, and the tattoos visible on her shoulders probably have a story or two behind them. They say that kids rebel against their parents, but in Noa's case, we're talking about a full on revolution.

    I try to put myself in her mother's shoes. She probably can't even keep one eye closed. The fear of the unknown is worse than knowing the truth, and you find yourself helpless, dependent on so many factors, that they might not find her in time. A parent's conscience. Did I make a mistake? Could I have done something different? Is my child suffering? Did they hurt her? Maybe she's been thrown in some ditch, injured and bleeding? You can't stop your thoughts, and you can't let them control you. It's too hard. It hurts to the ends of your fingertips, like a ball of worry stuck in your gut, pressing against your diaphragm making it hard to breathe.

    I go back to the paperwork in order to find something that will allow me to start working. Noa is seventeen. She's the baby, after two older brothers. The family lives in a community in the center of the country and she goes to high school in Kfar Saba. When she was in grade school, she was in the Scouts in her local chapter, and was a good student and sociable. In middle school, something changed. There was some blowup among the girls that led to her being ostracized, and the likeable little girl became quiet and introverted. Noa barely ate and started wasting away without a word. She was sent to a psychologist, but that didn't help. Her mother tried talking with the other mothers in the community and even talked to Noa's old friends, but nothing led to a breakthrough. Nobody knew what was going on inside her. Her silence was viewed as unreasonable stubbornness, and her friends disconnected from her.

    Noa was borderline anorexic, and she understood that if she didn't stop her hunger strike, she would end up in the hospital, and possibly worse. She went back to eating like before, but she continued to be a loner. She sat in her room, played guitar and wrote songs. Songs that were once short, gentle, and childish became angry and harsh. The guitar that lacked confidence in her small hands was sharp and clear, cynical and loud.

In high school, she made new friends. She chose to hang out with the kids who weren't mainstream – the ones who don't give a fuck. Slowly but surely, the girl who liked pink and blue became the girl in black. Clothes, shoes, nail polish. The heavy makeup around her eyes was dark and shocking. She began smoking, and even the cigarettes became heavy and strong. The smell emanating from her wasn't right for a young girl. Sometimes, she wouldn't go to school, and sometimes she wouldn't come home after school. A laconic message to her parents that she was staying over to sleep at a friend's tonight. Period.

At first, her mother was happy that her daughter was again connecting with kids her age. But her optimism changed when she understood which way the wind blew. As she consulted with psychologists, the opinions were split, and her mother chose to believe that her daughter would eventually figure it out. Her husband never helped raise the kids. Years of travel and hours and hours of work until he became head of the Mossad.

She put a band together where she was the soloist and they got a few gigs in clubs, mostly in Tel Aviv. There she met people her age who were on the same path as she was. A lot of people "made" music like this, screaming their pain to the world, talking about its cruelty and life being hard and stressful. Many of her new friends didn't join the army after finishing high school like most kids do.

When she was suspended from school, her father was forced to enter the picture. Turns out that Noa made friends with a group of kids who had decided that Israel was a colonizer, and just like them, she wasn't joining the army. She never told anybody that her father was the head of the Mossad, because she was ashamed and afraid she would be rejected by her peers all over again. Her father "owned a small insurance company in Kfar Saba." None of them met her real family.

Noa met an Arab boy from Jaffa who was studying international relations in France. His mother was French and she came to Israel in the seventies and fell in love with Muhammad, Avi's father. Avi was actively involved with movements dedicated to equality for Palestinians and hung out with a group of Muslims living in France. Her father found out about it after he hired a private investigator, Danny Cohen. The pictures and details that he laid out for him left no doubt about the mess his daughter was mixed up in, and it shocked and greatly distressed him. The head of the Mossad consulted with Boaz, a senior psychologist whose job was picking through new recruits, primarily those who were there for operational duties, who saw mostly a rebellious youth in Noa.

"Noa is looking for a way to stand out, to be special. Disconnecting from you includes a different way of behaving, dressing, different music, and differentiating herself. You have to try to disconnect her from the group that she has joined, but don't brow-beat her. Shower her with love and be supportive of her. She's a smart girl and will understand the logic of things if you do it right."

A terrified Noa came home one night because her father called and told her to come home immediately. "Come, sit," said her father, as he sat beside her mother. Both sitting straight up, expressionless looks on their faces.

"Did something happen?"

"Yes. Something did happen," her father said. "I discovered a number of things that concern me." He laid out before her what he knew, and she didn't even try to deny it.

"So what?" she said defiantly. "I have every right to live according to my values and beliefs."

"You aren't old enough to understand the consequences your actions will have on your future," he answered her decisively.

"What's so bad about what I'm doing?" She still didn't understand the significance of her associations and where this could lead.

"The boy that you met, he is active in an anti-Israel group in France," he told her. "If he knew who I am, and maybe he already does, we're in trouble. The damage to you, us as a family, and the country itself is massive. And therefore, starting today, you can't go out to Tel Aviv. You can't have any more contact with this guy, or the rest of the group. You're going back to school, and you aren't disappearing for another day without permission. If you disobey me, I'll see to it that you pay dearly. You have gotten yourself into trouble, and I'm trying to mitigate the damage from here on out. Do you understand?"

Noa, for the first time in years, started crying. Her mother went to console her, but Noa refused to accept her hug. She got up from her chair.

"Sit down," commanded her father. "You didn't answer me. Do you understand?"

"Yes, father. I understand. Now may I get up?" she asked without looking at him.

"Yes, you may. Go to your room and maybe take off some of that heavy makeup. It looks terrible." Inside, he recalled Boaz's advice not to cause her to despair and to shower her with love, but he didn't know how.

The weeks and months passed and it seemed to Noa's parents that things were working out, or at least improving. Noa didn't skip school. She began doing her homework, and her grades improved. The black clothes remained, but here and there she wore shirts with some color, she did away with all the makeup, and even took out the piercing in her eyebrow.

"Mom," Noa said one evening," I want to go to the class trip to Poland." Surprise. Noa hadn't gone on any class trips until now, and didn't engage in any school activities that weren't mandatory.

"Great," her mother said. "No problem, when is it?"

"Winter. The teacher said that you get the most authentic experience, to feel how the Jews in the freezing cold ghettos felt."

"She's right. If you want, I'd be happy to go with you. I have always wanted to see the concentration camps but I never had anybody to go with," her mother said.

"Let's not get carried away here. I don't want anybody to think I'm dragging my mother along with me."

Can't argue with that, her mother thought. No kid her age is going to want her mother along on the trip.

So, after all the preparations for the class trip, Noa went to Poland. When she landed in Warsaw, she sent a text to her parents: "We landed. Everything is fine." The delegation took a tour around the city and they situated themselves at their hotel. The plan was dinner followed by splitting up into smaller groups by classroom to listen to testimonials from Holocaust survivors. At dinner, she sat next to her roommate Michal, one of the quieter, less popular girls that she befriended.

"I'm going to the bathroom," she said to Michal.

"Shall I come with you?" Michal asked.

"No, it's just around the corner. I'll be right back."

Michal waited, but felt anxious when Noa didn't return to the dining room. She got up to look for her but couldn't find her. At nine, everybody sat in the meeting room. The teacher called the names of the group, and only Noa was missing.

"Has anybody seen Noa?"

No response.

"Whoever is staying with her in the room, please go up and get her."

Michal went up to room 402, hoping that maybe she came back. The room was empty and she went back down, worried.

"She's not in the room," Michal said. "She went to the bathroom after dinner and I haven't seen her since."

I flip through the paperwork and find the details on the Israeli Arab fellow who lives in France. His name is Ahmed (Avi) Araf. His family lives in Tayibe, and he's the youngest of six children. His father is a building contractor, and his mother teaches French at the local high school. His current address is in Clichy, a suburb of Paris. As far as I can tell, he's part of a group called "Black September Renewed."

The original "Black September," was named after the event in Jordan that occurred in 1970 titled "Black September," and was active at the beginning of the seventies. The group kidnapped and murdered eleven Israeli athletes at the Munich Olympics, and since its founding has maintained the highest level of compartmentalization of any other Palestinian terrorist organization.

Most worrisome, I think to myself. What a mess.

We don't currently have any information on the organization, its activities, or where they operate. We just have that guy's address, which is enough to get started. Sometimes, gathering material starts with a gut feeling, or a bit of information that comes up in a phone call or an operational call of one sort or another. From the letters, I find meeting places and phone numbers of the team that's arriving. Only the commander has been in the system for a while, and even he is a few years behind me. Udi was one of the younger guys who managed to standout both because of his skills and his handsome, European appearance.

I jot down in code the meeting locations and phone numbers and check the flight's arrival time. I will need to meet them at night. Tomorrow is Sunday; businesses aren't usually open on their day of rest. A lot of people are going to be at home – that is, we can walk around close to the object's apartment, but we have to be very careful. The area is known for having a large Muslim population, and they are suspicious of whoever doesn't look like them.

I decide to go home. Another weekend that blew up in our faces. But, an emergency is an emergency, and in this case, time is of the essence. The girls and Nathan rode with Hani, Joel and their kids to a restaurant called "Le Entrecôte" after the excursion. I arrived at the end of the meal and we returned home together. At nine in the evening, the phone rang. It was Udi.

"Hello... this is Paul speaking," Udi said. "How are you?"

"Great, finally you arrived. I hope your vacation will be enjoyable. Would you like to meet so I can give you some recommendations?"

I arrive at the meeting place a few minutes before Udi. "I assume you have read the file. I tried to find some more information about him, but couldn't. There's no mention of the man in the local phone book."

"I don't know any more about him than you do, other than his picture, which I assume you also have. However, I spoke with Saul who investigated along with the Polish police, and it turns out that Noa left the hotel with two guys. She was holding hands with one of them, and it didn't appear that she was resisting."

"Did somebody see where they went?" I ask.

"No. We didn't see anything at the airport or train stations. Her picture has been circulated to all relevant locations, including border crossings."

"Could it be that she wasn't kidnapped, but rather snuck out on her own accord?" I ask, mostly to myself.

"Anything's possible. We're still checking."

"What are you planning for tomorrow?"

"Tomorrow, we'll first take a vehicle to Clichy, and then I'll send a pair to figure out where we can sit and watch the house, any weak points, access points and withdrawal routes from the place, transportation, what we might need for cover in order to enter his building and find proof that we have the right address.

We'll see what we can learn about the apartment and about the guy."

"I suggest that we set a meeting for tomorrow at noon. The McDonald's at the Champs Elysees work for you? I hope that by then you learn enough to come up with a continuation plan. I wish I could come with you. If only I wasn't a diplomat in Paris." I'm itching to get back in the field on this type of mission.

Second Week

Sunday

It's seven o'clock on Sunday. I'm at home in Paris and it's nice being curled up in my comforter. I relax a bit and change positions, enjoying the soft pillows and the touch of the sheets between my toes. Sunlight flickered off the window. It was a beautiful day. Blue skies, and a deceptive sun smiling down. I roll over and lightly touch Nathan. He hugs me in his sleep. The years create behavioral patterns. His body heat feels nice, and I try not to think about the girls who, any minute now, will burst into the room, where the day will once again become another with just dad.

I'm reminded of the trip to Vittel we're about to embark on, the Mediterranean club on the outskirts of the village known for its hot springs. The vacation was planned well in advance. Suddenly, my work phone rings. On the other line is a colleague from Israel.

"I understand you're about to go on vacation. I just wanted to let you know that when you get back, you have to pack. It's been decided that you're coming to Israel for about two or three months."

The serenity disappeared. "Wait, wait, what did you say? I'm here with my family. What do you mean two or three months? Are you out of your mind?"

"There's no choice. Every option has been exhausted. It's imperative."

"Is this a request or an order?"

"It's not a request according to what I've been told."

"So send the message up the chain that it's not an order I can follow. After everything I've been through here, there's a limit. It's not fair, I'm not able to do this, and I won't." My heart was about to explode.

"I'll pass along your message and let you know," he answered calmly.

The feeling of being on vacation vanished and was replaced by the heavy feeling of a person who feels like they're a puppet in somebody else's game. Even Nathan felt like all hope was lost. We decide to try and ignore it; we try mostly for the girls.

When we returned from our vacation, there was a voice message waiting for me: "Call Ya'akov as soon as you return from your vacation."

"Miriam? What's up? They left a message telling me to call Ya'akov."

"Hey, how's it going?" Ya'akov says on the other line.

"All right." I don't feel like elaborating.

"You've been saved. We found somebody else to come to Israel."

"I see. That's what you wanted to tell me?"

"No, I wanted to tell you that you have to come to Israel in a few days because there's no choice. But we found a different solution. So that's it."

Twenty years in the system and they just move you around, as if you were an emotionless package without the need to even breathe. "Goodbye."

I turn over onto my back and fold my hands behind my head. How many hours, days, years have I invested – with love even – to the system, to the state, from a sense of duty, and how coldly and cruelly that love is requited.

"Mom, are you awake? Shir and I are going to the boulangerie to buy baguettes and croissants." Sunday morning tradition.

I go to the kitchen and make breakfast, hoping that the girls won't be too mad at me for working today as well. We all sit around the table, enjoying another few moments of being together.

I arrive at the McDonald's by the Champs Elysees. Udi is waiting for me, surrounded by hamburgers and French fries.

"Are you ever going to grow up?" I'm disgusted by the smell alone.

"What's your problem? These are so good."

I break out a salad and orange juice that I brought with me. "What's new?"

"No news from Poland. They may have left the country by car, or they're hiding out there. Nobody has taken responsibility yet. In Israel, everything's quiet. The school is continuing on its trip, as per our orders. We added additional security and confiscated all cell phones. God forbid word get out to the media. I'm still waiting for the summary regarding rental cars. If somebody took her out of the country, it's possible they rented a car for that and arrived in Warsaw with their car."

"Okay. We have to check on these things faster here. Maybe that's the right direction," I say. "What have you discovered here?"

"We found a few places where we can watch the house. It's not on a main street, but it's relatively long. There are two streets on either side, Gabriel and Landy, such that we can enclose the area from these two streets. Behind the object's house is a small park from which it's possible to watch the building and maybe even the apartment itself."

"I sent Sting and Barbara to do some reconnaissance on foot. The place is crawling with Arabs, but we'll figure it out. The people we brought in can assimilate themselves into the population. He is French-Moroccan, brown skinned, and she is also dark skinned, a new immigrant from Belgium. The building doesn't have a front desk so we can get in easily – we saw people walk in without even buzzing the intercom. It's an old building, four stories. Tomorrow I'll send somebody to see if there's an apartment for rent there. There's a "for rent" sign on the building adjacent to it, so they got a little confused. Maybe his name appears on a mailbox. Since we have a photo of the guy, I decided to leave the couple at the coffee shop to see if we get lucky and spot him."

"Nice," I say. "Send me the information so I can send it on to Israel."

"Okay, I've got it."

"Maybe we should bring in an expert in Arabic who will sit at the coffee shop, or a Moroccan restaurant in order to have a listen, get a read on the place. That way we can learn something about the new organization. I'll call home, see what they say."

"Good idea. Maybe there's somebody in the area, and we won't need to wait for somebody to arrive from Israel," Udi says.

"Yeah, I'll check..." I say, pensively. "You guys continue checking out the area, so let's meet tomorrow at three o'clock at the location of the third meeting and see where we go from there." I leave and find a phone to call David, who is in Israel, and ask him to consider bringing in a collection officer who is an expert in Arabic to help us out.

The second phone call is to Yaron, my boss in Holland. I'm sure they told him that I've been annexed away on another mission. As far as he's concerned, that means he has to take my place with my team. The team has to keep working.

"Hello?" Yaron answers.

"Hi."

"I've been waiting for your call. I understand that you have decided to take a vacation. All right, I'll try to take your place," he chuckled.

"Yeah. We can make do without me at the moment. The problem is that I have no idea how long I'll be away. And of course, there's the issue regarding the Old Man and Handsome.

"I read the material and the special requests. Don't worry, I'll take it from here. You'll join up when you finish."

It was clear to me that afterwards, in private, he'll go fishing for details to pry out of me. On my way home, I think to myself, *Fun, as far as things look right now, at least I'll get to sleep at home. Wait. What fun? A girl disappeared. Kidnapped. What's the matter with you? Enough, don't think about that, that doesn't help anybody.*

Everybody's at home. The girls are in front of the television in the living room and Nathan is snoring on the couch.

"How can you guys hear anything over your father's snoring?" I ask, smiling.

"We're used to it," says Lior and runs to give me a hug. "Are you done working for the day?"

"I hope so."

I sit down between them and hug them with an outpouring of emotion. We decide to stay at home today and not go out. The new operations telephone rings. The ringing wakes Nathan up from his two-hour nap. He was out cold.

"Hey, David," I say.

"Hey. Anton is coming to visit tomorrow. First thing in the morning, go over the material. Everything is there."

"Okay."

"There is some indication that Saul finished his role. He's tired." I understand from this that in Poland, there's information that shows Noa has probably already left the country, and they are on to her. Everything is written in the information to follow. "All right then, have an outstanding week and hopefully we'll hear some good news."

"Amen. For all of us," I say.

I return to my thoughts about Noa, trying to feel something. A snippet of intuition, maybe an idea we haven't thought of, but all I manage to think about is at the moment, the girl is in trouble and we have to save her. In my private life, I worry about Shir. A month after she was born, she was hospitalized and underwent surgery. More recently, she fainted in my arms and I was forced to travel for work and leave her with Nathan. Deep down, I fell apart – what kind of a mother am I?

We get up and prepare a family dinner. Sweet potato and pumpkin soup with an Israeli salad, cheeses, baguettes, and omelets that I make with Lior. Shir sets our small table. It's important to appreciate every day like this. Family. Kids. Love. Home. Another week has passed. What will tomorrow bring?

Monday

Nathan drops the girls off at school, and I make my way to the bus station. The Metro is faster, but the bus displays the whole city before me. I love taking the bus. Every corner warms my heart. I arrive at the embassy and go up to our floor. Even though my colleagues are surprised to see me here on a Monday, they don't ask too many questions. I enter the room. A pile of telegrams await me. If only one of them contained some type of lead, or news.

Telegram 1:
Re: Operation "Door Knock" – Anton
1. Anton arrives on Monday morning from London via Eurostar, arriving at "Gare du Nord" at 1020.
2. Meeting place: Lobby of the Concorde Le Fayette hotel at 1130.

Anton's job is to make contact with the Muslims in Clichy. To learn about the organization "Black September Renewed," and how Ahmed Araf is connected to the organization, with the goal of getting to the person who kidnapped or helped kidnap Lady D.

Telegram 2:
Re: Operation "Door Knock" – End of Operations in Poland

Below are the findings:
1. From security camera footage from the hotel, Lady D appears to be walking while hugging a man with a dark complexion, and next to him is another man holding a small bag. (Check with the Shin Bet and a private investigator to determine whether the dark skinned man is in fact her Arab boyfriend, Ahmed).
2. Two men and Lady D get into a black Jeep with a French license plate from Paris.
3. The two men sit in front and Lady D gets in the back.
4. There were no reports from witnesses about signs of distress. Lady D was chatting with the men.
5. Her bag and clothes were found in her room, but not her cell phone, wallet and credit cards, cash, her Israeli passport, a sweater, coat and toiletries.
6. Tracking her phone hasn't produced any signals. After a search, her phone was found smashed in a trash can near the hotel.
7. Lady D received five phone calls after she landed in Poland from a French phone number. Each of the conversations only lasted a few moments. An SMS message was sent to her about five minutes before she got up from her seat in the dining room and disappeared. The text read as follows: *Go now from the side entrance of the hotel and turn right. I'll wait for you on the first corner across the street.*
8. The phone the calls were made from has been neutralized and we can't track it.
9. Polish police checked the border crossings and a car with passengers matching the description of the three crossed the border on highway E30 heading to Berlin.
10. Questions that remain:
    a. The full license plate of the car is unknown, just that it ends "75."

I transfer the operations summary we have so far to headquarters. After taking a detour to see whether or not I'm being followed, I find a public telephone and call my team that I "left behind."

"Hello," Handsome says.

"Hi," I respond with a smile. "I see you arrived early. How's it going?"

"Just fine. Decisions have been made. When will you be here?"

"I won't be. Bruce will come in my place. He'll fill you in ("Bruce" is Yaron's code name).

"I see. I'll see you when I see you," he says.

"Tell everybody I said 'hi.'"

The next call is to the Old Man at his house. He's waiting with Dina for answers.

"Hello," Dina answers.

"How are you doing, my dear?" I ask.

"Okay. Reasonable. Waiting."

"Yeah, I know. My fingers are crossed. Where's Joe?"

"He's here. Wait. Joe... he's coming. See you later..."

"Bye, big hug, we'll talk."

"Hi," Joe says.

"Hi, how's it going?"

"Reasonable. Waiting. It's pretty tense here."

"I can imagine. We'll wait and hope for the best," I say. "Listen, I won't be home with the company for a while. But Bruce is coming. I'll call when I can, okay?"

"No problem, have fun. See you later."

Eliyahu is waiting for me in the predetermined meeting spot. A likeable guy, smiley and modest. Now he is Anton. The thin mustache he grows prior to every outing adorns his upper lip. He stands and shakes my hand, adjusting himself to his cover, moves his chair in my honor and waits for me to sit down.

Anton looks like a wealthy Arab, impeccably dressed in a blue pinstripe suit, tie, black shoes as shiny as mirrors. His clothes were purchased in an expensive boutique, and his watch and shoes attested to his financial status.

"How are you, my dear?" he said flashing a half smile under his mustache.

"I'm fine, good-looking," I say right back at him. "Let's say that you ran into me when you got out of your taxi and invited me to join you for a coffee, because you liked how I looked."

"Of course I did," he answers. "We like them curvy. We'll start with coffee and see where it leads... by the way, how's Nathan?"

"Relatively speaking, he's fine."

He and his family were sent on multiple missions abroad until his wife finally said, "That's enough! From now on you can go on short trips, but the kids and I are staying in Israel."

"I understand that you're up to date," I said.

"Yeah. What a shitty situation."

"The shittiest. Are you familiar with Clichy?

"Yeah. I'm planning on getting a hotel in the area and start sniffing around. It's a new organization, and if it's called 'Black September,' then it's probably going to try to recreate the success of that organization from years back. It will be hard to gather information," Anton says. "I saw pictures of the girl's boyfriend. I intend to be in the vicinity of his apartment twenty-four-seven and find out what he's up to. Since we're talking about the girl's life, I won't take even a moment's rest."

"Absolutely," I say. "You have my number. Any problems, questions, help, transfer of materials, I'm here. Let me know which hotel you end up staying at, including your room number."

He stood up and formally shook my hand. I headed out.

I want to go to Clichy, to be a part of the action. It's hard for me not to be. But that would be an operational mistake. I know the area, the feeling in the air is like a powder keg that could blow at any second. The French and Europeans know it, but can't do anything about it.

I have another two hours before I meet Udi. I decide to head in the direction of Gallery Lafayette in order to sever any connection between my meeting with Anton and the one with Udi. I walk to the number nine Metro line and head down the stairs. The subway isn't completely full, but it's crowded. I find a place to sit in the corner, where I can see everything that happens around me.

I arrive at my stop and get off the train and head into a mall called "The Gallery." Lots of clothes, bags and shoe shops. It's crowded. There's loud music blaring. It's a bit old fashioned for my taste, but I have time to kill. It's a sore spot: having to spend one or two hours (and sometimes an entire day) without actually getting anything done. Most of our energy is spent, primarily, being patient. I have two more hours. What am I going to do now?

I decide to go outside and look at the old buildings and the decorations in the display windows. Fresh, chilly air. I stop on the street corner where and old man is selling hot chestnuts. I pick up a bag, the wonderful smell steaming out of the paper, and I look for somewhere to sit. On the next street, I find a bench surrounded by bushes and flowers where I sit down and snack on the chestnuts that are burning my fingers as I try to peel them. Suddenly, I notice a movement out of the corner of my eye, something moving at a different speed that draws my attention. What was it? What did I see?

Around the corner, a face peeks out and then retreats. Maybe I'm imagining it? I keep sitting there. I can't ignore anything. Maybe somebody is following me? I continue eating and at the same time make a plan if, indeed, I'm being followed. I need to give the impression that I don't suspect a thing. I want them to make a mistake and get close to me so that I can get a read on them.

On the other side of the street, I notice there's a travel agency and decide to go in, sitting down by the counter. My field of vision was wide enough to see what was happening on the street. Across from me was a woman in her forties, meticulously dressed in a knee-length, tight blue skirt and her hair pulled back. Her neck was adorned with a scarf.

"Madame?" She looked at me politely and reservedly.

"I'm interested in a London getaway. What have you got along those lines?"

"Plane or train?"

"Train," I answer while looking outside. The pace of the people outside is normal, until a fellow who has a similar appearance to the one looking at me earlier peered around the corner. I notice the movement of his head turning toward his shoulder, like when somebody is talking into a microphone.

"How many days will you be going, and how many people? Do you need to book a hotel as well? We have specials..." She looks over at me, waiting for an answer.

"We're a couple, for the weekend from Thursday to Monday, with a hotel," I answer and continue looking over her shoulder. I see him. He has curly hair, dark skinned, wearing jeans and a blue shirt. He has a pair of white ASICS with red stripes. He's looking at the notice board, pretending to be interested in one of the advertisements, but his eyes and face are pointed towards the next street over.

"I have a phenomenal deal with a three-star hotel, passage on the TGV, which includes breakfast, for two-thousand francs."

"Where is the hotel located?" I ask, wasting time.

"Next to Buckingham Palace," she says.

Out of the corner of my eye, I see the fellow move. Since he's so close to me, him leaving the place while I'm behind him means that his activity has nothing to do with me.

"Ok, thank you very much. We're planning to travel in a

month, so I'll get back to you. Please give me your card? Thank you so much for your time," I say and get up.

I exit the travel agency when suddenly a large, blue Peugeot stops on the side of the road, and two guys run inside. One of them is my curly haired friend. I hear him say to the driver, "Go, go, he left in a car, license number..."

That's that, they weren't talking about me. It looks like a training exercise for beginners. Must be the French version, I smile to myself. I can proceed as planned. I look at my watch; it's time to meet Udi.

I enter the coffee shop in the Latin Quarter. It's five minutes to three. I order sparkling water and wait. There is always the possibility that one party doesn't make it, for whatever reason, so you always have to have an alternate meeting location sometime after the first meeting. But I'm not worried. Udi will enter any minute now.

"Howdy," he says quietly. "How's it going?"

"Am I imagining things or are you looking rather pleased with yourself?" I look at his goatee and his new look. Everybody is trying to adapt themselves to Clichy these days.

"Pleased is a matter of how you look at it," he said. "When the girl is back home with her parents I'll be pleased."

"Well then...?"

"It's like this: our couple managed to dredge up some details. Yesterday just before evening, they arrived to the area. The front door was wide open and the object's name was handwritten on the mailbox, apartment number four. Our friend lives on the first floor in one of the two rear apartments. There wasn't anybody in his apartment yesterday. There's a great vantage point from the park behind the building. No lights went on during the night. They marked the front door and nobody came in until today, late morning.

"This morning, Merlin made contact with one of the neighbors in the building. A local French woman who has lived there for many years. She complained that the Muslims made the neighborhood worse and told Merlin not to look for an apartment around here. Merlin remarked that the building looked nice and quiet, and the woman said that one young man lives on the first floor named Ahmed, a Moroccan family with four noisy kids lives on the second floor, and on the top floor is another family with kids. Not bad for a day's work." He smiled satisfactorily and continued, "We'll keep a lookout according to the schedule. We'll keep the mark on the door. That will keep us from having to sit there unnecessarily. Instead, we'll check the lights from the park at night."

"Good job," I say. "In addition, Anton arrived and is located in a hotel nearby. He intends to snoop around the area."

"I understand that the team in Poland has almost completely packed up."

"Yes," I answer. "The girl was seen leaving with two men heading to Germany in a blue Jeep with Parisian plates. Saul continues to follow up with the investigation in Germany. We're waiting to hear something, putting a lot of effort into keeping things from reaching the press. The girl could get hurt if the pressure around them gets too heavy. Let's get back to our business. Your friends know Anton? Show them a picture so they'll recognize him. So we don't get in each other's way by accident."

"Yeah, they are aware of his general existence. I'll show them a picture."

"Let's meet tomorrow evening. Set it for five. If we need to meet earlier, we will."

"See you then," Udi says.

Tuesday

It was a cold, rainy morning. I'm taking the train to Brussels. Since I didn't have any way to help out with the mission, I decided to visit my team and head back to Paris in the afternoon. Ludwig arrives first and I take the opportunity to see how he's doing.

"Not much news."

"Have you talked to her yet?"

"Sure, a lot. A weekend alone here, there's a lot of time to talk. I can't wait to see her, I miss her," he says, smiling. "I hope I picked a good one this time."

"Me too. You deserve it. Now you have to focus all your energy on the job. You have to push, to initiate, not to wait for ideas or their demands. You have a new mission and you can show everybody what you're worth."

There is a knock at the door. I go to open it. Laurie is standing there, rubbing his hands together.

"Hi," he says and gives me a kiss on each cheek. "I thought you weren't coming."

"I came just for a short visit to see you guys. Shall I make something to drink and we can sit for a bit?"

"Strong coffee, please, no milk, no sugar."

We sit on the armchairs in one of the rooms, leaving Ludwig alone to start working.

"Well?" I ask.

"Celina wants to go back to Israel. In Israel, with family seems to be the best thing to do for now, and there will be somebody to look after the little guy."

"Approved. That's the perfect solution for now. So it looks right, tell Celina to buy round-trip tickets. Submit them as part of your expense account."

"No problem. I want to help her pack and get everything organized, and maybe also take her to the airport."

"Not a problem. Right now, Bruce is responsible for you, but of course I'm in the loop... I haven't run off."

"What about Albert?" he asks. "Have you spoken to him?"

"Yes, they are waiting for answers. Tell me, how's it going with Ludwig?"

"It's been two and a half days since our conversation, but the guy has made quite the metamorphosis. Apparently love has bewitched him," he said, smiling. "He's already come up with a few new ideas."

"Fantastic."

"When Celina is in Israel, I'll be able to work harder to make up for Albert being away."

John ("Laurie") met Celina while he was still in college. They both lived in London in an area with a large Jewish population. Their parents were friends through the community and they met socially. John came from a traditional, Zionist family. They lived in the Golders Green neighborhood, which was predominantly Jewish. His mother was active in freeing Zionist prisoners from the Soviet Union, part of the group called "the thirty-fivers." They became famous for protesting in front of the prime minister's office at 10 Downing Street dressed in black and wearing chains. For her entire life, she sought ways to be actively involved in Zionism. Her father owned a small, private, non-rated hotel, and the family all helped him run it.

Celina came from a different kind of home. They lived in the exclusive St. John's Wood. A good Jewish home, but without a

Zionist background. Her father made his way in the *schmatta* business and owned a chain of fashionable women's boutiques.

At the age of seventeen, John and Celina started dating. Her father was pleased. Despite the fact that he had non-Jewish friends as well as family members who had married non-Jews, he didn't want that for his children. At nineteen, John decided that he was immigrating to Israel to join the army. When she finished her psychology studies, Celina flew to Israel to visit him just as John was finishing a commander's training course in the paratroopers' brigade. She decided to stay because she fell in love with the country and the lifestyle that was so different from the wet and cold in London. The two got married and moved to a kibbutz in the Galil where their baby, Bar, was born. Celina's parents also fell in love with the country. Her father sold most of his businesses and the family relocated to Ra'anana.

The service abroad made their lives difficult. Celina, independent and supportive of her husband, didn't like being alone at night and was forced to deal with her daily routine alone. She tried not to show how she really felt, but Bar absorbed her repressed anger and developed a dependence on her that only increased her frustration. Later on, a second troubled second pregnancy only added another level of difficulty to her plight. When I visited her in London, we sat in the living room with Bar sitting on my lap.

"You must miss them all the time," she said.

"All the time," I answered. "It's the one thing I can't get used to. Leaving at the beginning of every week is very difficult for me."

"So then how do you manage with this job?" she said, trying to understand.

"Celina, are you angry with John?" I said, changing subjects.

"Yes and no. I understand him, but it's hard for me. I'm mostly mad at myself. Maybe I'm not cut out for this way of life."

"I understand, and I think it must be very difficult to be alone with a small child and a difficult pregnancy. You're allowed to say that it's hard."

"It is," she said, lowering her gaze. "It is hard."

The phone in my bag rings.

"Hello?"

"Hi." It's the operation leader in Israel, David. "I understand that you went to Belgium. After some checking, turns out she left Warsaw with a boyfriend from Israel. So this whole affair is coming your way. Since the fellow was last in Israel, we're checking up on him, what we know about him and about whoever he was in contact with in Israel."

"I see," I answer. "I hope that he comes back to the apartment so that we have a thread, but if he has any sense, he'll stay away. In any event, we have to be prepared for the possibility that somebody else may enter the apartment, perhaps leading us to him. Maybe Anton should try to rent an apartment there."

"Right," he says. "I'm not sure you have enough manpower there. Four people surveilling might be problematic if they decide to head to Paris."

"Agreed."

"I'll check about an apartment and manpower and get back to you."

This thing has gotten more relevant as far as we're concerned. We have to get her back as soon as possible. Did Ahmed know whose daughter she is when he was in Israel? Or did he find out later, which made her that much more attractive in his eyes.

There's a knock at the door. Yaron is standing in the doorway wearing a suit that doesn't fit him.

"What gives, you going to a wedding?" I say.

"Very funny. I had an important meeting. I didn't have a choice."

I smile. "What's new?"

"We got the down low on the next meeting. I hope you come back quickly."

"What's the mission?" I ask.

"You remember that new computer technology we developed?"

"That's already operational?"

"Yes."

"We have to maintain the business connection. We are technicians trying to sell them the equipment and our maintenance as a package. A long-term mission awaits us," Yaron said.

"Of course. I get it." The team needs to learn the new system in-depth, not only regarding the system itself but also the financial side, so that they look and sound believable. My phone rings again. I take the call and move into another room, turn the radio on so the guys in the other room won't hear.

"Hello?"

"Listen. You have a green light to rent an apartment, preferably as a lookout apartment. In addition, two of Udi's guys are getting on a plane in the morning to join you."

My visit ended before it began, and I find myself hurrying back to Paris.

"Udi, how's it going?" I say.

"Good you called. I was waiting for the right moment to call you. Things have gotten interesting on my end. We have to be seamless so we don't miss anything."

"What do you mean? I'm not sure they've told you that two more will be joining your trip tomorrow afternoon."

"Fantastic. Have them bring another car when they arrive."

"Of course. Ask your friends to look for an apartment to rent. Leah Goldberg is looking for something with a patio where she can sit and enjoy the view..."

Anton will enter the apartment and solve two problems at

once: a place to keep tabs on the object, and to feel out the surroundings and start to situate himself.

"No problem. We saw one in the building next door. I suggest you be in the vicinity."

"Hello," I say to Anton.

"*Ahalan wa sahalan.*"

"I want to see you... buy you a cup of coffee?"

"It's a date. Kisses."

The meeting with Anton isn't far from the Gare du Nord, where my train stops. Anton gets up from his chair, shakes my hand and gives me four kisses as is fashionable. He pulls my chair out for me and only then sits down beside me.

"*Kif halak?*" he asks.

"Fine. Turns out there's movement in our apartment."

"Great." We all want to see results, especially when it comes to this mission.

"I don't have any information yet, but we got the green light to rent an apartment to serve as observation post as close as possible to the location," I tell him.

"I have to check, I didn't want to make too much noise, especially since we didn't have clearance until now," Anton says.

"Of course."

"Another couple is joining Udi's squad. We need to take into consideration that tailing him could take a while. Hard to believe that our friend would bring the girl to his apartment."

"I trust Udi. He's a real professional. A lot of experience. All right, I want to get this girl back home. It's heart wrenching," he says.

"From your mouth to God's ear," I answer.

"Listen, I met a young Muslim. He's not in the business, but his brother is. I sat in a coffee shop, but I may as well have been in a *casbah* in Nablus. I try to be there as often as possible. Some guy started spouting off while I was there, and I was able to sell him my cover story about wanting to invest in a company that wants to bring real change. He got excited and started talking about his brother and his group of friends. A group of fanatical students who want to change the power structure. As far as they're concerned, Black September is their philosophical model, because they didn't condemn violence, including against leaders. In 1971, the organization assassinated the prime minister of Jordan, Wasfi Tell, a murder where one of them bent down and licked the blood as he lay there dying, as a symbolic act. Then in 1972, they hijacked Sabena Flight 571 and in the end, murdered eleven Olympic athletes from the Munich Olympics. May they burn in hell."

Anton continues telling me more. "How did the fellow put it? They want to bring the State of Israel to its knees. To return the honor of the Palestinians and to gain independence. They are prepared to die and are looking for unconventional ways to terrorize Israel, the United States, and the world. In his words, the revolution in Europe has already begun, and it won't be long before all European governments join the struggle, making it very difficult on the State of Israel. What can I tell you? He's right. It'll be even more difficult with the Muslim conquest of Europe," Anton says, giving me his interpretation of the subject. "We have to understand that the Palestinians are stubborn and very hungry. They won't stop at red lights. It seems to me we've become overconfident, which has blinded us and caused us to underestimate their determination."

"Yes, I've been watching the occupation of Europe ever since I arrived here. It worries me. Evil won't be vanquished, and peace – at least the way that I wish it upon the world – won't happen," I summarize… "And back to our matter at hand, there's a reasonable chance that this guy getting close to the girl was planned back in Israel," I say, pondering.

"What's certain is that this guy came to Israel sniffing around and a golden egg fell right into his lap."

"Yes. I don't understand how the Shin Bet weren't on to him

already, and why he hasn't been questioned? Is it possible the head of the Mossad concealed information intentionally, or because he suspected something?"

"I don't know, but it's a question worth figuring out, because maybe we're sitting here because of concealed information," Anton says.

"The question about whether there were failures will almost certainly come up, but as far as we're concerned right now, that's irrelevant. I think that it's better to concentrate on the mission for now. We're lucky nothing's come out in the media. They'd have a field day." Neither of us would stop thinking about this. Each one saw an investigative committee in our future. "What do you intend to do with the brother?" I ask.

"For now, I'm waiting for him. It's better if they come to me. And with my cover story being solid, that leaves me with all the leverage. I hope they need the money and connections I have to offer, so that they have a reason to come to me. I don't have time to play hard-to-get, but I have to give it a chance."

"Okay."

Anton is one of the best in his field. He doesn't just give the impression of being loyal and honest, his track record speaks for itself. As a businessman, he has compiled a bunch of receipts over the years for his various identities. There aren't many like him in the system. There are a number of mythological identities, some of whom I've encountered. Their ability to play whoever is on the other side amazes me. They have to speak their language, be one of them, to know how to think a few steps ahead along the other guys' line of thinking and to be charismatic. Anton learned from the best until he branched out on his own.

Anton was born in Israel and grew up speaking Arabic at home. His father immigrated from Syria and his mother from Iraq. They met in Israel and got married. Eliyahu grew up in Bat Yam, where his family maintained their Arabic character and values. As a child, he was ashamed of his parents, but as he got older, the fact that he could speak, read and write fluent Arabic led him to Unit 504 in the army – the intelligence corps. Later, he was lent to the Mossad for operations and after he was discharged, he joined us.

"Done. You look for an apartment and continue gathering intelligence. Good luck." I stand up and smile. He gets up, gets into character, approaches me and kisses me twice on each cheek while escorting me out.

I leave the meeting. There's progress. I can feel it in my bones. I give Udi a call.

"Paul, *mon cheri*."

"Hi," he answers, "are you here?"

"Yes. Can you make time for me?"

"Always, can you come to me?"

"Of course."

This time I'm waiting for him, and I sit where I can see most of the people sitting or coming into the café. Udi's running late. I hope everything's all right. Almost a half an hour after I had already planned on heading to the alternative meeting spot, in comes Udi, who sits down in a frenzy.

"Sorry I'm late."

"Did something happen?" I ask.

"Our guys thought they saw the object leaving the house. We started following him, but since we didn't have a confirmed identification, we sent Merlin back to check the marking on the door and it turns out nobody has left the apartment."

I grin. "So tell me what's up. Start at the beginning."

"There wasn't anything new with the apartment this morning. Nobody has entered since we started watching it. When Sam went by the place, he discovered that the blinds were different," Udi said. "Then Gail went in and discovered that the mark wasn't in place, the implication being that somebody was inside. We started watching from the street. We don't have the manpower to do a double watch at this point. About thirty minutes before we were supposed to meet, we thought we saw the object exiting the building, like I told you."

"Okay, so a false alarm this time. Next time it will be for real. Whoever is in that apartment will have to leave it sooner or later."

"That's right. I'm glad that Bill and Monica will be joining us," said Udi. "I'm not leaving the area until we see who enters or leaves that apartment. By the way, there are two apartments available that work well as observation points. We're lucky that the apartment can be seen from the park as well as the main road. The bedrooms in the back and in the living room face the street."

"Anton's also checking things out and said he'll look into the apartments immediately. He'll probably call me soon. Do you have a preference for which one?" I should have answers for Anton when he calls.

"The one that is to the west of the apartment is better."

"Gotcha."

"Are the cars ready for vehicle surveillance?" Udi is the man here, but I also have experience in this area, so I give myself permission to ask.

"Yes, both of them are ready to move out immediately. Each one is facing a different direction. Since we only have information about the Peugeot that hasn't been seen in the area, we have to be prepared for anything. One possibility is that, when the object leaves the apartment, he'll take a taxi in some direction or will walk to the Metro," says Udi.

"What does Merlin have to say about the woman she first spoke with about renting the apartment? Can we contact her again in order to get some information about the object out of her, or whoever is currently in the apartment?"

"Might be able to," Udi says. "The question is not only if we can, but who will make contact. Anton is the enemy as far as she's concerned."

"Maybe Merlin. Can she do it? What do you think?"

"Merlin's a badass. She can definitely do it, and I think it's worth a try."

"Let's wait on this until tomorrow morning. Tomorrow, late in the morning, she can approach her with the same cover story," I tell him. "I hope that Anton turns something up. He made contact with the brother of one of the operatives and threw out some bait. We're waiting for them to get back to him."

Patience. It's an important word, but sometimes opportunities are missed when the right steps aren't taken on time. *What if additional measures are necessary?* I ask myself. I've got a bad feeling. My instincts are talking to me. We don't have time, and we can't wait. I decide to call Israel.

"Hello?" It's David, the mission commander at headquarters.

"Hi," I say. "I have to fill you in on our progress to date. I have a bad feeling about this," I say, and tell him chapter by chapter on where Udi and Anton are.

"I understand. Some light progress."

"Yes, only light. I feel like we have to take additional measures in order to flesh out some details about this guy."

"Are you suggesting we enter the apartment?"

"Yes but for now, somebody's in there, though it might change. We have to do several things at the same time. If somebody leaves the apartment, some of Udi's guys will follow him while the others simultaneously go in, and get a heads up before they come back."

"I get it. We'll need to get approval and check their friends' activities."

We're talking about a professional team – this is what they do. I'm convinced we'll get a positive response, if they think it will help us. There's a lot of pressure at home – I wonder who knows about what's going on. We've all been prohibited from talking about it, and none of us are. I assume that the situation in Israel is similar.

"Okay. Check it out and we'll see where we go from here. I hope that we'll be able to return to normal soon."

"Yeah. It's hard when missions become personal," David says.

That's exactly the point. Usually, nothing is personal. They give us assignments. Names and places that aren't connected in our private lives. We look at things from the outside. They don't touch us.

"I'm always thinking about the parents," I say, and keep myself from asking questions about the head of the Mossad. I know that they're worried sick.

Noa's mother walks around her spacious home. Outside, the world operates as usual while at home it's deadly silent. Her husband went to the office. He tossed and turned all night just like she did. They barely speak, and try to fine some comfort.

How did this happen? She thinks to herself. She takes a sip of coffee, her second cup, trying to stay alert and focused, despite the fact that she didn't sleep all night. She goes back upstairs again to Noa's room, looking around, looking for clues but finding none. She rifles through her desk drawers and her closet. Nothing. Her computer was taken back to the office to be searched. She sits on the bed, whose black sheets send her back to Noa's "black days," where she seemed to have returned to recently. Could she have been playing a game with her parents, her family? She picks up the pillow on the bed, stifling the scream erupting from her throat, the first time she has allowed herself to scream since receiving the news. It was a scream filled with terror and immense despair. Her crying goes on unabated as she screams her daughter's name into the pillow until she collapses on the bed, exhausted.

After about a half hour, she sits up in the unmade bed. When Noa gets back home, the bed will have been made up. Noa doesn't like people going into her room; she likes her privacy. She smooths out the sheet and blanket, puts the pillows back in place and fluffs them a bit. Suddenly, she feels something hard in the bottom pillow. She pulls out a thick, black notebook from the pillowcase and starts flipping through it.

In the beginning were angry songs, rebellious and dark. Further on, Noa turned the notebook into her diary. Things that happened to her. The falling out with her friends, the friends she played music with, the Tel Aviv crowd. The opposition to the occupation and resistance to enlist in the IDF, and a feeling of being estranged from her family. The disdain that she felt towards her father and his position, the disconnect from her parents and brother, who didn't understand her.

She keeps reading...

Today I met an amazing guy. Avi. He's part of the new group that I sit with and discuss the need to change the face of the country in this cruel world. Avi is tall and dark with big eyes and a mischievous smile. It's obvious he'll be a leader one day. He came from France for a visit. His family lives in Tayibe, right next to us. I told him we're basically neighbors.

"We are, are we?" he answered with a smile.

The next time we met we already talked about our beliefs and values, and our goals in life. He's amazing. Smart, mature. Different from the kids at school that are only interested in goofing around.

Today I decided not to go to school and met up with Avi in Tel Aviv. Just us. We sat at a coffee shop. He paid for me. It's fun talking to him. I told him about my music and about my shows. He promised he'd come listen. He gets me. It's weird, my whole life, I've never really talked to an Arab, except for the cashier at the store or the gardener. Why? Is it really impossible to solve the conflict and live in peace, side by side?

Avi told me that his goal in life is to put an end to the status quo, to return to the Palestinians their lost dignity. He is motivated by mutual respect and has no intention of using force or harming anyone, because he doesn't believe in that. If I would tell my father, he'd say that Avi is naïve, and that you can't trust an Arab... but my father is wrong, he's too extreme. Maybe he has to be that way because of his job. I wonder what Avi would say if he knew who my father was. He never asked, and I never told him.

Avi came to one of my shows. I stayed the night in Tel Aviv with one of my friends. We were hanging out at her place. It was the first time I realized the actual meaning of the expression "butterflies in my stomach." I sat next to him and all I wanted was for everybody else to go away and leave the two of us alone. He excites me. He looks at me and sees me. I think he cares. The fact is, he was interested enough to come to hear me play and wants to be my friend, because of who I am.

I got up to make coffee for everyone and Avi came with me. He hugged me and we kissed. My first kiss – until now, I hadn't let anybody touch me. I'm falling in love with him. I want to be with him all the time.

I didn't go to school again. What's the point? What does it even do for me? I can study for tests outside of school. The kids at school are immature and annoying. They don't get me and make fun of me. Avi said he'd meet me at eleven, so I took the bus to school and from there walked to the central bus station and headed to Tel Aviv. Nobody will know. Tomorrow I'll bring a note from "mom." What's the big deal?

Yesterday he said to me that he's crazy about me. He just asked that I stop painting myself black because it hides my beauty. So I took off my makeup and underneath my black shirt, I put on an old pink t-shirt. I'll take the shirt off when I get to town. I want him to like me, to think that I'm pretty and that I look good. I hope he loves me.

Yesterday was so much fun. We walked on the boardwalk above the beach. We went all the way to Jaffa. We walked around the flea market there, where he bought me a necklace with a heart on it. Afterward we walked back and sat down on the beach. Avi spread out a towel that he had in his backpack. We hugged and kissed. He told me that he never felt this way about anyone. I told him that I hadn't either. I told him about my relationship with my parents and my friends. He was interested. I feel like I can trust him, tell him everything. He understands and doesn't criticize me like everybody else.

He walked me to bus stop to catch the last bus of the night. We stood at the bus stop holding hands. I'm happy. I can't tell anyone. My father would kill me and my mother would give me non-stop lectures. My whole life is one big secret, so here's one more.

I asked Avi today if his family would accept me if they knew we were in touch.

"Are you crazy?" he answered. "No way. They want me to marry my neighbor's daughter. But I'm not marrying anybody at the moment. I'm too young and I have a lot of things to do before then."

I was a bit hurt by his response. I thought he was serious about me. "You don't think we could be together?" I asked.

"We're together now, aren't we? But I have to go back to Paris soon. I'll miss you. Will you miss me?" he asked and kissed me on the lips. His lips are so nice and soft. When he kisses me I forget about everything.

"I'll miss you like crazy. I'll come visit, okay?" I asked.

"I wish. I don't think your parents will let you."

"They won't know about it. You're my secret. I'll travel to Paris on a trip with my friends. They don't pay attention to me anyway."

"We'll talk on the phone all the time and when you can, come visit," he said. "We have two weeks until my trip, let's think about it." How can we not think about it? The whole way home I cried silently. My love is leaving. What will I do? I have to be creative. To plan. I got home. Everything was black.

I told my parents that I'm spending the weekend with my friends in Jerusalem. I just made something up. I have to hang out with Avi on *our last weekend together. Just us. I want to sleep with him all night. I want to have sex with him. I'm a bit scared, but feel like I have to before he goes. Almost all the girls in my class have already done it. I hear them talk about it all the time. I want to give myself to him and let him know that I'm his and not just my soul. My body and my soul. He arranged a room for us at his friend's place, who went out of town.*

What an incredible weekend. We didn't leave the house. I finally understand what everybody's talking about. He was so gentle with me. Understanding. How nice and exciting it was. It didn't hurt at all. I wanted him more and more. I know that it will all end soon.

We talked non-stop the entire weekend. He told me what an Arab guy feels like in our country. How sad, how unjust. I trust him to bring change. He is smart and open-minded and convincing. One day he'll come back and lead a revolution. I'll be right beside him. An Arab and a Jewess bringing peace and equality. Even though he's my first boyfriend, I'm certain we'll get married and be a family. Everybody may hate us for it, but that doesn't bother me. The main thing is to be with my love.

What a dark day. Mom and dad were waiting for me at home. They know about Avi. My dad and his bullshit. He's mad at me and Mom is quiet. I'm not allowed to see him anymore, nor my friends from Tel Aviv. I have to go back to school and I'm not allowed to skip anymore. I talked to Avi and told him. He calmed me down and said, "Don't worry. Do what they tell you. I'm going back to Paris in two days anyway. I'll call you. We'll talk and plan something out. They'll get used to it. Everything will be fine. Remember, do exactly what they tell you, be a good girl, listen to them, do whatever you have to do to make them think everything is all right. I trust you and love you. Don't forget that I love you, my sweet."

My love, he's wise. He always knows what to say and how to say it. What does my father understand? He thinks he's so smart. I'll turn into the perfect little girl.

So boring. I went back to studying every day, without missing even a second. I did my homework at home and studied for my tests. My grades improved. I decided to drop the black look entirely, both to prove to my parents that I'm changing for the better, but mainly for Avi, who loved me without makeup and just wearing a little color. I'm lucky I have a guitar. It gives me hope. I stopped performing, disconnected from all my friends, and stayed in my room with just me and my songs and my notebook full of stories.

Avi thought of a great idea. I won't even dare write it down here, though. I don't want anybody to find out about it ahead of time. The plan has to be carried out, nothing must interfere. Soon I'm going to be a very happy girl. Avi said that I don't need to prepare anything ahead of time. He'll take care of everything. I dream about him at night. I feel his body inside me. I am excited about meeting up with him. In my dream, we're sleeping together, eating together, going back to the Jaffa promenade and friends. My love. I miss you.

Noa's mother closes the notebook. These were the last lines. She calls her husband and tells him what she found.

"I'm sending a driver to pick it up," he says. "I have to go over all the material on my own."

"She's with him. They planned it. I'm beginning to hope that he actually did fall in love with her and that he won't hurt her," she whispers.

"Fell in love with her? Is that what you think? A seventeen year old girl?"

"Maybe... I hope so. At least he won't hurt her."

"My dear, what is it that you don't understand? How can I explain it to you? You heard which organization he belongs to. There's no way he didn't plan this from the beginning. I'm convinced that he also knew who I am in advance. I hope that we catch up with them, and the sooner the better."

She starts crying. She understands the import of his words.

He kidnapped her, and if he feels like he's in danger, he'll kill her without batting an eye.

"Don't cry. You have to be strong, for me as well."

"The silence is killing me. The inability to tell anybody, even the boys, leaves me stuck at home in an unbearable state of loneliness."

"I know. Even here, most people don't know, and I can't just disappear. There are moments when I have difficulty breathing," he tells her.

She, who has known him for so many years, knows that underneath the tough exterior is a sensitive man with a big heart who simply doesn't know how to express it.

I decide to go home to see my family, especially the girls. I need to hug them even if only for a moment. I have a feeling that this isn't over for today. I raise my hand to hail a taxi.

"*Bonsoir, Madame,*" says the driver. I give him the address and he starts driving.

I am just getting out of the taxi when my phone rings. David is on the line.

"Good evening. We found Lady D's diary. Now we are convinced that the business was planned. The event isn't explicitly mentioned, but there are enough clues. Even though there isn't much news, this gives us legitimacy. We can say that the love he showered on the girl, as she describes in the journal, was a big show for him. We assume that he knew who her father is. The fact that we haven't heard from him or his people is troubling. Are they waiting for the event to go public in order to increase their bargaining power for her return? Do they have any intention of returning her at all, or just to make threats or apply pressure?"

"Wow..." This story is becoming a real problem.

"Yeah, wow. We are sending a technical team this evening. They'll arrive before midnight. Let your people know that they need to be ready for action by tonight. They know the area, having been here before, and they have the equipment. Make sure that you get the information and be prepared to meet with them tonight."

I need to get to the embassy and take out all the telegrams, or to make sure somebody brings them to me. I'll ask Nathan to see who's on duty, maybe I'll be able to avoid having to go to the embassy. I enter the house without prior warning.

Lior jumped up. "You're back..." Shir also comes running over and jumps all over me.

"Hi, girls," I say, hugging and kissing them. "How're you doing?"

"Good. Dad's making us pizza." The unmistakable smell of cheese wafted through the apartment.

I make sure that I can actually stay and eat, and won't need to run out in the middle and disappoint everybody. I head into the kitchen. Nathan is wearing a silly apron we bought somewhere. He's covered in flour, as is the counter and the floor.

"Hi," I say and give him a kiss, wiping away some of the flour stuck to his face. "Who's on duty at the embassy tonight? I need some help."

"Dov, why?"

"Can you call him and ask him to bring me the telegrams?"

"Okay. It's pressing, I understand. Are you staying?"

"I can stay but I'll need to leave at some point. I have an idea I need you to help me with later on."

"Ah, really?" He's intrigued. He likes the idea of being a part of this whole fiasco.

We sit down to eat the pizza and devour every last crumb. I offer to clean up, a chore I haven't done in ages. The girls shower and get ready for bed in the meantime.

"I have to meet some people who are arriving from Israel. It's going to be later, and it won't make any sense if I leave by myself. So can you come with me, and as soon as we start speaking, go to the bathroom? Is that okay?"

"I'll ask for overtime," he says. "I'm exhausted, but I'll shower and freshen up."

"Excellent. Thank you. In the meantime, I'll wait for Dov and the telegrams in order to know where we're going, who's coming, and how many."

The telegrams arrive. A team of five men. I only know the commander, who started working years after I did. They will enter the apartment and exit without anybody knowing. They have to scan the apartment, to photograph everything, and if they have time, to plant bugs in the phones and in the apartment itself. Some of them will stand guard outside, and one of them will leave with all the material and equipment we pick up in order to send it home as soon as possible. It's not likely that anything will happen tonight, but if the conditions are right, they'll try. The meeting place operates twenty-four-seven, is always crowded and noisy, and the air is fogged with cigarette smoke. We tell the girls that we're going out after they fall asleep; they're old enough to stay home alone. Next to the landline phone is a list of numbers if necessary.

At eleven, Nathan and I head out. I don't want to arrive at the last minute. It's better to walk around the Champs Elysees a bit, buy something to eat on the way, and then arrive. Suddenly, we also have some quality time together. We find parking close to the place and we walk in the direction of the main boulevard in our warm coats and scarves. I enjoy the cold weather. We look at one another and smile.

"Remind me of your name again?" I ask Nathan. It's our standing joke that we always have to get to know each other all over again.

"What's going on here? How is it that you're working here in Paris? I didn't think this was a very good idea."

"You're right. But we're talking about something extraordinary. Maybe after the fact I can tell you. Not even Yaron knows what I was called away for, and he's taking over for me."

"Really? He's probably not happy about that."

"That's his problem," I answer. "But I hope that this ends sooner than later. I have to travel to Israel in a few weeks, unless I get delayed here and if I do, then Yaron will travel in my place."

"So then I hope you get delayed," he says. "I like having you here. Being alone kills me."

"No. If you only knew, you'd take that back," I say quietly.

"I see," he says. "So if you need to travel to Israel, the girls will kill you."

"Time passes quickly. Living abroad will end, and then they'll have me full-time and then we'll see how they like it," I say with a smile. "And what about you? You'll have to get used to having me around again, and you won't be able to sleep diagonally anymore."

"Maybe this isn't the right time, but your schedule irritates me. Maybe they are taking care of your team, but they forgot about you a long time ago. Have they forgotten what they promised you when you left for this mission? If I would have known, I wouldn't have left Israel for all the money in the world."

I don't say anything. The feeling that I've been trying to ignore has returned. I'm at their beck and call. Promises are one thing, reality is another. Why don't they treat me the way I treat my people?

"Nathan, it's not the time. Believe me, I'm dealing with something that's taking everything I've got right now. I need quiet right now. Please." We both continue walking in silence, stopping to look in the display windows.

A little before midnight the call comes. Thomas is on the line. "Good evening."

"Good evening to you, too. Are you on your way?"

"I'll be there in half an hour."

"Good. Nathan is with me. I brought him as an escort."

"I gotcha."

Little Thomas. Short and thin, baby faced, a man you

wouldn't look at once, let alone twice. But when he opens his mouth, you can't take your eyes off him. He doesn't care about anybody if the circumstances dictate. A strategist, creative. Daring. He always says, "Whoever doesn't try will never fail, but he also won't succeed."

The rest of the team makes fun of him. "Little Thomas buys his suits in the kids department at Marks and Spencer." But if you ask them one question: who's the one member you want with you on a mission? His name will get most of the votes, and by a wide margin.

He arrives about a half-hour later, together with another guy, his support.

"Hi." We shake hands and sit down.

"How was your flight?"

"It was fine. What's our story?"

"You arrived from Israel and got my number from Nili, a mutual friend."

"I'm going to the bathroom, I'll be right back," Nathan says getting up.

"I understand that you are aware of what happened and what's being planned," I say. "Anton is walking around gathering information. He has already made contact and has laid bait, now he's waiting for the fish to bite. Udi and his guys are waiting to follow whoever is in the apartment as soon as they leave. As soon as the apartment is empty, and it's clear they won't return immediately, they'll get the green light to go in. We aren't talking about an operation that has been adequately planned. We just don't have time and we're very concerned."

"Obviously."

"Do you have my phone number and Udi's?"

"Yes," Thomas says. "If nothing happens tonight, and I imagine nothing will, I'll ask you to set up a meeting with me and Udi in the morning. I have to touch base with him about a few things."

"Of course."

I give him two possible meeting places, and the rest of the details will be discussed between them tomorrow by telephone.

"What about in Israel? Does anybody know about the matter?"

"No. It's incredible. Absolute silence. I'm shocked. What a crazy world, they aren't afraid of anything." Thomas' opinions are known to lean towards the far right. The system is comprised of people who run the gamut in terms of their politics.

"Okay. I'm here for whatever you need or want to ask. Be in touch and hopefully we'll be able to dig something up."

"From your mouth to His ear," he says, looking up.

Nathan comes back, we talk a bit more and then leave. I take the long way back to the car. We have four days before the delegation to Poland is supposed to return home, before somebody leaks something to the news.

One last call to Udi. I tell him that the guys arrived and are getting themselves organized. He sets the meeting place for tomorrow. The light is off in the apartment, but nobody has left the building. It looks like tonight will be quiet.

It's two in the morning by the time I get into bed. I close my eyes and imagine the pair chosen to finish watching the object's apartment. Thank God it's not me. How many nights have I burned waiting? I'll never forget the time I couldn't stay awake. There were two of us in the car. Tzvika sat next to me. We split the time between us. In the middle of my watch, I found myself dozing off. Tzvika saw that I was asleep and was forced to take over for me while I slept soundly.

Wednesday

I wake up. It's six o'clock. Everything is still dark. I check the phone to see that I didn't miss any calls during the night. Everything was quiet. I enjoy the silence, my quiet solace. I close my eyes and see Noa's picture in my mind. She was thin, introverted, and there was something melancholy about her.

I get up and go to the girls' room. I watch them sleep, pull the covers over Shir, then go to the kitchen where I put on the kettle to make myself a cup of tea and step into the shower. I let the hot water wash over and warm my body, enjoying the feeling of the steam, which has fogged up the mirror. It's a new day. I interlace my fingers and smile. Positive thinking creates a positive reality. I'm sitting in the kitchen, a cup of tea in hand, writing telegrams that I'll have Nathan send to Israel. I'm summarizing yesterday.

Lior will get up first; she likes to be early. Shir is harder to wake up; she has her own pace and we try not to annoy her in the mornings. Sometimes it annoys me, but today, I feel like everything's fine and there's no stress. Nathan opens a watchful eye and is treated to a cup of coffee in bed. He smiles as if to say, "Where did this come from? Am I dreaming?"

The morning rush has started. Sandwiches, bags, clothes, morning beverages and an apple on the run. Kisses all around. Nathan takes the telegrams and heads out with the girls.

Anton calls and requests to meet this morning.

"Bonjour, Monsieur," I say to Anton.

"Bonjour, Madame."

We sit down over coffee and croissants.

"I have something to tell you…"

Finally, I think to myself.

He continues, "Yesterday evening, I was sitting at the coffee shop in Clichy. Suddenly, the fellow I told you about comes over to me, Daoud, the guy whose brother is in the organization. He was with another guy who he presented to me as Mahmoud. Daoud spoke with his brother, who is very interested in meeting with me, but right now is busy with another thing and isn't in Paris. The whole group is involved in something, that's how he put it."

"Were you able to get any more out of them?"

"I said that I wasn't going to wait around for them because I'm very busy, and that it was too bad nobody could make time for me. And then the second guy said that they understood, but they were in the middle of something that will make all of us feel good. I looked at him and said, 'Come on, what could possibly do that? They've already tried everything, and nothing doing.' They looked at each other and said that they were serious, that there's an important operation happening and he can't tell me about it, but he might be able to arrange a meeting if we can get physically close enough. I said to him, 'Daoud, I understand. But I'm a busy man and every hour that I spend here costs me money. Tell me where and, if I can make it work, I'll be there. And if not, some other time.' He shifted in his chair and said, 'They're in Holland. More than that, I don't know. But I can find out for you.'

"'Excellent,' I said. You have my phone number, let me know. I'm going to be in Belgium and Holland anyway, so give me an address and I'll be there.'"

"Nice. Now the question is, are they there with the girl?"

"Wait. After that, I asked him who I'm supposed to meet with, and he said that his brother Youssuf will be there, and maybe his higher-up, Ahmed. I told him that would be fine and asked if he had a picture so I could recognize them. He took out his phone and showed me a picture of our "friend" Ahmed."

"My dear," I say, excited, "You nailed it. We have to meet the team and decide what we're going to do. The question is, do we still go into the apartment here as planned, besides just to verify the information on Mahmoud and Daoud? Should we take into consideration the possibility that the conversation with them might be a smokescreen?"

"Right. I think we have to go into the apartment. Obviously, we can't pack up and leave, but need to spread out here, and there as well."

"How did the meeting end?"

"He said he'd call me after talking with his brother, Youssuf, and will give me a time and place to meet. I paid, left a fat tip, and got out of there."

"Nice. I'll call home, and also to our friends here. I'll set up a meeting with both of them on the other side of Paris so we can touch base. After the guys in Israel make their decisions, I'll let you know as well. Put the apartment for rent on hold in the meantime."

I leave the meeting with Anton and feel renewed. I walk along the streets, cleansing myself from the meeting and then call Israel. "David…" I tell him about what's going on with Anton.

"Wow," he says. "I'm sitting here with some people, I'll call you back. Also, I think you're both correct and that we need to go into the 'lover's' apartment. Maybe there we'll find something important. It may be that the meeting is a diversion and they want to check out Anton. Give me an hour, even half-an hour."

"You got it."

I call Udi and Thomas and set up a meeting for the three of us in another hour and a half. In the meantime, I sit at a nice little café and treat myself to a cup of hot chocolate, sweet and creamy the way I love it, despite the fact that such love is unrequited. The phone rings. David is on the line.

"Already?"

"No. I updated the head of the Mossad before we do anything, and he wants to speak with you."

"Hello," I hear a British voice.

"Good morning," I answer formally.

"I wanted to tell you and to all your guys that I very much appreciate all that you're doing," he says quietly.

"I hope that everything will end quickly and as well as possible. This is personal for each one of us."

"I thank you all very much. It goes without saying that my wife and I are very, very worried."

"Of course you are, we're all thinking about you all the time, and I, as a mother, completely understand. I wish I could do more to help in these difficult times. We send our support from here."

"Thank you, thank you. I hope we can meet soon in order to raise a toast."

"Me too."

"Goodbye and good luck. David will be in contact soon."

The sweetness of the cocoa makes me slightly nauseous, and I have a bad feeling in my stomach. Everything is dwarfed by this phone call, not because of what the head of the Mossad said to me, but more what he didn't say. He let me know his and his wife's state of mind without putting it into words.

I don't really know him that well. I have spoken to him a few times, either professionally or in passing in the hallway. When I started working there, we were like a big family. Everybody knew everybody, we ate lunch in the small lunch room, everybody in line with trays, directors and low-level employees together. A sense of brotherhood and belonging. I leave the cup of cocoa almost full, take a sip of cold water that was served alongside it and leave.

I meet Udi and Thomas at the Café de la Paix next to the opera house. Most of the people here are tourists, and a mix of languages can be heard all over. Udi is waiting and Thomas enters a minute later. I start updating them on what Anton told me and from there move on to the decisions made in Israel. I look at the two of them. They didn't fall out of their chairs when they heard what Daoud told Anton; any mission can change on a dime many times before it's finished.

"David called me. We have to go into the apartment for verification and to get any other details that we can find. Thomas, your team stays here. Udi, you leave two people here to help out with outside security and take the rest of your team and meet up with Anton, who will get to Holland on his own. We have to keep Anton safe – he's going to meet with Youssuf and Ahmed and keep tabs on those two."

"Okay," Udi says. "Just to update you: yesterday, there was somebody in the apartment. A light was on until after one in the morning, and nobody has left the apartment since then. Somebody will have to come out sooner or later. I suggest that Bill and Monica stay in Paris and that everybody on Thomas's team meet at our safehouse for instructions on tonight, when we will hopefully be able to go inside. Until then, I'll keep Merlin there so we don't miss anybody who leaves."

"I'm good with that," Thomas says. "Usually, as a rule, the team works independently. Partnerships exist, but they aren't as good in my opinion. In our team, we understand one another without talking, but it is what it is and we'll make it work."

"No choice. By the way, the head of the Mossad called me and told me to tell everybody "thank you" personally, from him. It was a very touching conversation. I'm sure he wants to be here himself."

"Yeah, that's the basic instinct of anybody in his situation. What a shitty situation," Udi says. Thomas nods his head in silence. What more needs to be said?

"All right, let's get to work." I grab Udi before he leaves. "Udi, we need to coordinate meeting locations in Amsterdam. Give me a few options that you know of, and I will give them to Anton before we get there."

He writes the name of three places in the center of town on a piece of paper. "We wanted progress and we got it. Hopefully, she's still under the illusion that she's found the love of her life and that she's all right."

"Yeah, hopefully they won't treat her differently from how she imagined they would until we can get to her."

Hopefully, hopefully. How naïve this girl is and all she wants is a little love and attention.

In my conversation with Anton, I ask him to pack it up in Clichy. Better he not hang around there right now. I let him in on the decisions made and on the team members who would be joining him in Holland. He isn't supposed to tie himself to them, except for a meeting with Udi where they will coordinate vantage points, communication protocols and meetings when necessary. I hope I can get to Holland and continue to coordinate the operation.

"Take care of yourself there," I say to Anton, meaning that he shouldn't fall into some trap they might be setting for him.

We have to protect our people when necessary. There have been mishaps, like in the case of Chaim. A humble and likeable fellow who went out to meet with an object in Paris. The other side was onto him, and sent somebody to shoot him in the café. He was hit in the gut, stopped working in the field, and taught field work to the younger generation.

"Don't worry, I'm always careful. There's a price I'm not willing to pay."

Despite that, I suppose we are all highly motivated and on occasion cut corners. I hope that these guys don't try to get cute – that they aren't planning on exposing the girl as well as a few Mossad agents. Suddenly, a thought occurs to me, and I have to tell headquarters.

"David, it's me again," I say to the operation commander in Israel.

"News already?

"Listen, I think that maybe we made a mistake by not publicizing the girl's disappearance. It doesn't make sense if you look at it objectively. If they know who she is, they understand that we, the Mossad, are looking for her, and they are waiting for us to expose as many of our people as possible."

"Look, the decision to keep the matter quiet came about for two reasons: first, we didn't want to cause a panic in the media that would create a lot of noise in places where it isn't appropriate for us to do that right now. By the way, we told the students that the girl has been found and sent home. The second reason is that their organization is new and we assume they don't have manpower or serious resources in order to pull off a scheme like this. Time will tell. As far as we're concerned, we need to be careful. Anton has to watch out. He can't meet those guys in a non-public place, and we need to protect him while doing so."

"Okay." It's hard to think that something bad will happen to one of us. Over the years I've worked here, I was never concerned for my life. Perhaps I'm too old for these "games?"

I close my eyes. Stop! Let it go. Shake it off. It will be fine. Thought dictates reality! We'll get them, and everything will work out in the end.

"Nathan," I say into the phone. "When will you be home? I'm buying a few things for lunch. Shall we all meet at home?" I need my family and have to make the most of the fact that they are close to me right now.

"I'm on my way. The girls are home."

"See you soon..."

I stop at the neighborhood market. Chicken schnitzel and mashed potatoes, comfort food. That's what I feel like right now. I buy chicken breast, potatoes and some vegetables. Maybe soon I'll need to leave. It seems like the business in Paris is about to conclude.

I go into our apartment and the girls are in front of the television waiting for their father. "Hi, Mom," they say and jump up. "We forgot you were here."

Great, just what I wanted to hear. It's so nice to feel like such an unimportant part of their daily life. They've written me off already.

"Hi, I'm here. Who wants to help me make schnitzel?" I know the answer.

"Me," says Lior and jumps up. She likes to cook.

"I'm tired, I don't feel like it," Shir says. The world is functioning normally.

"So then rest in front of the television; afterwards you can wash the dishes." I smile to Lior, who is satisfied with the work orders.

"Oh, fine..." Shir says.

She'll probably try to get out of it later.

Nathan arrives home with a smile. "How are my favorite girls?" he asks and hugs and kisses each one of us. "Have we gone back to Israel?" he asks.

"Very funny," I say and make a face.

But, it's true. I hope that when we all go back to Israel, I'll remember how to cook, clean and sit quietly at home without running around.

We sit down to eat and Shir comes up with the idea that will save her from having to wash the dishes. "Dad, you didn't do the dishes today, so why don't you wash and I'll dry."

"You're sneaky, you know that?" Nathan says. "I'll think about it."

In the afternoon I receive a call from Udi.

"It's happening. A guy left the apartment with a backpack and took a taxi to the north train station. He bought a ticket on the fast train to Amsterdam. The train is leaving in fifteen minutes. We're also going, and Bill and Monica are on lookout near the apartment in Clichy. Thomas's crew as well. As soon as it gets dark, we're going into the apartment. So we part ways here, perhaps we'll meet up later."

"Good luck. Take care of Anton. I don't want to think for a moment that these guys planned everything to catch a couple more birds."

"Yeah, okay. I won't let him out of my sight. We'll meet there and establish guidelines."

"Don't forget to report, even if you need to make a long distance call. Don't start being cheap now," I say, joking.

He chuckled, "Call home, tell them I won't have time to call them."

"No problem."

In ten more minutes, they'll board the train. Merlin apparently will travel in the same car as him so she can see everything he does. The rest will wait in the cars in front of his and behind. When he gets off the train, they'll continue following him. They aren't many and so they have to be very careful, and must not lean on the fact that this guy isn't a professional.

Two are left to watch the apartment. One of them went up to mark the object's door, to make sure that nobody has gone in or that there isn't anybody else still inside. They don't have keys to the door, and they can't let them know, even after the fact, that somebody was in there. We have no idea if the apartment has an alarm, and the team can only check that at the entrance. We have to wait for a few hours.

Thomas calls to update me. "I went into the object's building and, as luck would have it, each door has its own alcove, so we can stand there without anybody noticing. There's a noisy elevator and a narrow, rickety staircase that makes a bunch of noise. So it's easy to know if anybody's coming."

"Too bad I don't have a walkie-talkie so I can listen in," I joked, but I was serious. A reminder of the days when I was a part of all that. The excitement, the adrenaline, the expectations and the satisfaction. I miss that, though perhaps I just miss my youth? "Good luck to us."

Evening comes. Darkness. The lights in Ahmed's apartment are still off. In the apartment above his and in the apartment next door, light could indicate that the television is on. The number of cars driving on the street dwindles. There's almost nobody around. The park behind the building is empty and the time to try to enter the apartment approaches.

At eleven at night, the apartment above the object's has been dark for half an hour. A faint light emanates from the apartment next door. Thomas sends L to knock on Ahmed's door to make sure nobody's there. She goes up slowly, trying not to make any noise on the stairs. Nobody on the team uses the elevator.

She's at the door. A light knock doesn't bear any response. She knocks harder. Silence. She gives the signal over the walkie-talkie for her partner to come upstairs. He arrives with equipment for opening the door. It's delicate work and requires a lot of luck. The light in the hallway goes out, so we need a flashlight.

He's an expert locksmith, and while he's working on picking the lock, she helps him and mans the communications while simultaneously listening and checking out what's going on in the building. The spotters are outside. A car and driver are waiting in case we need to make a quick getaway. Everybody is waiting quietly, answering only when asked, and only when necessary.

A half hour goes by, another ten minutes, and L announces that the door is open. They go into the apartment and scan it to make sure there aren't any alarms or surprises. S is sent up to help catalogue and photograph. They have to return everything exactly as they found it. The door locks behind them, and each one heads in a different direction to scan the living room and bedroom. They don't talk. Flashlights on their heads.

The lights in the hallway of the building go on. They stop and turn off their flashlights. A neighbor went down with his dog, took a walk in the park, and they're waiting for the spotters outside to let them know when he gets back to the building. They hear the elevator ascend, the door to his apartment close, and then they wait a few minutes for L's call, turn their lights back on and continue to work. They go through the drawers, closets, under the bed, in the sheets, the kitchen cabinets and refrigerator. We need to get inside the head of whoever lives in this house to know where they would hide something.

Another hour goes by and the team finishes up. They check that everything has been put back exactly as they found it and wait for the spotters to tell them the coast is clear before exiting. S leaves first, followed by A and then L. After A locks the door behind him, the couple goes downstairs embracing. All the team members are wearing dark colors so as not to stand out. They walk to the car that is waiting for them a few streets over and get out of there. Udi's team leaves as well. Everyone drives to the operational apartment to touch base and to prepare material to be sent back home.

Everybody arrives and sits down in the room. Excitement is in the air.

A begins. "There wasn't much material. We found pictures of the girl, mostly with Ahmed. The pictures were definitely taken in Israel, in Tel Aviv. We found lists. Among other things, there are names of members of her family there, including the big boss. The private address and workplace of the mother. There was a lot of material in Arabic and French. But we did find material on the new organization – its essence and its goals. There are a number of addresses on a piece of paper, both in Holland and in Belgium, which I wrote down on a piece of paper for the team heading there. We photographed everything, including things that didn't seem important."

L continues, "I found pictures of our friend and a few more

trainees. Apparently at a training camp in one of the Arab countries. I found pictures of the guy together with a girl, and no doubt they're in a relationship. It could be that's his girlfriend, or ex-girlfriend. I photographed other notebooks that might have been college study material."

S reports on material that was found on his computer. He copied all the relevant information. "I photographed the whole apartment and put a bug in the phone."

"We didn't find phone numbers or names of anybody else, but it seems as though there was some thought put into what to leave out and what to conceal," says A.

"Yeah," says Thomas. "Maybe that's a point of caution we should consider for the future."

The meeting ends. Whoever is responsible for the equipment stays behind with Thomas to organize everything to be sent back to Israel on an El-Al flight leaving that afternoon. The teams disperse. Udi's team and Bill and Monica, who are staying in Paris, split up. In the morning, Monica will fly to Holland armed with the addresses we found in the apartment. Bill will stay in Paris, next to Clichy, to make sure that the apartment stays empty, in case this was a diversion. Thomas and the members of his team will go back together with the equipment and the material on the plane.

I receive a telephone report that night and update headquarters about the main points. I have a hard time falling asleep, and so I get up and pack my blue suitcase. It's clear to me that tomorrow I'm also going to Amsterdam.

Thursday

Thomas and his crew submitted the photographed material from last night to me during a morning meeting. I leave them and head to the embassy. I call Israel. "Well, how about that?"

"Good job. We'll check out the addresses. Might already be in the system. You're going to Holland, keep coordinating."

"Okay, of course. We have another day until the kids come back," I say. Another day and the kids who come back from Poland will know that Noa isn't there. One more day until the information makes its way to the media and blows up.

"Yeah, I know. We have a meeting in one hour. The material will arrive in the afternoon and we'll go over it. If we have an indication that Noa is in a specific location, we're considering bringing the Dutch in on this. We don't want an altercation on Dutch soil, best if the Dutch free her."

"Fine. I'll wait to hear from you. I'm getting on a train at twelve."

"See you later."

I go down to the floor where Nathan works to say goodbye. I won't finish or come back even for the weekend.

"Nathan, I'm heading to Holland. What was here, is continuing there," I say. "I didn't say goodbye to the girls, I'll call in the evening."

"Okay. What else is new?" he says sarcastically. Nathan always had a hard time, like the girls, accepting the basic fact that I don't have any control over where they send me. "Are you sure you're not enjoying this?"

"I'm sure that I want to say goodbye nicely, so that I won't have to spend the whole trip in Amsterdam feeling guilty."

"You're right."

"Thank you for understanding."

"We'll hear from you this evening. Maybe you'll still manage to get back by Friday, Shabbat?"

"From your mouth to God's ear."

I wish I could tell him. He would support me and gladly let me go.

I'm back on the train again. We leave the station and its graffitied walls. The sky is blue. The sound of the train's wheels make a monotonous rhythm that intersperses with the roar of the wind once we reach top speed.

The streamlined team is in the office waiting for material to arrive. The head of the Mossad is sitting in his office on the top floor. His hand is on his forehead, eyes closed. The more time that goes by, the more difficult it is. He is reminded of the first conversation he had with the prime minister about the fiasco in the Jerusalem offices. They confined themselves behind locked doors, just the two of them, by request of the head of the Mossad.

"Did something happen? Did we fail the mission? Was somebody caught?" The prime minister looked at the cold and disciplined man and saw that he was more pale than usual. Stress. He sat hunched over and told the prime minister the series of events of the last few days, starting with the trip to Poland and her disappearance and going back to her meeting Ahmed and the findings of the private investigator, and explained to him the next plan of action.

"That's awful." The prime minister leaned his elbows on the table and leaned his face towards that of the head of the Mossad.

"Just awful. I can only imagine what you're going through. Your wife's at home?"

"It's difficult. Very difficult. Nobody knows about this. We decided that we can't let this get out to the press. Even in the system, very few people know. It's all as secret as can be."

"I understand. Talk to me, day or night. Just don't let it become an international incident."

"Thanks. I hope that this will end quickly, this nightmare."

Every morning he had a conversation to update the prime minister. During one of the conversations the prime minister suddenly asked, "When you learned she was involved with an Arab fellow, did you mention it to the head of the Shin Bet?"

"Only to see if they knew him. And when I learned that he was leaving the country, I left it alone."

"Mistake," said the prime minster.

"Indeed. Mistake," said the head of the Mossad.

Silence.

"Well, forget about it, let's focus on fixing it," said the prime minister.

"Yeah," answered the head of the Mossad.

He doesn't need to hear it again to know that, when it's all said and done, there's going to be a discussion.

The last time he received an update was over the phone about an hour ago. "A little more, hold on just a little more to maintain your strength," he said to himself over and over, hoping that it would indeed give him strength. Every part of his body was being drained of energy. It started in his legs and continued to his hands that found it difficult to hold even a cup of coffee. His stomach began to flare up. He took a deep breath, trying to get his strength back from the oxygen in the air. "Let this thing be finished already, just get it over with!" He slams his fist down as hard as he can on the table.

His wife is in the back room adjacent to his office. A suite built for him so he could rest and shower after exercising in the employee weight room. He has a closet there with shirts, ties, even a suit or two. Sometimes he has to spend long hours there.

He and his wife had a hard time staying at home. The loneliness and the secrecy. Tomorrow the class will come back from the trip and the cat will be out of the bag. Here, they are safe from the outside, from the need to try to hide it all as their world threatens to come crashing down. She sleeps most of the time and he quietly opens the door; the television is on, quiet songs in the background, and she is in the same position. He turns and closes the door behind him.

In the meeting room, he sits down at the head of the table and waits for people to join him. He has never waited before, always working on something until his secretary informs him that everybody is present and waiting for him, and only then would he arrive. Why waste even a minute's worth of work?

The trains leaves its final station in Brussels. The ride is slower. I'm sitting with a bottle of water that I bought from the coffee cart. I have no patience. In a moment, the view will change to green and blue, and the cows will return to pasture.

She lies in bed. Her husband comes in quietly and she closes her eyes so he'll think she's asleep. She's aware that his energy is dissipating rapidly, but she isn't interested in talking to anybody, not even with herself. To lie there without moving is less painful, less difficult. When she closes her eyes, everything is transparent. Empty. Is this how it feels to be dead? While waiting to die? Is there a heaven? Hell? Will I meet my mother and father again?

At the bank, they must certainly be wondering what happened to me. Me, who never missed a day of work, who arrives five minutes before everybody else and is the last one to leave. I don't like it when people talk about me. Nosing around in my life. I caught his secrecy bug. I need someone to hug me and tell me that everything will be all right. I need my mother, my father. I don't have anywhere or anyone to turn to. To sleep, just to sleep.

We arrive. I book a room for a few days and get in a cab. The hotel is fine, on a side street. The room is small but pleasant. I call Anton and Udi and tell them I've arrived. We arrange to meet for lunch or dinner at a restaurant in a residential area known only to the locals. I discovered it on one of my trips years ago. Beyond the need to update people and stay updated, I was hungry. I don't like Dutch cuisine, but I have gotten used to French and Belgian cooking. But when you're hungry, it doesn't really matter.

The other two arrive, each on his own. I begin by filling them in about last night. The verification of the girl with the fellow, about the addresses, about the material sent back to Israel.

Anton reports that he has a meeting set for tomorrow morning at ten thirty in the center of Amsterdam. A café in a busy part of town chosen by the other side. That suits us. Udi and his guys can watch Anton without a problem, they've already gone over all the possible seating arrangements and the team will be waiting there when the meeting takes place in order to keep an eye on things, who is in attendance, and the people coming and going. At least two of them will be armed. Anton will wear a bullet proof vest, even though he hates to feel encumbered.

"This time I'm also going to be there. Do you have a spare walkie-talkie?" I ask Udi.

"Yeah, we do. Bill's is here, he's in Paris. You can sit in the café next door," Udi says. He and his team have secured the area. "Sit next to the window because from there you can see almost everything. Sting and Barbara will also wait there and follow them after the meeting ends."

"Okay," I say. "We might have additional information from Israel tonight, will be interesting what turns up."

"I hope for something useful. We've already been to all the addresses. There are Arab names at two of the four addresses, just from looking at the mailboxes. All the addresses are outside the city center, but not far from it. The entrances to the buildings, and also to the apartments, are very narrow. Everything is so compact that you need to be an acrobat to climb the stairs."

"The Dutch are so tall and light, it's a good thing the population is mixed, otherwise we would stand out in the field to the point where we wouldn't be able to work."

We exchange information about all the team members. Udi hands me the written report about the addresses we checked out. Later, Ami will arrive from the embassy in The Hague in order to get the information and send it to Israel in an organized fashion.

"Is there anything anybody needs from the embassy?" Udi asks.

"Anton, who called you in order to set up the meeting?" I ask.

"First Daoud called to tell me his brother would call me, and later Youssuf actually called, at least that's how he introduced himself. He sounded friendly and serious. He said that they'll only be free Friday morning. I told him that I was here until Friday evening, and afterwards I had to go to London," Anton says.

"Good, let's say that if there's nothing to report, we'll meet tomorrow before we head out to the field."

This time I'm talking about the place where Udi's guys meet. Anton will also be there.

"In case of an emergency, I'll be in touch. And if not, let's leave the updates for tomorrow morning."

The meeting ends, and we get up to go our separate ways.

I use the time to wander around the city. I walk past manicured public gardens, colorful flowers, small bridges and houseboats on the murky canals. I arrive at Rembrandt Square, where the nightlife is. Cafés, restaurants, clubs and light drugs. In the middle of the square is a statue of the famous painter. From there, I continue to Dam Square, which has the floodgate. It's a giant square, and in its center is the palace, the first church, and a statue in memory of those who died in World War II. This square is on every tourist's itinerary, and so it is packed and noisy all the time.

I take advantage of the time and call home. As expected, I hear about it from Shir. "I'm sick, sick, sick of it! God!"

"Mom? How are you?" asks Lior.

"I'm fine, sweetie, what about you guys?"

"Fine. I have an English test tomorrow. No problem."

"I see. You'll do fine, you know English."

"When are you coming back?"

"I still don't know. I'll try to be home as soon as possible. I'm sorry that I left without saying goodbye."

"It's okay, Mom. Dad's here, you want him?"

"Yeah, sure. And give Shir a hug and a kiss for me. Okay?"

"Okay."

"Hello," says Nathan.

"Hi, how's it going?"

"Fine, what about you guys?"

"Hoping to finish soon."

"I see. Okay. Shall we talk tomorrow?"

"Of course. Good night. Kisses."

I sit at a small café on a side street, potted red gerbera in full bloom. I think about Anne Frank. Her story has guided me my whole life. I have read her diary many times. Every Holocaust Day, her small face peers up at me. Anna – Noa, Noa – Anna. Both of them hidden away here in the city, each one for different reasons, in different times. I wonder whether Noa wants us to look for her, or if she's still convinced that she has found the love of her life.

I'm waiting for Ami to take my telegrams to the embassy. He arrives running. It's the end of the day and he's dying to get home; his kids are also waiting for him. Evening falls, I go into the supermarket and buy a bottle of water, two sandwiches with gouda cheese and salad. I need a good shower. I just want to sit and stare at the television and hope that tomorrow arrives quickly, and that I sleep well.

David is on the line.

"Did you get my message that tomorrow morning there's a meeting?"

"Yes. They brought me a note into the meeting," he tells me. "The boss is encouraged. I understand that you guys are organizing for tomorrow with Udi's guys."

"Organizing in accordance. We hope to arrive at the address in the end."

"About the material you sent, there's a whole notebook on the organization. No mention of its members. We never got to any names, addresses or phone numbers. We found a few emails that the guys here are still working on. There's coding that should lead to a breakthrough. We saw the pictures of the trainees and that will take time to figure out." He continued...

"What is clear is that the girl is with him. In the materials, it is stated that they aspire to things that will draw the world's attention. In the notebook, there is a caricature where you see the prime minister on all fours like a dog and on top of him is a man who represents the Palestinian people with a whip in one hand and a bowl of food in the other that he withholds from 'the dog.'"

Nice bunch, I think to myself. But there are extremists everywhere. Those are the rules of the game. Control and power. A waste of energy and resources. What ever happened to "each man beneath his own vineyard and fig tree?"

"At this stage, we don't have anything helpful. In our estimation, we have about twenty-four hours until the media feasts on the news."

"I don't want to think about that at all," I answer. "Okay. So we meet tomorrow at nine a.m., our time. If there's news, let me know."

They have all night to work on the material.

"Good luck."

I'm tired. Tomorrow's a new day.

The head of the Mossad enters the suite. His wife is sitting on the bed, pillows behind her head, the blue light of the television lights the room. She raises her glance to him expecting some tidings. He sits on the edge of the bed, holding her hand. She leans her head on him and closes her eyes.

"How do you feel?" He doesn't know what else to ask.

"I don't feel anything," she answers. "Make this nightmare come to an end, please."

"We're trying." He tries to cheer her up, but she starts crying quietly. He hugs her, and all he wants is somebody to support him, to give him strength.

I must not break... I must not break... I must not. He repeats the mantra in his mind.

"What do you think will happen?" she asks, knowing he can't answer the question. She tries to talk, to not disconnect. She knows that he feels the same and needs her support. She holds up her hands and strokes his face, crying. He looks at her and is filled with a feeling that he hasn't felt in a long time. He hides his face in her shoulder and starts to cry, vocal and tormented. She holds him, finding the strength for a moment not to completely fall apart, until he is comforted in her arms.

"It's going to be all right," she says. "She'll come back."

"Yeah. She has to come back. She has to come back." He goes to the sink in the small bathroom, washes his face, fills a cup with water and brings it to her.

"Let's go eat something. They left food for us in the refrigerator. We have to keep up our strength. Tomorrow is an important day. We should tell the boys."

"Yeah. On the one hand, I'm concerned but, on the other, it will be a relief. Maybe we can stay here for a few days."

"We can. But the kids can't. That'll kill them. I'll make some phone calls and we'll all go to a friend's house, without the media finding out." He has a few friends, all willing to help out. He picks up the phone.

"Yitzhak, good evening."

"Hey, what's up? I finally hear from you."

"Yeah. Listen. I don't have time to talk, but I need a private place for my whole family for a few days."

"Something happen?"

"Not now. I need your help. Do you have a place for us?"

Yitzhak on the other side understands. The man on the other end of the line needs help.

"Of course there is," he answers. "Listen, come to my place, I'll wait for you. When do you want to come?"

"Tomorrow afternoon, more or less. May I be presumptuous?"

"Of course you can. Up to half my kingdom. What's mine is yours," Yitzhak says.

"I don't want anybody else in the house. Is that possible?"

"I understand. I'll send the staff on vacation. I'm planning on being on vacation anyway. I'll make sure they stock the refrigerator, and Friday night dinner will be prepared in advance."

"Thank you very much. I'll let you know when we'll be arriving."

"See you later."

"It's all arranged," he said, turning to his wife. "We'll go to Yitzhak's tomorrow afternoon before the media starts hounding us. We'll stay there until we decide to leave."

"At least we'll be with the boys," she says. "Call them. What will we tell them?"

"I'll tell them that we're going on vacation for a few days and they should cancel any plans they may have had. Period."

Friday

There's light coming in from the window. A new day. It's seven in the morning. Still early. I turn on the television hoping to hear some relaxing music on MTV. I'm lying in bed, recovering. A night devoid of thoughts and dreams, just like I asked for. I have enough time to shower, eat breakfast and walk to the apartment where we have our meetings. I put on clothes that will be comfortable to walk in.

"Good morning," I say to Merlin, who opens the door before I have a chance to knock.

"Good morning." She's always smiling, optimistic. The entire team likes working with her. She's serious, intelligent, and speaks wonderful French, outstanding English and can even get by in Italian. She looks good and is in shape, and doesn't wear makeup or doll herself up. In the field, she's a shapeshifter – with a wave of her hand, she becomes a different person. Udi's team has quite the asset.

Udi's team is busy dealing with the walkie-talkies, and Anton hasn't arrived yet.

"Any news?" Udi asks.

"No. Nothing substantial that can help us," I respond.

Anton enters looking tailored as usual, and I am reminded of an instructor that liked to deliver his courses on cover stories wearing an expensive suit, Rolex watch and shiny leather boots. Lesson number one: you have to look like who you want them to think you are. Afterwards, dive deep into the content. On the first day, we laughed, but later we understood that he was right, despite his being dramatic and annoying.

"How are you doing this morning?" I ask.

"I'm good. Slept well. We're going over everyone's job. Anton won't have a communication device and, so we have to come up with signals if the need arrives. The most important are signs he's in danger."

Udi continues to brief the team about the conclusion of the meeting. The team will track everyone who arrives, hoping they reach the desired address. If everything goes smoothly, the team will deploy to the new address just like in Paris, until a decision is made. I give Anton a hug and whisper, "Good luck, take care of yourself."

"Thank you, my dear." He smiles and walks out.

The team has already left, and I go to Dam Square, and from there to the coffee shop next to the meeting place. I sit next to the window where I have a wide viewing angle. Barbara and Sting are already situated near to me. Each one in charge of a different field of view. I'm able to see some of the people sitting in the other café. At present, there's a team member waiting inside, the rest are waiting for Anton and the people he'll be meeting with, so they can get a good spot from which to guard him.

I order a cup of tea and a small piece of cake, which gives me a reason to sit down so they won't hassle me about it. At 10:25, Anton enters the café.

At 10:35, two Arab-looking guys enter the café. One of them resembles Ahmed and I get a little excited.

Anton extends them his hand and says to the short one, "Youssuf?" He nods. Anton extends his hand to the other fellow and introduces himself, and he answers him, "Ahmed." They sit.

Yes! I think to myself. *Yes!*

They order coffee, and Anton asks if they'd like something to eat. They politely decline. Anton explains to them, "I have made a lot of money in my life, and now I want to be part of something that will have a long-lasting impact after I'm gone. I want to leave a legacy for my children and grandchildren so that they will value what is theirs, and will fight for what they deserve."

"So do we," says Ahmed. "We believe in being proactive. We must take matters into our own hands and remain steadfast. We don't like what's happening with the Palestinian leadership. We are projecting weakness, don't you think?"

"Absolutely. We need to unify all of our forces, and also to prove to the other side that they need to be afraid." Anton doesn't elaborate.

"And now we must let both sides know that we are the new leadership," says Ahmed. Youssuf is quiet; it's obvious who the boss is.

"I see. But who is 'we?'" asks Anton, straightening his glance.

"We are a small group that started out in Paris. We met at university and have spent hours talking, arguing and coming to conclusions. We decided to become activists. We established a team to work on the ideological part of things, a team responsible for recruiting members and resources, and an operations team. We chose leadership and handed out roles. We have a chairman, secretary-general, and a treasurer. Each team presents their conclusions to the group. Over time, we added new members, each to a different team. The operations team went to Lebanon to train with professionals. We have about one hundred soldiers, and each member has pledged to recruit at least twenty new members every year." Ahmed looks at Anton proudly.

"What would you like from me?" asks Anton.

"What can you offer?" Ahmed asks him back.

"I am a businessman. I work in Europe, and I am connected to many businessmen across the Middle East. I can help raise money and make connections."

"That's exactly what I need."

"But, first things first. I need to verify that what you're selling me is the truth, and not just some group of dreamers. I beg your pardon in advance, I have no intention of insulting you."

"Of course," says Ahmed. "You'd have to be an idiot to just hand me money. You're welcome to come to the next meeting this weekend in Paris."

"Let me know the exact place and time, and I'll do my best to make it. My schedule is quite full, and I travel a lot," Anton answers. "Just one question, with your permission. Have you managed to come to any arrangements with any wealthy people who have connections?" Anton is trying, carefully, to extract information.

"Yes. The group that trained in Lebanon was completely funded by businessmen who pledged to finance other groups in the future."

"Very nice. And what do they ask in return?"

"To be part of the leadership, to take part in authorizing the operational plans."

"I'm also interested in having some influence, particularly regarding planning and policy. I'm already too old to understand or take part in operations." Anton chuckles.

"Why? You're not that old, you've got a lot of good years left in you," Youssuf says, speaking for the first time.

"Thank you, thank you." Anton smiles at him. Youssuf is the sorcerer's apprentice, apparently. "If I may know, what is your place in the organization? Which team are you part of?"

"I'm the head of the operational team. I was in Lebanon. We received training and started working."

"Really? How long were you in Lebanon?"

"One month. Including everything." Ahmed is pleased with the effect of his words on Anton, who has decided to show some excitement for the first time. "The first mission I was part of was a trip to Israel. I was born in Tayibe, Israel, so it was easy for me to enter."

"I see. So we're talking about Israeli Arabs as well?" Anton asks.

"Yes, why not? You'd be surprised, not everybody prefers the good life in Israel. There are many Arabs in Israel who want to see Palestine stand on its own two feet."

Ahmed was momentarily reminded of his father, who got rich in construction and prefers to remain under the occupation, to be a law-abiding citizen who looks down on his Palestinian brethren from above. "Yes, you're right. You know what they say? A Jew who is afraid, packs a suitcase and runs, but an Arab, as soon as there is danger, plants an olive tree in the ground."

"Yes. They just need to be convinced. We are here to persuade all Palestinians, and to scare the Jews so that they pack up their suitcases and go back to wherever they came from."

"Others before you failed. How will you succeed?" Anton asks.

"We are not afraid. We are prepared to die for the cause. For every one of us who dies, two more spring up in his place."

Anton leans back in his chair. "But in the meantime, you haven't mentioned a single operation. I take it that you are still talking and preparing."

"Not exactly. We are in the middle of an important operation. When you hear about it, you'll see that we don't just talk, and you can put money on the table. You'll be proud. You'll be running after us."

"*Inshallah*," Anton says.

"That's the reason we're here in Holland. Our headquarters are in Paris, where we live and meet. Better to do it here." Ahmed tells him.

"So then it's good you had time to meet with me," Anton says.

"Yes, our time is limited. I hope you understand," says Ahmed.

"You're very persuasive; now I feel like joining," Anton says, trying to fish for more information.

"The only thing I can tell you is that we have taken a valuable hostage. A bargaining chip. We will bring it to Lebanon. We are just waiting for the final arrangements before we leave."

"Impressive, I must say," Anton says, looking at Ahmed with reverence. "Bless you. But I don't understand, if you took a hostage, how come we haven't heard about it in the media?"

"That's part of it, you'll understand later." Ahmed shares the secret.

Anton feels like it's time to stop. He places his hand on Ahmed's shoulder. "It's better if we don't talk anymore. We should maintain confidentiality. So, you will be in touch about the meeting, and we'll continue from there. Good luck with your mission. I will pray for all of our success." Anton leaves a respectable amount of money on the table, gets up, shakes their hands and leaves the café without looking back.

Ahmed and Youssuf remain seated. Sting and Barbara get up after a couple minutes and leave after Anton, to keep an eye on him from behind. One can never know. Anton catches a taxi, and Sting and Barbara follow behind. Youssuf and Ahmed get up, pay the bill with Anton's money, and Ahmed pockets the difference. The team goes on alert. Youssuf leaves the café after him and they walk to the cab stand to wait for a cab.

The rest of them organize themselves into two cars, one looking out to see when the two get into a cab, and to then describe it to the team. Color, license plate. The taxi leaves and so does the team, whose words I continue to hear on the walkie-talkie. In vehicular surveillance, things happen fast, and a wrong turn can leave you out of the picture. I go outside and walk to the team's apartment. Anton will arrive the moment he feels everything is in order. The couple safeguarding him will join Udi.

I enter the compact apartment. Table, sofa, armchair. Dutch minimalism. I call David in Israel.

"Hello, my dear," I say. "We're following them. I'm waiting for Anton to come back to the apartment. We'll call soon."

"Thanks for the call," he says and hangs up.

It's hard to sit far away and wait. I take out the communication device and turn it off. I can call Udi, but I won't bother them in the middle of their work. He'll call when he can.

Anton knocks quietly on the door. I open it and give him a hug.

"Good to see you."

"Thanks," he says and sits down and takes a deep breath, letting out some of the built-up tension.

"Coffee? Something cold?" I ask.

"Coffee. Make it strong, please."

I make him a cup of strong, real Turkish coffee with a heaping teaspoon of sugar.

"Thanks, just what I need," says Anton. "Come sit."

He tells me about the progression of the conversation.

"I have no doubt they are going to send her to some hiding place in Lebanon, assuming they told me the truth," says Anton. "It isn't clear to me how they will get through border control with her, but they are capable of anything."

"Yeah," I say. "Wait. Let's call home. David said they're considering bringing the Dutch in if we get an exact address." I call Israel. "Anton is with me. He's fine. Udi is tailing the two guys. One of them is absolutely our lover-boy. They're talking about a new Ron Arad,[3] and the need to get her out of the country as soon as they can."

"I understand. Call me as soon as Udi calls or gets back."

He understood. No need to elaborate. A little more patience. Anton and I look at each other.

"A real son of a bitch, that Ahmed," says Anton. "He realized she was the Mossad chief's daughter before he approached her, and he started hanging out with the same crowd because of her,

---

[3] Ron Arad was a pilot whose plane went down during a mission over Lebanon and was captured. He was killed, and his body was never returned.

for sure. He's cold and cruel to find a seventeen-year-old girl, to convince her, to cause her to fall in love with him, to bring her to Europe, that motherfucker. May he burn in hell."

"The question is whether anything goes in war. Are there red lines or not? Sometimes, being humane brings disaster," I say to Anton.

"I can't believe that you, as a mother, are saying this," he says, annoyed.

"Wait, wait, understand. I'm not for it. I sometimes even hate what I do. In my heart, I'm a liberal, but let's be real. If you believe in the goal, in the world today, you have no choice but to go all the way. Look at what people did in the Holocaust. Human life in modern society isn't worth much. Arab society is known for being cruel, also to its own. This doesn't blow my mind. They're willing to do anything in order to succeed, including blow themselves up."

"You're right. I just find it difficult to understand how it's possible to be in such an intimate relationship with a young girl, and then do something so evil to her like that, and in such a cruel way."

"Heart of stone."

"I hope we get to her on time. Maybe we'll get lucky," Anton says.

The Mossad chief sent his assistant to the main gate and made sure to bring his two sons into his office. On Friday, the rooms are empty, and only people on duty are in the war room, which is always operating. On the top floor, one could hear a pin drop. They enter the suite. First time visiting here. They see their mother on the bed.

"Dad, is this what you've been hiding from us all these years?" He smiles at his father.

"Yes. Sit down. We have to talk," he says in at tone that silences everybody. They look at their mother and understand something's wrong. "You guys know that Noa went to Poland, right?"

"Of course. She's coming back today. Is she going to join us?" the younger one says, and then is quiet, understanding that it's better if he doesn't speak.

"She traveled to Poland a week ago, the first night she disappeared."

"What?"

Their mother began to cry. The Mossad chief tells them the sequence of events. The older one gets up and goes to hug his mother. He asks why they haven't told them until now.

"I'll explain why. Imagine that everything was out in the open, in the media. How would we be able to get to where we are? This is the only chance to return your sister back home. Do you understand?"

They lower their heads, trying to understand. The younger one gets up and also goes to hug his mother. They stand together, tears streaming from their eyes. Their father is looking at them in pain. He isn't used to displays of affection. His wife reaches her hand out to him, inviting him to join them, and only then is he able to muster the strength to go over and hug them. They stand there like that for many minutes.

The Mossad chief's wife is the first to regain her composure. "We aren't giving up. She'll be back. You'll see. Everything is going to be fine."

The boys look at her, ready and willing to believe that. It doesn't matter that they'd been feeling distant from her in the last few years. Right now, she's their little girl that they raised and nurtured.

"What now?"

"We are going to Yitzhak's house in Savyon. I have no doubt that the story will explode on the eight o'clock news, and I don't want the media after us."

"Fine by me. Let's go. I don't like being here," said the younger one, who only recently was discharged from the army. It gave him a feeling of being in an enclosure, instead of free.

After an hour, Udi came in in a frenzy.

"We arrived at the address," he said. "It was one of the four addresses that you gave us. Two went inside. We don't know what floor. I left the guys there, waiting. We have to inform headquarters immediately; we have to decide what to do."

We relay the information back home.

The decision had already been made to ask the Dutch to go in and grab the whole group and get Noa out of there when they discussed the options that would come to light as a result of Anton's meeting with Ahmed. The head of the Mossad called the prime minister to report to him and request help.

"Whatever you think is right, do it," said the prime minister.

"We want special forces to go into the apartment get my daughter out of there," said the Mossad chief. "There's only one problem. We don't have the exact apartment. The building has nine apartments in it. They're definitely in there somewhere."

"Understood. We'll make sure they do what is necessary and without delay."

"Thank you, Mr. Prime Minister."

The prime minister called the Dutch prime minister, who understood the severity of the situation. He is not prepared to be responsible for the girl getting hurt on his watch.

After about an hour, Ehud, the Mossad representative responsible for foreign affairs, arrived at Udi's apartment to get the full picture. He received a photo of Noa and Ahmed, a description of Youssuf, and the address of the building where the three of them supposedly are. From there, he went to meet with the commander of the police department's special forces, which had already received their orders from the Dutch prime minister. Two teams were summoned and were just waiting for details in order to head out to the field. The guys already in the field received instructions to remain there until the police enter, and were told to keep a low profile in order to keep an eye out and to make sure that they don't disappear anywhere.

At the same time, there were already rumors popping up in Kfar Saba and the head of the Mossad decided to activate the censorship protocol. Have to allow the Dutch to work without distraction; the information can't get out. There will be time to talk after it's done.

The boys and girls that returned home were in an uproar. Parents began calling each other, the teachers and the school principal. The school principal received instructions to quiet the matter, and decided not to ask unnecessary questions and instructed his teachers to do the same. The answer given to everybody was that the girl is here and everything is fine. The parents demanded an urgent meeting with the teachers and the school principal, which was scheduled for eight the next morning.

The problem has been delayed, for now.

The special forces of the Dutch police department are sitting in the briefing room. Their commander is standing before them.

"We're talking about a very sensitive incident. I received a request from the prime minister to take this matter personally. The girl is the daughter of one of Israel's senior leadership, and she was kidnapped by an Arab fellow while on a class trip to Poland. She's known to be with at least two guys in one of the apartments in the building at 13 Noordstraat. Please pass the photographs of the girl and the young man among you. Take the photograph on the mission. We also have a description of a third fellow. About twenty-seven, five-foot nine. Very thin, dark skinned. Black, short hair. He wears glasses and has big ears.

"Pay attention! These two were seen today in town wearing blue jeans. The fellow in the picture, Ahmed, was wearing a dark blue sweatshirt and black jacket. The thin fellow was wearing a black shirt, black sweater, and a dark brown jacket.

"Team A will leave first and find observation posts. Each apartment will be identified by team members from the outside. You should be prepared for gunfire. Be aware, do not injure any innocent civilians, I don't intend to turn this mission into a bloodbath. In the second phase, Team B will enter the building. Three people will stand outside each apartment door and, when we give the call, break down the door and go inside. All teams will act at the same time and take advantage of the element of surprise.

"In addition, physically oversee all possible exits from the building, emergency exits and the roof. In the event that we have a positive ID on the apartment, the team outside that door will go in, with the rest of the teams falling into defensive positions, or attack positions if necessary. Understood? Questions?"

"Are we going to close the street off to vehicular traffic?"

"In the first phase, no. We don't want to ruin the element of surprise. At the moment of the break-in, we'll close off the street to all vehicles."

They aren't excited about the mission. A girl was kidnapped. There are many like her throughout the year.

"I want to remind all of you that this isn't just about us. We're talking about an international incident if we fail. Act wisely and with determination, and let's not waste time. Good luck to all of us and we'll see you when it's all over."

The first team spreads out along the rooftops in the area and on the object's roof to prevent any escape. They report on the two-way radio about angles of view. Good thing the Dutch regularly leave their apartment windows unobstructed, which allowed the team to eliminate some apartments as irrelevant. In the end, there were three possible apartments, numbers one, five and six. In apartment six, there were curtains that prevented all visibility. In apartments five and one, there is light but no way to see anyone inside. It may be that they are in closed rooms.

The second team gets organized at each of the three apartments. After each unit signals that they're ready, the order to break into the apartments is given. At once, the thundering noise of three doors being broken into could be heard. In apartment one, no one was home; the apartment was empty. In apartment five, there was an elderly Dutch couple who were startled, to say the least. The old man was sitting in an armchair, pale, and his wife fell on the floor in a panic.

In apartment number six, there were three men. The two men mentioned in the briefing and another man were sitting in the living room, drinking coffee and smoking. They jumped to their feet, panicked, and surrendered immediately. In the rest of the rooms, there was nothing. The police handcuffed the three and took each one in a separate vehicle to headquarters. There, each one was put in a different room.

The commander of the special forces made a phone call to the Dutch prime minister and reported the results of the mission. The prime minister then called the prime minister of Israel and detailed the events. The prime minister of Israel requested from his colleague to allow his people to attend the interrogation.

"No problem. Send me whoever you want. We're beginning the interrogation immediately."

The prime minister called the head of the Mossad to update him.

"Yes... yes. I understand... thank you... good night."

He looked up and said to his family, "They caught that son-of-a-bitch Ahmed along with two others. Noa wasn't with them. They're interrogating them in Holland. The prime minister asked that our people be allowed to join the interrogation. I have to make some phone calls."

The head of the Mossad reports what took place to the operation commander at headquarters and asks him to make sure that Aharon, who was a police interrogator and in the Shin Bet before his current position working for the Mossad, leave from Brussels to join the interrogation. Aharon speaks Arabic.

"In addition, I want to find out if we can also send Gideon

from the Shin Bet." Gideon is known across the whole community as somebody who can break anybody under interrogation. "David, I will call the head of the Shin Bet to ask him to release Gideon, and you'll take it from there."

"Absolutely. I'll take care of everything."

Aharon was activated out of Brussels; he would be briefed in Amsterdam. Gideon packed his suitcase. The material would be given to him by a driver who would take him to the airport. The only problem was that there aren't any flights from Brussels to Holland on Friday evening.

"I'll ask one of my friends to help me out. I'll get the prime minister's approval on the matter," says the Mossad chief and again called Yitzhak, who is hosting his family. He explains what is required, and makes sure he understands that it's a matter of life and death.

"I'll see what I can do. I'll get right back to you."

The Mossad chief sits down in an armchair. His arms and legs are sprawled as if they don't even belong to his body. His older son sits down on the edge of the chair and gives him a hug. He feels like his dad could use some support. He has never seen him like this.

The phone rings. Udi's guys report that three men, two of whom were at the previous meeting, were taken from the building and apparently transported to the police headquarters, each one separately. The girl was nowhere to be found.

"Stay there. Pay attention to all movement entering or exiting the building. Maybe somebody who doesn't know what happened will show up. Which apartment was it?"

"Apartment number six on the second floor."

"Do we have forces in the area?" Udi asked.

"No, everybody left."

"Two of you go up to apartment six, if you can, with one going in and the second one keeping watch. The third will stay downstairs and secure the area. Enter and see what you can find out.

Anything that looks important. Do it before somebody comes to fix the doors.

"Hundred percent. Five minutes and we're in."

"After you finish, drive to the second address that we found on Sunday and check out what's going on there. You'll have to wait there until you hear otherwise."

"Gotcha."

Udi briefly summarizes everything for us. We all nod. It's dangerous, but we have to take the risk, without approvals and without bureaucracy. The second address suddenly became relevant. Perhaps the girl is there.

"Go for it," David says when I request his approval. "I hope we don't get in trouble for this. Are the locals aware of the second address?"

"No."

"I'll make sure the police gets the address. You need to get over there immediately. Those three are being interrogated. I called Aharon in Brussels; he has no information. I sent him your phone number so he can contact you when he gets to Amsterdam. Brief him."

"Got it. It'll probably happen within the next three hours."

The events are occurring in rapid succession. We usually work carefully, step by step. At the moment, we have the pedal to the metal. Udi isn't comfortable with the notion of sitting here in the apartment, and I unfortunately, am forced to sit and wait.

"Udi, pay attention to the second address. The police will arrive shortly. Don't forget to let us know what happens."

"See you," he says, the door slamming shut behind him.

One hour from the moment Udi left, Barbara returns. She sits down next to us and tells us that everything went smoothly. Merlin went in and went through all the rooms. She put everything she thought was important in a bag. At the end, the team continued on to the second address, and Barbara was brought back here so we could work on the material and report back to Israel.

The three of us sat and contemplated the paperwork. Three pictures of Noa. Her black hair covered, her face pale, her clothes wrinkled. Inside a white envelope we found a Lebanese passport with Noa's ID photo, apparently taken from her Israeli passport. "Nour Qatar" was the name chosen for her. The implications of the name weren't clear, but there might be a reason for the last name.

"There are two options for when they reach border control. One is that she is cooperating and wants to go to Lebanon. The second is that they drug her and declare her sick and unable to speak, and that they need to get her 'home' to Lebanon."

"There's a third option," Anton says.

"Yes," I answer, "there is a third option."

On a computer printout, there's a hand-written note in Hebrew with the phone numbers for Dad, Mom, and the house. We assume that Noa wrote them down because they asked her to, intending to use them in the future as part of a scheme to extort the family and the country.

"Good thing Udi sent them to the apartment," I say, turning to Anton.

"Yeah. The Dutch will be pissed if they find out," he says.

"True. But I'm a bit surprised that they didn't gather the information themselves. Not very professional." I point to the paperwork and pictures on the table. "Let's hope that this is just a bonus that will be useful for other things." Maybe in order to show the world the level of cruelty, absence of red lines and waging war on the backs of children.

Udi calls from the field. "We're here. It's quiet inside. A small building, four apartments. There aren't any names that would give anything away. Dutch names on the mailboxes. In one apartment there's a family with small children, in another there's an elderly couple in front of the television. The other two are dark. I'm staying here for the time being. I assume that the police will arrive soon."

"Yes, I hope so. I figure they'll be there any moment. Keep an eye out."

I call David to update him on the findings of the bag.

"Right, those fuckers. The police are supposed to arrive any moment at the second address. Are the guys there?"

"Yes, just spoke to them. There are four apartments, two are dark. Would indicate that nobody's home."

"Maybe by design, maybe they're aware of what happened to their friends, and maybe they took off. Who knows? Let's hope for the best. Have the team back off when the police arrive, but have somebody pay attention to what happens."

"Of course."

The head of the Mossad receives an update.

"I understand," he says.

"What, what do you understand?" the boys say, jumping up. His wife secluded herself in the room, unable to bear the waiting. He summarizes the events for them.

"Cold hearted bastards," the big one says. As the hours pass, he feels growing anger welling up inside him. At everyone. His parents, Noa, himself. How could we not have noticed? How is it nobody told us? How did I allow to get involved with this man? Why didn't Dad think that it was necessary to handle this through his office or the Shin Bet from the beginning?

"The Dutch police are supposed to be breaking into another address in Amsterdam. I hope she's there, sitting and waiting for us to get her out," says the head of the Mossad to his sons. Deep down, he hears his own voice say, "Just a little longer... a little longer..."

"They're here," says Udi into the telephone. "I'm sitting in the car."

"Try to keep me on the line." I put him on speaker.

"The civilian police are approaching at a fast walk. One team is deploying around the building. I see that they have good angles for a sniper if it comes to it. They're going behind the building and onto the roof. Now another team is arriving, about fifteen guys are going in. Hold on..." We listen and pray. Let her be there. Let them find her. I can hear noise in the background...

"Did you hear that noise? They broke in, but I can't see anything. I don't have a vantage point. I'll call when they come out." He hangs up.

We're all pacing around the room without saying anything. We don't have any words left. The last week will come to an end in these next few minutes. Or not? Maybe she won't be there either and we'll have to keep searching. I'm already trying to start thinking about what comes next. Maybe we'll find some new information? We have the passport, so she certainly hasn't left. She's here, in Holland. But where?

Udi calls again. "They just took a guy and a girl out of the building and put them in separate cars. I couldn't tell if it was our girl or not, sorry," Udi says. "Shit. They didn't let anybody get close. When they went in, they closed off access."

"Stay there. It's not over yet. Maybe there are other people inside?"

"Yeah, I'm waiting. We'll do the same thing we did last time, if we can, of course."

"Okay."

"Are you calling Israel?" Anton asks.

"Yes, in a moment. Let's wait a little more. Maybe it's her and maybe there are more people coming out. It's not over yet."

There's nothing unequivocal yet.

The phone rings. Aharon has arrived from Brussels.

"Hi, I understand that we're supposed to meet up. Have you arrived?"

"I'm at the entrance to the city. Shall we meet?"

"Yes. But you're going to have to wait for me," I say.

"Okay. I'll wait for you at Dam."

"I'll finish and call you. Bye."

I hope that by the time we meet up, this story will already be behind us.

Udi is back on the line. "Can you hear me?"

"Yes, we all can."

"We heard a single gunshot, then quiet after that. Then two guys with equipment rushed inside."

"What do you mean? What could it have been?" I ask.

"I don't know."

Maybe they shot one of the kidnappers. It could be that whoever they took out first isn't connected to our deal, I think to myself. Better to wait for information.

"An ambulance is on its way. I can hear the siren. It's parking near the entrance to the building. I've gotten out of the car and getting closer. I have to see."

I hear him breathing hard while walking. "Be careful, don't get too close. Don't annoy anybody."

"Don't worry," Udi says, "I'm not a child."

I don't say anything and wait.

"The paramedics are coming back with a stretcher and... wait... I can't see what's on it... a corpse covered by a sheet. I don't know, no idea," says Udi.

"Wait, maybe now Noa will come out of there. Stay in the area."

"We're staying here."

Should I call David? Should I call Ehud, my contact? Yes. That's what I'll do. He'll know.

"Ehud?"

"Yes?" He's trying to recognize my voice.

"Are you at the police station right now? I'm a friend of David's, from today..."

"Ah, okay. Yes. I'm here."

"Are you up to date? They took two people and a body out of there."

"Yeah, only we don't know who's who. I'll call you back when I know."

"Thanks, and by the way, Aharon arrived, I'm supposed to send him to you later on."

"Okay. Right now we're all busy. Have him get a hotel room in the meantime," Ehud suggests.

He's right. I call Aharon and suggest that he check in. We'll meet up later.

"You're not going to believe it," Udi says. "They're taking another body out. Another ambulance arrived. One shot, two bodies? Are you thinking what I'm thinking?"

"Yes."

We all lean back, unable to believe the implication of what we just heard. Could this be the end? Or not? Maybe there's still hope? Maybe she actually was the first one out.

I have to call David.

"Hello?" David answers.

"Hi," I say, followed by silence, hoping he'll talk instead.

"Well?"

So he didn't hear anything. Shit.

"They brought out a man and a woman. We didn't see who they were, we were too far. They left. After a few minutes, there was a single gunshot. An ambulance arrived and took out a body. We have no idea who. After a few more minutes, another ambulance arrived and took out another body. Ehud is aware of the facts, but is waiting to find out who's who, and who left there on their own two feet." There, I said it. I take a deep breath.

Silence.

"I'm sorry. I know what you're thinking. But we should wait before you pass the message on, so we can be sure."

"Yeah."

The three of us pace around the room.

"Coffee?" I say, turning to the others.

"Yes, coffee," they both say and follow me to the kitchen.

Each one wants to make coffee. To do something, to keep busy. It's hard for us to just wait around. We stand in the kitchen holding cups of coffee.

"Who would have believed it," says Anton.

"As fast as we were, we weren't fast enough," I say.

"Wait. Maybe everything is all right. We haven't heard anything. Just hang on," Barbara says.

We nod.

Please... please... please let...

"That's it, it's over," David says on the other side of the phone.

"Oh no. We're very sorry to hear."

"From what I was able to clarify and understand, there were four people in the apartment. At the entrance, a guy and a girl, who were brought outside and immediately taken into custody. In another room was a guy with a gun. He was going to shoot anybody who came inside, and a sniper killed him with a single shot. The police went into the bathroom, and inside Noa was laying there in a pile of ice. She had apparently been murdered a few days prior. We were a few days too late. You did your best."

Udi and his team arrive to the apartment, heads hung. We all sit down in the small living room.

"There isn't much to say," I say, and tell them what David told me. I see in my mind's eye the girl, tired and in shock, in a bathtub full of ice. What a sad end. I shake myself out of the thought, erasing the unpleasant vision from my mind. "I want to tell all of you, to all of us... thank you. This time wasn't just another job. This girl became our daughter, too. We hoped so badly, we tried. No dice. All of you, book flights home first thing in the morning. I'll write a summary report tomorrow. When you get back to Israel, prepare a detailed report. I'm going to a meeting with Aharon, so I'll say again, thank you, and have a good night."

We hug and say goodbye without any extra fanfare. I go downstairs, tears streaming from my eyes, and I can't do anything to stop them. I catch a cab and arrive at Dam Square. I head to the café where Aharon is sitting, waiting for me. I sit down next to him.

"I'm sorry for the long wait."

"I understand that there has been a change." He looks at me and apparently sees a tired woman – very tired, and sad.

"Yeah." I briefly tell him everything from the beginning until about an hour ago.

He's shocked. Like all of us.

"I'm sending you to Ehud at the police station. The three of them are locked up there. Interrogate the fuck out of them, get everything you possibly can. Everything. How was the operation planned, what is this organization, who are their people, how do they operate, what are their sources, connections. E v e r y t h i n g. Be in touch with Israel for special requests. Ehud will help you. There's also supposed to be an interrogator from the Shin Bet, but I'm not sure. I'm tired. I have to go to sleep. I'll call Ehud and set it up. Okay?"

"Yeah. I get where you're coming from. It's a real shame," Aharon says.

I pick up the phone to call Ehud and set up a meeting.

"Good night."

I get up and walk to the street where the taxis are waiting. After a ten minute ride, I go up to the small room. It seems like it's been forever since I left it this morning. I get into bed without even taking a shower. I don't have the energy or desire. I suddenly remember that I didn't talk to my family today, and then I fall asleep.

Shabbat

It seems that I woke up in the same position I went to sleep. I look around me and then at myself. I fell asleep in the clothes I wore yesterday; I didn't even brush my teeth. I'm reminded of yesterday and I lie back down and close my eyes. I never met Noa, but over the course of the last week, she was kind of like my child, and I lost her. I feel a type of mourning. For as long as I can remember myself, this is the first time I ever cried at the end of a mission because we failed. I cry for her, for me, for her parents and family.

I get into the shower. The water flows over my body and I decide to snap out of it, to come back to myself. I need to go to my family. To my girls. They are my life, them and Nathan. That's the only thing that matters right now and, in all honesty, at all.

I go down to the lobby, check out of the hotel, get into a cab and head to the train station where I buy a ticket, sandwich and something to drink. I let Nathan know I'm on my way. I let David know that I'm heading back to Paris, and I'll write my summary report from there. I tell Yaron that I'll be back in the apartment to continue working on Monday.

I board the Thalys train from Holland to Paris. After four hours, I arrive at the North station in Paris, get in a cab and go home. Five hours without thinking, memories, feelings, no criticism, no pain.

I walk into the house. The girls jump on me and I hug them and try to conceal my tears.

"Mom, are you crying?" Lior asks, catching me.
"Just a little. It'll pass," I say and try to smile.
"What happened? Dad!" she calls Nathan. "Mom's crying."
"I'm fine. Give me a moment to calm down in my room. Okay, sweetie?"
"Okay, Mom."
I go into the room and Nathan comes in after me.
"What happened?" He gives me a hug. "What happened?"
"Long story. Sit." I sit on the bed and tell him the story, starting from the picnic on Shabbat until today. He sat there quietly; only by his facial expressions can I tell just how shocked he is.
"All that happened to you in a week? I don't believe it. Forgive me if I was hard on you," he says.
"It's okay." I flash him a sideways smile, "I'm okay. Think about the big boss and his family."
"Yeah, an awful tragedy."
The girls knock softly on the door. They understand that something happened and that maybe they aren't allowed to bother us, but they need their mother and I need them.
"Come in, come in," I say. Shir and Lior lie down next to me, each one on either side. They stroke my arms and hair and I'm grateful to them for being a part of me, my own private girls, for us being a family.
Nathan strokes my face, gets up and comes back with a cup of tea and some cookies he baked. That's all I need. Anybody looking for more doesn't understand the meaning of life, and love and happiness. It takes some perspective in order to see that. The last week brought that home to me.
In her room painted pink, a reminder of days long gone, when pink was her favorite color, Michal is curled up with her big comforter, shocked and hurting. Ever since she got back from Poland, she finds it difficult to speak. The seven days that they spent walking through the concentration camps was difficult, but not only because of the disaster that befell the Jewish people.

Noa's disappearance shocked and angered her, and mostly left her feeling lonely. The whole class rallied around each other. They cried and laughed together, and only she stood on the side without anybody noticing. Nobody asked or paid any attention. She felt invisible.

That Friday night when Noa disappeared on her, the whole grade was in an uproar. The guards and teachers explained to everybody that they were doing all they could to find her. They asked that nobody call home and tell anyone about it, but Michal knew in her heart that Noa wouldn't be found. She recalled the things Noa would throw out there: phrasings, clues. She didn't sleep all night. She opened Noa's bag, went through it looking for clues left behind, but didn't find a thing.

When they planned the trip, Michal was up in the air about going. She asked Noa why she was going, and since when did she care about class trips?

"The trip to Poland is just an excuse."

"Excuse for what?" Michal wondered.

"To be away from home. Freedom. Independence," she had said.

The next morning, Michal opened her toiletries kit to brush her teeth and was shocked to find a small note: I'm fine. Not a word.

She choked off a scream. *I was right, it was all planned.* She ran away. She's crazy. How did she do it? To where and with whom?

She wanted to take the note and tell the teacher. Instead, she folded it up and returned it to her toiletries kit, hidden. Noa asked her not to say anything. It was their secret. She felt close to Noa again, to somebody. The feeling of loneliness that she had been feeling since yesterday evening subsided a bit, for a moment.

She went down to the dining room where everybody was sitting, quiet. The teachers were confused. She sat in silence. Nobody came over to her, nobody said a word. The teacher accompanying them on the trip addressed the class at the end of breakfast, stood behind Michal, and rested her hand on her shoulder.

"Guys, today, a difficult day awaits us. We are continuing on our trip, as well as looking for Noa. Don't worry, we're doing our best." She then bent down to Michal and asked, for the only time on the entire trip, "Are you okay?"

"Yeah. Yeah, I'm fine." She didn't understand where such a stupid answer came from. How could I possibly be okay? The only person that ever paid attention to me disappeared. The kids tried asking her, but she pushed them all away. She didn't answer, looked away. She was the weird kid, just like they expected her to be.

She sat on the bus in the same place she sat with Noa on the first day of the trip. Nobody sat in her place. She did what everybody else did, quietly, without uttering a word. When they got to the hotel, exhausted after endlessly walking the streets of Warsaw, they got everybody together and told them Noa had been found.

"She's on her way back home, and everything will be explained when we get back. One thing, though: don't talk about this when you call home. Cases like this could jeopardize the trips to Poland, so please take responsibility."

The kids started discussing the matter and the noise in the room was horrendous. She sat there, staring. Sad for herself, and sad for Noa that she missed an opportunity. When they got back home, her mother and grandmother came to pick her up from the school courtyard. Quietly, without saying goodbye to a soul, she got into the small car and sat in back. These women, who called her 'Miluchka,' were her entire family. They came from Russia when she was eight years old. The only things she knew about her father was that he wasn't Jewish, and that he was a drunk and a bum. Her mother and grandmother, gifted musicians, played the violin. In Israel, her mother gave private violin lessons. She didn't have many students, and she was forced to take on another job caring for the elderly and infirm. Her grandmother, who never learned Hebrew, almost never left the house; she was responsible for cleaning the house and preparing food. Michal was her whole world until she stopped communicating with her altogether. The house was a very quiet place. Each one of them in their own private world. They didn't even eat together, and each one went to their room early.

On the way, when her mother asked her how the trip was, she answered, "Good," and was quiet.

"Was it difficult?" he mother asked.

"Yeah. Difficult."

She watched the road and the people. Nothing had changed. The world was operating as usual. When she got to her room, the first thing she did was call Noa, but there was no answer. *They probably punished her and took away her phone*, she thought to herself. They'd see each other at school.

The next evening, her mother entered her room.

"Noa's dead," she said quietly.

"No way!" Michal said and looked at her. Dead? No, no. She was found and returned home.

"The teacher just called. She said that Noa was dead. Something terrible happened on your trip."

"What? What exactly did she tell you?"

"She said that during the trip, she was kidnapped by Arabs and that, after a lot of searching, she was found dead in Holland in an apartment with those men. Why didn't you tell me when you came back? Why didn't you tell me she wasn't there for the whole trip? Why, Miluchka?" her mother said and looked at her, not understanding.

Silence.

She felt like her head was going to explode. "Leave the room, please," she said and lay down on the bed, shocked.

Later on, she turned on the computer. There must be something on the Internet. Her father is an important man. Everything was there. The whole story. The trip to Poland. Her disappearance. The search. Her return home in a casket. Her picture, her parents and her brothers, looking at her.

She turned off the computer. What does any of that matter now?

Noa is dead. Noa is dead. Noa is dead. Gone.

If I had told them, would it have ended differently? Would they have found her faster? Been able to save her? How did this happen? Why didn't she tell me where she was running off to? Why didn't she trust me?

Michal is curled up in her bed. Tomorrow afternoon is Noa's funeral. Tomorrow will be her last chance to tell her "goodbye." She shuts her eyes tightly, trying to stop the disturbing thoughts.

Unsuccessfully...

Third week

Sunday

The head of the Mossad and his family wake up Sunday morning to their new life. The sky is blue, the wind outside is chilly. In Yitzhak's house in Savyon, they feel somewhat safe from the crowd forming outside. Only a few people know where they are. It's all over the news and the media is causing a stir. Friends, colleagues, the whole community is at attention. Sooner or later, they'll have to deal with it.

Saturday, Yitzhak and his wife arrived to embrace and support them. The head of the Mossad's parents had passed away long ago, and his wife's mother lived in a nursing home with a full-time caregiver. Her memory had betrayed her, swinging from childhood to adulthood for no apparent reason, not knowing where she is, from crying to laughter, between pain and tranquility. There was no reason to tell her what had happened.

On Shabbat, the boys called their aunts and uncles and explained that their parents needed to disconnect from everybody until the funeral, which will take place on Sunday. They had a strong family connection, even if it wasn't frequent or particularly warm. And, of course, they would respect their wishes and understood that this new reality required special treatment.

At night, they cried and screamed, conversed and laughed, but mostly, they were quiet. Each doing their own bit of soul-searching. The head of the Mossad answered a few phone calls. The prime minister expressed his condolences, as did the defense minister, head of the Shin Bet, and other close friends and colleagues. He answered curtly, politely, and with a heavy heart. For almost forty years, he never took a break. He wasn't there when his kids were born and almost missed the bar mitzvah of his oldest son. He preferred work over any kind of leisure activity. The theater wasn't his cup of tea, he preferred eating at home rather than going out to restaurants, no matter how good, and rarely read books.

He had a few friends that he'd known forever, mainly friends from the army, some of whom saw commercial success, and some of whom were just regular folk. They stayed in touch over the years and got together as a group a few times a year. When he spoke, they all listened. He wasn't accustomed to expressing his opinion, but when he did, it was accepted. A man who didn't show emotion, but always tried to help and lend support. A special man.

The rest of the night, he sat in the dark living room with his thoughts. How did this happen to us? How did I let this happen? Specifically my own family. Why didn't I follow up and get the full story just like I do at work? How did I let her run off like that? Why didn't I see her distress? How, after everything I learned from the private investigator, did I choose to simply forbid her from seeing him? How did I give up on my little girl? How did I abandon her? Did I do it based on my wrong interpretation of the situation, or was I simply ashamed? Was I afraid to admit to my colleagues and myself that my daughter, a part of me, got into such a predicament?

All night, his wife lay curled up in bed. She has nothing to look forward to, just the tremendous physical pain and heart-wrenching grief: a sense of loss mixed with pangs of conscience. Noa was abandoned, humiliated and ostracized, which led to her extreme behavioral shift. We looked into it, consulted. On paper, we did what we needed to do, but we chose to listen to advice that didn't prove to Noa that we were on her side, that we wouldn't abandon her, that we loved her no matter what.

How was she able to plan everything without anybody knowing or even taking an interest? When and how did the two of them plan what she decided she was going to do? How is it that we didn't hear anything about it, not a clue or even a sign? How did she spend her last week? Was she terrified? Did they hurt her? Did she know that her end was approaching? Did she suffer? Did she think about us that week, and during her last moments? Did she think about me? Was she angry? Did she forgive us? Did she love us?

A large funeral was planned for the small community. Some of its residents were known, government and Knesset officials, army officers and members of the security establishment. The cemetery on top of the hill is small and intimate. Trees and flowers surround the graves and in the winter, cyclamens and windflowers are in full bloom. There are many children buried there. At three in the afternoon, they will all go up to the top of the hill with a police escort and guards.

Early in the afternoon, the family arrives back at their home. A driver takes them in a fancy black car. They get out quietly and go down the steps to their home. The guards have been there since yesterday evening. They don't let the newspeople get close.

She won't sleep here anymore. Her tough tone won't resonate through the home anymore. The four of them felt a sense of betrayal, both in the sense of having betrayed her, but also having been betrayed.

At a quarter to three, clouds covered the blue skies, further emphasizing the feeling of pain and sadness that everybody coming to the funeral felt. They stood at the lower entrance to the cemetery. Those who attended streamed in en-masse, shaking hands, exchanging hugs, wiping tears. Silence. Nobody is speaking.

At three-fifteen, the car from the burial society arrives carrying the casket. The eulogies begin. The first to speak is the prime minister, who chooses to address and consol the parents and brothers personally. He goes on to praise the head of the Mossad, that his life is woven into the fabric of the country, devoted to its security and safety. He spoke of the enemy for whom nothing is off limits, and finished with the hope that Noa would be the last victim.

The deputy chief of the Mossad spoke of the Mossad and of its chief, about the attempt to bring her back safe and sound. He asked forgiveness for the establishment's failure, particularly now, despite many successes. He finished by saying, "We mustn't let our children pay the price for this struggle."

The head of the local council spoke about the community, about the family and about Noa. About the community, about solidarity, and about the flower that was plucked in its youth. He called on leadership to stop its cruelty and to bring in its place the peace that he hoped for.

The school principal spoke of the trip to Poland. He discussed the symbology of the last week, the path of the six million, and at the same time, the last week of her solitary life that led to Noa's cruel death, may she rest in peace.

The last to eulogize her was her oldest brother. He approaches the microphone hesitantly. He holds a piece of paper upon which he had written some of what he wanted to say.

"Our Dear Noa, before I say anything else, I want to ask your forgiveness. I apologize that I wasn't there for you, that I wasn't the big brother that I should have been. We are all standing here shocked and in pain. You, our little sister, Mom and Dad's little girl, you walked your own path. Music was the essence of your life, your greatest love.

"The first few years of your life, you were a happy little girl. A girl who loved being outdoors in the neighborhood. Us, your big brothers, taught you how to ride your bike, we showed you the windflower fields, the avocado orchards, we took you to and from afterschool activities and scouts. We took the place of Mom and Dad, who came home in the evening. The three of us did everything together.

"Everything was so good, until you experienced your crisis. Perhaps this isn't the place, but perhaps it is, to say that you experienced something difficult. Your friends who lived here in this neighborhood that's supposedly protected, the exclusion and humiliation that, as far as you're concerned, never ended until today. An experience that changed your life, that changed you.

"We weren't able to understand the implications. We hoped that it would pass, that music would turn you back into a happy girl. But, despite finding happiness of some sort or another, you found it in the wrong place, which led you and all of us to this moment, here and now, where we are forced to say goodbye.

"Your room, Noa, remains vacant, hiding away your secrets forever. I feel like a failure as a big brother, a failure that I can't undo." He is unable to stop the tears from building up in his throat, and he begins to cry audibly as he reads the words in his broken voice. "Noa, I hope that this isn't the end of our journey. We will meet again sometime, up above. Make it a better place for us up there than what we made for you down here. Peace be upon you, my sister."

He goes over to his parents and brother and hugs them. They stand like that for many minutes, with sounds of crying heard all around them.

Six of her father's friends stand around Noa's remains, raise her and carry her to the hilltop. The family walks behind them on Noa's last journey. The head of the Mossad hugs his wife while the boys stand at their side, red-eyed and crying, hidden behind sunglasses. They arrive at the grave that was just dug that morning. The view is so beautiful, breathtaking. Noa is put into the ground and covered with clods of earth. The representative from the burial society takes scissors and makes a cut in the shirt collars of the parents and brothers, as per Jewish mourning customs.

The head of the Mossad stands with his sons at his side and says the mourner's prayer for his daughter:

"May His great name be exalted and sanctified in the world that came into being by His will. May His kingdom reign, and may His salvation flourish and bring His savior near, in your lifetime and in the lifetime of all of Israel quickly and speedily, and let us say, 'Amen.'

"May His great name be blessed forever and all time,

"May it be blessed, may it be praised, may it be glorified and exalted, raised and honored, uplifted and lauded, the name of the Holy One Blessed be He, beyond all blessings, songs of praise or consolation, and let it be uttered throughout the world, and let us say, 'Amen.'

"May the great peace of heaven and the good life be upon us and on all Israel. And we say, 'Amen.'

"May He Who makes peace on high, make peace over us, and over all Israel, and we say, 'Amen.'"

Amen.

The funeral procession ends with the prayer "God full of mercy." Heart-wrenching.

People come and lay wreaths on the fresh grave. A wreath from the prime minister. The Knesset. The Minister of Defense. The Mossad. The Shin Bet. The town. The school. The bank where the mother works. The Scouts. Next to the wreaths are vases full of water. Whoever wants can place a flower in them, which will become a huge bouquet as they pass by. A mound of small stones, as per the Jewish burial custom, becomes a large mound of stones.

Everybody bids farewell to the grieving family and walks back down in silence to the bottom of the hill.

An hour after all the mourners had left the cemetery, she went up to the hilltop. A young, lost girl. She came to say her final goodbye. She wasn't able to be part of the ceremony, she wanted Noa all to herself, her only friend.

She arrives at the grave that is covered in flowers and sits down and stares in wonder. Noa got so much attention. Where were all these people in her life? She was so lonely that she chose me as a friend; was it because nobody else wanted her either, or perhaps she didn't want them? She certainly understood that people, especially kids, can be mean and harsh and can't be trusted. What's life worth? What's my life worth now that my only friend is gone and won't ever come back? How will I return to school? To home? To life?

She lay down next to the grave, her head resting on the wreaths. She looks to the sky, imagining Noa peering down among the grey clouds that, in a few minutes, will be covered by the blackness of night; smiling at her, consoling her, understanding her, accepting her as she is.

She gets up and takes out a notebook and pen from her small shoulder bag, sits and writes, every so often stopping to look around. At the end, she puts the notebook and pen in her bag and takes a sip from her water bottle, still unwilling to leave Noa's side.

Sunday in Paris is a day of rest. Most of the shops are closed, and we decide to make a day of it.

"Let's go have a picnic in the park," offers Nathan.

"Yeah!" say the girls.

We stop at a supermarket on the way and buy baguettes, a variety of cheeses and cold-cuts, fruit, vegetables and a cake for dessert. We take a tablecloth, cups and plates and silverware and head out. I'm happy to be here today. I have to get rid of the feeling of sadness and failure. For everybody who took part, put their heart and soul in the operation, it was a failure.

It's difficult for me to think of the bereaved family. About the funeral. I also need to ask Noa for forgiveness and to say goodbye, to hug her father and tell him that we tried. The girls are jumping around me and Nathan protects me from them, protects me from myself.

After we buy what we need, we head east towards Reims. There are tons of great places on the way, and we'll find a nice area that we like and stop. I open the window all the way, the fresh air penetrating my body, refreshing my soul.

"Mom... it's cooooold... are you crazy?" Shir yells from the back.

"Sorry, just a little wind, it's not going to kill anyone," I say, and I'm reminded of things my mother used to say, things I told myself I would never say. Over the years, we mature and get old like our parents did, and we start to talk and think like them. The generational gap will always remain the same. Kids will always feel that their parents don't understand them, and parents will always feel that their kids are inexperienced and need to listen to them. The world operates the way that it operates.

Nathan's hand is on my knee, rocking it back and forth, trying to shake me from the thoughts that keep coming back to haunt me. We look at each other and I smile, trying ineffectively to hide my doleful thoughts.

"I know," he says to me. "It's all right."

"What do you know, Dad? What's all right?" Lior asks.

"Nothing. It's between me and Mom."

I turn to them. "Come on, let's play a game." I have to push these sad thoughts away for now and enjoy my girls, my family, the moment; tomorrow on the train to Brussels I'll have plenty of time.

The house is full. People from the office made sure to bring chairs, hot water urns, drinks and food. A mix of people wanting to hear, to console, to lend a hand, to be for and against peace, to be angry and to hurt, to laugh and to cry.

Starting at around four o'clock in the afternoon, people have been coming and going. The door that had always been closed to the public was suddenly wide open, breached, and it seemed as if it would never be shut again. The head of the Mossad feels tired and weak. He apologizes and goes into his bedroom on the top floor, goes to the bathroom and locks the door behind him. He sits down and leans back, hands on his head, feeling like he can't see another person, or hug or shake hands with anyone. He is frustrated, full of despair and anger, mostly at himself. He takes a towel and, screaming into it, muffles his cries.

He lies down on his bed, and after an hour, his wife opens the door and peeks inside.

"Are you sleeping?"

"I wish I could. I can't remember how long it's been."

"Almost everybody has gone. I didn't notice that you'd slipped upstairs.

"I couldn't see another face. To think that this is how it's going to be for the next week. I'm going to explode."

"No choice. It's what everybody does. They say the *shiva* is therapeutic."

"So they say," he says, scratching his head. "How am I supposed to explain the last week? The last six months? How can I, the head of the Mossad, even admit it to myself?"

"Honey, you have to let it go. You'll go out of your mind. You have to forgive, her and yourself as well. Let her rest in peace," she said, lying down next to him, her head on his chest. "What will we do? How will we get past this? How do we move on? Is it even possible?"

"I don't know, honey. Let's take it one moment at a time. One hour at a time. There's no other way right now. You'll pick me up, and I'll pick you up. We have two kids out there."

He is aware of the significance of his words. He mustn't break... he mustn't break. "Come on," he says, getting up. "Let's say goodbye to our last guests. We'll go to bed. Maybe we'll be able to fall asleep. Tomorrow we'll think about everything all over again."

He smooths out his clothes, and they both go down to the living room. The living room is empty.

"Where are the boys?"

His wife says, "I have no idea."

They hear voices coming from Noa's room and freeze for a moment. The boys have decided to sit on their little sister's bed.

"Here of all places?" he asked them when he opened the door.

"Yes," answered the older one. "Who would have believed it. I'll wake up from this nightmare and there will be another tomorrow..." They got up from the bed and went to their rooms.

Tomorrow, they would think about tomorrow.

Monday

I wake up early and return to my routine. The previous events are still echoing in my mind, in my heart but, for now, I have to get back to my regular team. A new mission. Preparations. Trips. Ongoing problems. Unforeseen problems. Personal affairs.

I miss my crew. They have been like family to me these past few years. I left them for a week, which for them was also difficult. The Old Man is waiting for answers about his wife's illness and tough decisions await them. Handsome sent his pregnant wife and son back to Israel and Ludwig, who is in love, misses his new girlfriend in Israel.

I arrive in Brussels in the afternoon and hope that Yaron is in the apartment. I'll be able to get back into the swing of things quickly. I have no idea about training and when we'll go back to Israel. How much time for preparation and execution? I enter the apartment and hear the men conversing.

Everyone's here including the Old Man. Great. I give everyone a hug and am excited. This last week brought up emotions that I'd kept hidden. All these years I have tried not to allow my emotions influence me. It doesn't always work. This time, I feel great sadness and helplessness.

We sit and have a cup of coffee. The Old Man brought cake.

"The tests came back. Carcinoma. The situation isn't great, but we can live with it. She needs preliminary radiation therapy to shrink the tumor and then an operation. Later on she'll undergo radiation and hormone therapy. To prevent any recurrence of the tumor."

"What about little Celina?" I ask Handsome.

"Celina is resting and has let me know that she's not willing to come back here."

"Careful, it might happen in the end," I answer him. "It's not funny."

"I wasn't laughing."

Ludwig enters with a smile. I'm shocked at the change. The man is simply radiant.

"What's cookin', good lookin'?" I ask.

"We're going to Israel. What could be bad about that? I'm thrilled. I can kill two birds with one stone. Roi and Galiah – fun."

"Yeah. Just take into account that we're going there for work. We'll start early each morning and finish in the evening. We aren't going on vacation."

Yaron pops his head in the door. I motion for him to come in.

"Hey, what's up, how are you doing?" He shoots me a look with multiple overtones – he understands what I did, he understands that it was difficult, and that it ended up with the worst possible outcome.

"Fine. I'm fine. You?"

"Give us a few minutes alone?" The guys get up and exit the room.

"Fine, I won't force you to tell me about last week... to our business at hand. Are you up to date?"

"Yes, I'm up to date."

"Great. So we are starting to work beginning on Sunday, in Israel. We have a training program, go over it. You'll be in Israel for about two-and-a-half weeks."

"Gotcha."

"I suggest that you finish today, however long it takes, then go home. In any event, all the material is in Israel, and you'll have enough time to learn it."

What happened that has caused Yaron to be so generous? Giving us vacation days?

"Okay."

"Yes. Your team has become problematic regarding personal affairs."

"Totally. I need my own personal affairs officer," I say, grinning.

At home, he sits by himself. It's three in the afternoon. There's an afternoon break between those who have just left and those who are about to arrive. His wife went to lie down for an hour and the boys disappeared. Maybe down to the basement; they also need a break.

Forgiveness. That's the word that echoes in his mind.

Forgiveness, forgiveness, forgiveness.

Forgive me, my dear girl. Forgive me for not understanding. Forgive me for not acting correctly. Forgive me for screwing up. Forgive me for not saving you.

If only I could trade places with you. Let God take me here and now. I don't deserve to be here.

Punishment, that's what I deserve. To be accountable. To pay the price for neglecting my duty.

The doorbell rings and gets him out of his chair. Who could be arriving at this hour? He walks to the door, not wanting his wife to wake up. There are a few people standing outside, the head of the local council and two police officers.

"Hello," he says and waits to see what it is that brings them to his door.

"Hi, we're sorry to disturb you. Something happened, and we wanted to check with you."

"Happened? What more could happen?" The worst has already transpired.

"Do you recognize the girl in the picture?" He holds up a passport photo of a young girl.

"No, why should I know her?"

"Perhaps she's a friend of Noa's?" asks one of the officers.

"I have no idea. I never met any of Noa's friends."

"We found her lying beside Noa's grave," says the head of the council with a look whose intent wasn't quite clear.

"Did you ask her what she was doing there?"

"She committed suicide. An ambulance arrived at the scene and pronounced her death. In her bag we found an empty bottle of pills."

Oh God, it's not over. "Who is she? Do you know?"

"Her name is Michal Weinberg. Do you recognize the name?" asks the officer.

"No, but maybe my wife does. I'll go ask her, she's sleeping. One moment." He went inside and quietly entered the room. His wife was lying on her back, eyes staring at the ceiling.

"Honey…? Are you sleeping?" he asks quietly.

"No, what happened?" She sits up.

"Tell me, do you know a friend of Noa's named Michal Weinberg?"

"I've never met her but yes, there's somebody by that name in her class. They'd became friends recently. Why?"

They found her next to Noa," he says, having difficulty saying 'cemetery.' "She apparently committed suicide."

"Oh my God! Why?" she says, her eyes opening wide as she holds her head in her hands. "What happened, what's going on here? The Book of Job?"

"They have no idea right now. I am going back downstairs, the head of the council and the police are here." He went back to the living room.

"She knows her only by name. She was a friend of Noa's from school," he says to the three of them. "Is there a letter or something that explains why she did it? Have you notified her family?"

"We told her mother. She lived with her mother and grandmother in Kfar Saba. Immigrants from Russia. She was very connected to Noa. I supposed her death hit her hard and she didn't feel she could recover from it," says the officer.

It's dark by the time I get home. I let Nathan know that I'm going to Israel on Shabbat. I didn't want it to be a surprise.

I opened the door. "Who's home?"

"We're all here," the girls answer.

The girls hear the news and get upset with me.

"I have to go. Please, don't make it hard on me," I say quietly.

"How much longer will this go on? You're our mother, yet we see the neighbor more often than you," Lior says.

"Tell them 'no' and that's it. They can't make you," Shir says, and starts crying. I try to give her a hug, but she pushes my hand away in anger.

"Shir, Lior, it's not Mom's fault. This is her work, and it's only for two or three weeks. It will pass quickly."

"I don't care. I want my mom at home. Quit and that's it," Shir says defiantly.

"It's not that simple, sweetie," I say. Now I want to start crying. "I started something, and I have to finish it. It's my job, it's how we put food on the table." I know that's the last thing they care about at the moment.

"So find a different job, like everybody. A job where you're home and not traveling," she answers without skipping a beat. She cries and hugs Nathan.

"She's right, Mom," says Lior. "I understand you work hard, but how long can we live like this? We're all suffering, even Dad."

"I know," I say. "I promise that Dad and I will think about how to make things better for all of us, but for now, that's the situation. So let's make the best of it. We have a few more days until I leave, so let's have fun."

"It's hard to have fun when we're sad and angry. What do you want us to do?" She stomps her foot in frustration.

"You're right. Come here for a moment. Come on."

"I don't want to. I'm used to Dad."

Lior looks at me and sees my sadness and comes over to give me a hug. "We know it's not your fault. We understand. We'll get over it, Shir too. You know how she is, just let her calm down."

My angel who takes care of me; she thinks about me before she thinks about herself. It should be the other way around.

Later, Nathan says quietly, "I don't know how much longer I can take it the way things are going."

"It's not like I have a choice. I have to see things through. I understand and hear you. I'm angry, too. As far as they're concerned, the main thing is that the business keeps ticking. I'll go to Israel, and we'll decide what to do when I get back."

"Okay. We'll talk it over. Maybe we'll finish out this year and then that's it. Three years is a long time. Your commitment was only for three years."

"It's hard for me to request to come back."

"You took this on with the understanding that the conditions would be different. They changed the rules."

"Do you know what they'll say if I come back?"

"The'll say that the woman is problematic. That we were wrong about her, that mothers have a hard time functioning outside the home."

"Yeah, I suppose you're right. Management prefers that I suffer in silence. Turns out that not every team leader functions as they should. Everybody's human, some are better than others."

"I don't care about them. You know what you're worth, so do I. That's what's most important."

"Okay, I'll go. I'll look into my options, we'll weigh them and come to a decision. It's always possible to say 'enough.' Let's just, for now..."

"I just hope that we haven't done too much damage to the girls."

It's Shabbat, and I'm on a plane. It's funny – as soon as people sit down on a flight to Israel, it seems like they behave as if they're already in Israel. Noisy, rude, demanding, general chaos. But as soon as the Tel Aviv beachline and lights are visible, it feels like coming home. I flip through the weekend edition from yesterday's paper and discover a huge article on Noa, her parents and her brothers. Some of the details are accurate, while others are insane. Who gave them the right to invent their own facts? The story of Michal Weinberg appears on the same page in a framed column.

She left a suicide note:

My dear Noa,

You were my good friend who saw me when everybody else simply ignored me.
You're the only one who listened to me and didn't think that I was weird or invisible.
You were a friend to me, you decided to do something, but you didn't tell me a thing. You left me alone in this world, and I wasn't prepared for it.
You chose me to be your friend.
You chose me, but not a friend to the end, not really.
Apparently nobody will ever see me, not really.
I have no place left in this world.
I ask your forgiveness and my mother and grandmother's forgiveness, but I don't have the strength anymore.
I don't want to invest in a world that doesn't understand me, where I don't fit in.
I give you one last hug, Noa.

Michal

In another column, they interview psychologists about the connection between the two girls, scrutinizing the reason for suicide. The media has become hostile, intrusive.

I take a cab and go to my parents' home. The weather is warm and pleasant, which is expected during the mild winters here. I'll spend the night in my childhood room, which seems small and uncomfortable. Despite the late hour, my parents are waiting for me. In the last few years, we haven't seen much of each other. Even when they come to Paris, I'm too busy to devote my time to them. But they aren't complaining. They're happy to see me, they worry about me, but the main thing is that they love me.

Not far from my parents' home, the head of the Mossad and his wife are sitting together on comfortable armchairs on the porch after the last of the visitors have left. It's over. Tomorrow they will go up to the grave, and their home will be closed to visitors again.

"You have to give it time, for the emotion to subside, for your conscience to rest," his wife says.

"I've been thinking about it all week. I don't think there's a way back," he says, determined.

"Not that I'll be sorry about it, but I think that, ultimately, you'll change your mind."

"Maybe. But that's life," he says. "This quiet is good for me, to forget about what happened."

"Yeah. But it's only temporary. I'm not sure I'll be able to fake it and keep waking up every morning to this reality," she says.

"I have no idea. I think that it's a choice."

"There are women who lose their sons in war and decide to have another child. It seems absurd to think about such a thing at our age," she says, smiling. "But we have two other children, and for their sake, we need to infuse ourselves and the home with life."

"True. And so we have to get back to our routine and hope that over time, the routine will fill our lives back up again."

"There are stories of bereaved families that immediately decide to get back to living, rather than give up and let grief take over. I always thought I knew what they meant, but now I know that I didn't understand a thing," she says.

"My whole life, I believed that I was acting properly. Now I know that it was all nonsense. I did the things I was good at, and ignored everything else. Because I didn't believe in my ability to parent, I chose not to be around."

"Is that what you really think? What about me? Do you think that I was a good mother?"

"You're definitely better than me, but I was never around enough to even judge you. This question needs to be posed to the boys. Noa already made it clear that we failed big time," he said. "So much so that she was prepared to go off with that Arab, just not to be here, because she believed that he would love her more than we do."

"How could we? Is that the price of failure? We're serving a life sentence with no possibility of parole," she says.

She isn't sure that she can choose life, that she even deserves to choose life. Maybe she needs to accept the punishment for abandoning her daughter and dwell in the pain of mourning until her last breath. Her fountain of tears has run dry. The crying is cathartic, and she doesn't deserve that either.

"I suggest that we give ourselves a little more time before we decide. Tomorrow we go up to the grave, maybe there we'll get an answer. Maybe she will be with us and tell us what she wants us to do," he says.

They go inside. It's cold and late. They have a tough night ahead of them.

Week Four

Sunday

After noon, after I was able to get to the office and have a few conversations, we gather in the apartment where our instruction takes place.

"Folks," I say to my group of three. "Welcome to Ramat Aviv. We have another important mission in front of us. Our time here is limited and we have to learn a few more things. Tomorrow morning the professionals will be here, so I expect you to arrive after a good night's sleep, focused and ready. Don't hesitate to ask questions, even if it means that the day runs long. Usually, we are all here and our families are abroad, so nobody is in any hurry to finish the day. This time, it's the opposite – our families are here and want to see us. The temptation is great, but we have a lot to do." I look at each one of them.

"Okay, okay," says the Kid. "We get it. Tomorrow we'll get down to business, but when are we going home today? I have to let my wife know."

"Each of you will sit with me before you go home, I want to understand your schedules and needs." I feel like a personal affairs officer who needs to protect her chicks instead of dealing with the operations. It's the first time that I'm not certain that the team is suited to the mission with which they've been tasked. Maybe I need to say something to management?

"Say, is this mission too much for us? Maybe we should pass for now. Until all of us are on board?" I ask, seriously.

"I've kicked that question around a lot," says the Old Man. "As far as I'm concerned, it depends on Dina. We have to see how the therapy affects her. If she feels terrible, I imagine my performance will drop."

"I don't have a problem. But it isn't me that needs to physically perform the mission. I have less responsibility," says Ludwig. He stays in the office while they go into the field.

"I'm fine. Celina is here for the whole time that I won't be around, so I'm taken care of," says John.

I'm not convinced that he'll feel that way when it comes to it, especially if Joe isn't with him. I need to go back to management. This job will require all of us to be completely focused. If we can't guarantee that, we've got a problem.

At ten in the morning, the family goes to the cemetery. Most of the town's residents are at work, their kids at school. The four of them make their way to the fresh grave without any additional family members, as per their request. The flowers have dried up by now, the mound of stones having collapsed at the hands of the paramedics, a sign of the tragedy that occurred here after the funeral.

Noa's mother imagines Michal's body lying beside the grave, crying, despairing, hopeless, confused. But maybe she lay there peacefully, decisively, clear-headed, quietly departing from Noa and from the world. She bends down and gently feels the ground where she apparently lay in torment.

Noa's father says. "My dear Noa, we have no choice but to say goodbye, at least for now in this life, and to ask your forgiveness that we weren't able to understand, that we thought you'd be okay. We were wrong. We were too busy with our own lives, and it's criminally sinful what we did to you, and for that we will one day pay.

"Your departure weighs heavily upon us. We have been left grieving, but hopeful that you will be happily received in the place you're going to, that you'll find peace and tranquility, that you'll wrap yourself in the love that you deserve, that you never had. Your friend Michal chose to go with you. I'm sorry for her mother and grandmother.

"Yet we remain here, and we will try to come to the right conclusions. They say we have to make the decision to choose life or death. My heart tells me that I have no right to smile or enjoy life again. On the other hand, your mother is here and so are your brothers, who need to continue on with their lives, to raise families, give us grandchildren. They also deserve that we live for their sake.

"The dilemmas, Noa'le, are difficult. I hope that from up there you can help me, support, forgive and love me. I can't imagine why they chose to hurt you, my dear girl who never hurt anybody. How in the hell? How?"

He lowers his head, unable to stop his tears. They all gather around him, and he takes them in his arms and erupts in a heart-wrenching cry. They all start wailing, joining him, eyes closed.

And Noa looks on from above, her spirit enwrapping them in love. "It's nice here," she says. "You don't have anything to worry about. I forgive you and ask that you forgive yourselves. Continue on, love and be happy, remember that family is all for one, and one for all."

Her mother reads the lyrics to one of the songs she found in her desk drawer:

Before I leave I just want to tell you folks,
I was here for a moment and I chose to let it go.
They say that man's soul is rotten to the core,
But I say that it's basically a choice.
Every person chooses their own way,
For good or bad or even more or less.
I prefer to hold my tongue, to forgive and go my way,
Even if they say that I was wrong to go.

Farewell, people, but that's how it is sometimes,
People make mistakes, and are allowed to do things differently.

The boys play the last song that Noa recorded from one of her last performances with her band. They listen until the very last note, and at the end, they hug again and tidy up the grave. They remove the dried-out flowers, the remnants of the paramedics and rearrange the mound of stones. Without looking back, they head down to their car.

On the way home, the father says to his family, "I've made a decision. I'm quitting immediately. As soon as we get home, I'm calling the prime minister."

"What?" his wife says. "Are you sure? Why haven't you said anything until now?"

"Dad, are you sure you're in a position to make such an important decision?" the older son says.

"Dad, we'll support you, but wait a bit," the younger one says.

"I've had enough time to think," he said, smiling. "I feel like I can't do it anymore. This won't go over quietly, and I don't want to have to put anybody in the position of having to make a decision. I should have done things differently. From the beginning, when I asked Danny to check up on the matter for me, I should have sent everything to the Shin Bet."

"Do you think anybody would dare say that?" his younger son asked.

"Whoever says that would be one-hundred percent correct. Of course they will; after the period of mourning, they'll have a field day at my expense. The opponents of the prime minister will claim that appointing me was a mistake. Inside the organization, those who want my position will know how to say the right thing at the right time. I don't want to be there when the poison that people start fomenting begins to spill out of their mouths."

"So what will you do?" his wife asks him.

"You and I will go on a little trip, a month or two. Australia,

New Zealand, or wherever you want, and then we'll decide. By the way, I'm also thinking about selling the house and moving somewhere else. What do you guys think?"

"And leave Noa here alone?" she said, looking at him astonished.

"We can come visit her whenever we want. I just feel that I don't want to live in a community that behaved like that to our daughter. I don't want to live in anger. But there's time. We'll take things as they come."

I called the head of the operations department and requested that we meet immediately. I left my three team members to go over the material before the technical stuff they'll need to review for tomorrow morning. It was new technology, a system that remains top secret.

I'm not convinced that my team of three is enough. Maybe we need to add somebody to the team to fill in for the Old Man. I don't believe in burying my head in the sand. "Trust me" and cutting corners are not how I do things.

In the office, I go up to meet the head of the department. About fifteen minutes later he enters the room.

"Pardon me, I was called in for something urgent," he said.

"Did something happen?" I ask.

"Happen? I should say so. Boom, the chief just quit."

"What?" I don't believe it. "Why? He's one of the best. Finally, one of our own."

"Maybe because of the tragedy," he says. "We never got an explanation. He sent out a brief letter to the division heads and asked that they pass it on to all the employees. Everybody's in shock."

"Yeah. Shock would be the appropriate word." I think about the last ten days. How much he and his family have become a part of my life.

"So, what did you want to talk to me about?" he says, changing subjects.

"Are you aware of the personal issues with my guys?"

"Yes, of course."

"During the last week while I was busy with that other thing," I assume that he knows that I was part of the last operation, "I got the feeling that we're making a mistake. The Old Man isn't mentally available for work. It doesn't make any sense."

"What does he say?"

"He's not sure and we need him one-hundred-and-ten percent."

"I see. The problem is that your team are experts with computers; it's their baby. Okay. I'll think about it and consult with some people. Let's meet tomorrow afternoon. In the meantime, keep on as usual."

"No problem, good night."

I exit the building. The sky is painted with shades of pink, magenta, purple and orange. A spectacular sight. A cold wind blows. I get into the car and start driving. I'll go to my parents, shower, and call home, perhaps go meet Aharon, a childhood friend who was like a brother to me, or Yael from high school. My friends from way back, they're friends forever. The phone rings before I reach the exit gate.

"Hello?" I don't recognize the number.

"Good evening." I recognize but don't recognize...

"This is the head of the Mossad." Again? What does he want from me? "How are you? I heard that you were back in Israel."

"Yes, I am," I answer.

"Could you come to my house for a short visit?"

"I'd be happy to. I'm so sorry about how things ended up. We so badly wanted to bring her home safe and sound." I feel like I'm choking.

"I know. That's exactly why I want you to come over. I want to hear about it first-hand. Please, if you aren't too busy, would you mind coming over?"

"It will take me about forty minutes at this hour, I imagine."

"We'll wait."

I drive to the neighborhood where many of my friends live. It's beautiful, trees and flowers on every corner. There's something clean and pleasant. The boss's house is on a dead-end street, his yard facing the open areas, alone on the distant hill. Quiet. Pastoral.

I park the car and get out. I go to the main gate, which is protected by fences and alarms. I press the intercom.

"Hello," I say.

"Come in, we're waiting for you."

I go down the stairs at the main entrance to the house. In the doorway, standing and waiting just for me, is the head of the Mossad. I extend my hand to him, and he takes it and then wraps me in a big hug. I hug him back and start to cry. I feel him getting emotional also.

"I'm so sorry," I say to him quietly.

"I know, I know," he says. "Wait a moment while I call my wife and two sons, they want to meet you."

I sit in the living room. There's a blown-up photo of Noa on the counter, and next to it is a picture of the three kids. The house is clean and in order.

Everyone shakes my hand, and his wife gives me a hug. They sit down across from me, and he sits down next to me on the sofa.

"I've asked you to come because I wanted everybody to hear how things unfolded. That's important to me. Beyond the fact that I wanted to say thank you, to all of you, for the effort."

I tell them everything up to the very last detail. I tell them about my feelings as a mother and how much Noa entered my heart, how much I hoped, and how I came back to see my girls every opportunity I had. When I finished, I looked at the man who I just now heard was quitting and said, "I've been pondering this for a week, and I feel like I have done a great injustice to my family. I've been in this business just a little bit less than you, but enough time to know what it takes. The system has been my entire life since age twenty-one, the job more important than almost anything, I have no doubt about that, but the price is too high."

I tell them about abandoning my kids during sad times and happy times, and I use the Old Man as an example.

"I ask myself whether it's worth it? The answer is clear, but it leaves me feeling empty." I finish and am shocked at how open I was being in front of strangers. Maybe I said too much.

"You're so right," his wife says. "We've been going through this for years. As a mother, I have no idea how you do it."

"I'm sorry, we came to talk about Noa and I'm talking about myself." If only the ground could swallow me whole at that moment.

"I quit today," he says. "This dilemma is definitely part of my reasoning. I paid a heavy price, the heaviest. We cannot give up on everything. Maybe we don't have to, but that's what happens eventually."

I look at him. Our commanders never spoke like that. Is it the death of his daughter or his conscience of all the years away from home that made him quit?

"This dilemma is part of our being. The system needs its soldiers to be ready to go on a moment's notice. Part of the job, the demand for experienced, mature and responsible people with seniority, and the lack of ability to deal with or consider anything about the soldiers themselves, aside from the demands. The families become victims against their will," I say.

"I understand and even accept that. But we still haven't found a way to strike a balance between the operations and the operators," he says.

"You know, I don't think that anyone on the outside can really understand. Nobody hears about the successes, either, only the failures," I say.

"Like our story with Noa. What do they know? That we failed. It's important for me that you understand that we don't see this as one person's failure. You did everything you could and more. This was something that was simply unavoidable," says the head of the Mossad.

"May I be rude and ask to see her room?" It suddenly feels like the right thing to do.

"Yes, come with me," his wife says and puts a hand on my shoulder. "I want to personally thank you for all that you did."

"There's no need, really. I can just say that Noa really got into my heart."

One wall is painted a dark gray, the other magenta, with symbols drawn on it that undoubtedly have meaning. Two guitars are leaning on two large speakers and a sophisticated music system. An old armchair is in the corner of the room, like one passed down in an inheritance. A writing desk crammed with papers and musical compositions, a reminder of the hours she spent in her room.

I imagine her on the chair, holding her guitar and singing. Or perhaps on her bed leaning against the pillows, composing songs, mulling over her thoughts, mad at the world and writing down her feelings. Her mother and I understand each other without speaking. I hug her and she hugs me back.

"Thank you," she whispers.

"Thank you for letting me into her room. I needed to visit her here also."

The head of the Mossad sees me out after I say goodbye to everyone.

"Thank you for having me, it's been an honor."

"Thank you for making the effort to come," he says. "It's too bad that you're here under these circumstances. I would have preferred during a celebration."

"Me too."

I get in my car and leave while thinking about my girls, who are so far away, and I make a decision. I arrive at my parents' house and before I sit down to talk to them, I call home.

"Hi, honey." I feel a huge relief when I hear his voice.

"Hi, how's it going?"

"Fine. It's just great, in fact. I've made a decision. We're coming home at the end of the year."

"Are you sure? What caused you to decide?"

"I visited the big boss at his home this evening."

I describe my visit and the approval that I received from him even before I made the decision.

"Enough. I want to go home. I've been in this business more than half my life. I've done my part."

"Fine with me, and I'm happy to hear it. I think that it's the right thing to do for the sake of the girls and our marriage."

"Don't tell the girls, wait until I get back. Wait until I run everything by my managers. I don't want to disappoint anyone by having to walk it back."

I know that I first have to get approval for this.

On Monday morning, I sit with my parents in their small kitchen. My father spreads the newspaper out before me.

"Look," he points to the front page. "The head of the Mossad quit! What brought him to quit?"

Next to the headline is a big picture of the boss. The article sprawls over several pages. I flip through the paper and find the article. Noa's story is told in detail. Her life and her death. How the hell did they get this information? An interview with students from her grade who went on the trip appears separately.

On another page is the story of Ahmed from Tayibe. In summary, the writer asks a few questions: Why didn't the head of the Mossad inform the Shin Bet about the contact with his daughter? Could he have prevented her murder had he acted earlier against Ahmed? Did the head of the Mossad quit on his own, or did somebody tell him it was time? Can we trust somebody who isn't capable of administering basic judgement?

Basic judgement?

I refold the newspaper in annoyance. I'm not surprised.

"Well? What do you say?" my father asks.

"Too bad," I answer. "Too bad that they don't give a person a few days grace, after all he has done for the country. It's too bad that the media spends so much time on the bad and almost nothing about the good. Failures, for whatever reason, are what sell newspapers more than successes." I get up from the table. "Okay, I have to run."

"You didn't drink your tea; you didn't eat anything," my mother says.

"I'll eat something in the office, I have a long day. I prefer to start and finish early," I say, dodging the issue.

I make my way to the apartment where we're training. Today, the team wasn't able to concentrate because of the recent news. We've got three weeks here, and then hard work in Europe. That will be my last operation. Despite my decision to return to Israel, I have to finish out the year as if it were my first day – enthusiastic and paying attention to the details.

Epilogue...

The Old Man
Three weeks after the team returned to Europe, Joe and his family returned to France. Dina was hospitalized for a few days and then transferred to the cancer center next to the city of Fontainebleau. The treatment she underwent in Israel significantly reduced the size of the tumor, so the surgery was simpler and easier. After a week in the hospital, Dina went back home, and life slowly returned to normal. The office decided to send an *au pair* from Israel to live in their home and lend a hand with whatever was needed – shopping, cleaning, taking care of the kids and cooking. Dina enjoyed having the young girl from the kibbutz around, who made the house happy and joyful, and also reminded the kids where they really belonged. The music of Shlomo Artzi and Arik Einstein could be heard in the background, and the young girl's stories about high school and the army made the home Israeli.

Joe returned to work for a shortened week. Despite not intending to travel on the upcoming operation, he helped whenever he was asked, especially with Ludwig and the office and marketing preparations. He was like the tribe elder giving advice to the two younger men. To the Kid, and his young replacement.

When I visited their homes about a month after the surgery, I found Dina strong and beautiful, with light in her eyes. We hugged for a long time. There is no greater joy than a person recovering from a serious illness.

"How's it going?" I asked. "You look wonderful, my dear."

"Thanks, sweetie," she said. "I feel wonderful. Sometimes it seems to me as if this illness was a gift."

"Are you serious??"

"Completely. A non-cancer survivor wouldn't understand it. Suddenly, life took on a whole new meaning. Since this is a second chance, I have to grab it with both hands, to fix what needs to be fixed, to be happy with all the things that I have, to get back to my basic beliefs and, most importantly, to love and to smile."

"Too bad one needs to get hit so hard to realize that, huh?" I'm reminded of the last conversation I had with the head of the Mossad.

"I made a vow. I set rules for myself. I won't try to live my life without my partner anymore. I have to remember and remind him that we are one family: my husband, me and the kids. Being together gives us strength and purpose. Health is a way of life, and we have to make sure to eat healthy and exercise. To smile because the world will smile back at you. From here on out, I live by those rules."

"Yeah." I think that makes sense, simple and easy. If a person goes through a difficult experience, when they gain the upper hand, they come out strong. "Seems like it's possible to add one more small rule, and that is not to take life for granted. One should be thankful for each day that passes and each one that comes in its place."

I look at Dina and think of Joe. He stopped complaining about his pay and a promotion and was calmer at work. He ate according to his wife's rules. The Kid kept tabs on what was allowed and what wasn't. Joe was much more modest and quiet and talked a lot about Dina and the kids, about where the family went and what they did on the weekend. No more fancy restaurants and secret cigars, but instead, nature walks, exercise and picnics. He even took Dina to a few concerts and the opera that she so loved despite him never having been a fan.

A year passed, and Dina received notification that she was completely clean; she just needed to get checked every six months as part of the monitoring process. At the end of that year, they returned to Israel and got used to their home all over again. Joe put in a request to continue working only at headquarters. He wanted to be at home as much as possible. Every so often, he would participate in training sessions and make short trips, because the system wasn't ready to give up on his skills.

Dina volunteered to counsel women who became ill and began to feel helpless. She lectured in front of crowds of sick women, their spouses and their families, and even organizations. And when Joe asked her to rest, she would say to him, "They need me."

"So then quit your job and devote your time exclusively to this."

Dina did indeed quit and became a full-time volunteer. In addition to helping out at the hospitals, she taught courses on healthy living, eating right and exercise, and she has been a mentor to many women and families.

The illness never returned. I won! she thought to herself every night before falling asleep.

Tuesday morning was a particularly hot and insufferable summer day. Dina was in the kitchen making sandwiches for everybody, sourdough bread from whole wheat flour, avocado, tomato and cucumber.

Joe came out of the shower and, before having a cup of coffee, went out with the old dog for a walk. Dina put the sandwiches into the kids bags. Suddenly, she heard a noise outside. This noise was different from any sound she had ever heard. She was shaken from her thoughts and went to look out the window. What happened out there? She saw one of the neighbors carrying their dog in his arms. *Oh, what happened to the dog?* she thought to herself and ran to the door.

"Need to take him to the vet and fast."

"What happened?" Dina asked the neighbor.

"There was an accident," he explained, shaking. "Dina, it's Joe..." he answered, not able to look her in the eye.

"Joe?" she asked. "Joe?" How could she not have thought about him? He was the one who took the dog out. What happened to Joe?

"He was injured, the ambulance is on its way."

She ran to the road. Around the corner a large crowd had gathered. She approached, her heart pounding like a hammer on a drum. He was laying half on the side of the road, half on the sidewalk, his eyes closed, his face pale.

"Joe?" she whispered, stroking his face. "Joe?"

The ambulance arrived. On the way to the hospital, they were able to resuscitate him. A medical miracle. After months of recovery at the hospital, Joe came back home, paralyzed from the waist down, and had difficulty using his right arm.

Joe refused to accept the evil decree. "I don't want to live like this," he said to Laurie when he came to visit him.

"Don't say that," he answered him. "You're the strongest man I know. You'll beat this, too."

One day, not long after Laurie's visit to their home, Joe was found dead in his bed. He chose to end his own life, and people were left with no choice other than to respect his wishes. All his friends and acquaintances from the office, friends from the army, high school and their mutual friends came to the funeral. The eulogies were touching and there wasn't a dry eye in the crowd.

Dina hung a big picture of him in the living room and decided to continue on with her life, despite the difficulty.

Our Old Man is no more.

Every so often, we would meet and reminisce, expecting the door to open and for him to walk inside in a frenzy, impeccably dressed, a fragrant cigar at the edge of his mouth, and a smile flickering in his blue eyes.

"Have you heard the one about the…" he would say.

May he rest in peace.

The Kid

Celina gave birth to their daughter about three months after they returned to Israel. John wasn't at the birth, but arrived that night on a flight. In the morning, he arrived at the hospital before they had even opened the doors for visitors. He quietly entered her room, kissed his wife and stroked her cheek.

"Hi, Mom."

"Hi," she said with a smile.

"How do you feel?"

"Great. We have a little girl, and this time she looks like me."

"As it should be," he whispered to her.

"I actually wanted your face and my intellect," she said with a smile.

Gali was a healthy little girl and quickly became the princess of the house. Now they were a big family. Four. After a month, they went back to London. Celina hired someone to help her with the kids and the house and didn't give up on her studies. Her goal was to be independent. She devoted time to her son and little daughter. She lost weight and took care of herself, and wasn't about to let any frustrations get in her way.

John came back every weekend and liked what he saw. A mature, confident woman, active and independent, warm and loving. Celina was a beautiful woman, the mother of his children. He was proud of her and his family.

At work, he was a successful team leader and eventually came back to Israel to take over one of the operational departments. Joe's death accompanied him every day. His picture was hanging over his head in whichever office he moved to in his many roles.

Many years later, he walked Joe's daughter down the aisle, as per her wish. He was excited and did so gladly, tears streaming from his eyes, holding the arm of the blue-eyed bride with her mischievous smile. So much like her beloved father.

Handsome

Ludwig continued to fly from Tel Aviv to Brussels, each time staying one week in Israel. About six months after the training period, he received a phone call from his son, Roi.

"There's something wrong with Mom. She's always crying," he said and started to cry.

"Don't cry, honey, give me grandma."

"She's depressed. I took her to a psychiatrist, and she's taking medication."

"How is she doing with the meds?" I asked, shocked.

"A little bit better, but it's hard for her to sleep. We're hoping for the best."

"What about Roi?"

"He's fine. Sad. He misses you."

"I'll try to get there quickly."

Ludwig flew home and the Old Man took over for him. He went straight from the airport to his ex-wife's parents' house. He was greeted with a cup of coffee and a slice of cake; his mother-in-law was waiting to have a serious conversation with him.

"What happened? How did it come to this?"

"The psychiatrist says that it's something she's predisposed to, but it's just coming out now," she explained. "Lately, we've seen a slow decline in her mood, more frequent outbursts, but we thought that it was just a difficult phase that would pass. I don't remember anybody in the family that was ever like this, but this is a different generation."

"What did the doctor say about what's to come? Will she be able to take care of Roi?"

"He said that it will take some time, but she'll be fine. I've got my finger on the pulse here, and since they live with us, Roi's taken care of, don't worry about that." She rocked uncomfortably in her chair.

"I'm not saying that as a pretense to take Roi. I'm simply concerned."

"I know. We didn't just meet yesterday. You're a good man, I just think that if we were to take Roi from her, she'd completely fall apart."

"If you think that Roi's situation requires that I take him for a while, I'll do it. I'll come home immediately. I won't cut her off from him in any way. She's the mother of my son, and I don't forget the love that I felt for her. I know that you're providing Roi with everything he needs, emotionally and materially. His friends and school are here."

"Everything will be fine. We're taking care of both of them."

"Yeah, she's lost on her own. But our main focus from now on needs to be what's best for the child."

Ludwig was happy with his work, in love with Galia, and he wanted to get married and have her be with him in Europe until his service was over. But he didn't want Roi to suffer for it. He met with Ariela. She didn't look good. Grey and tired.

"I've ruined my life," she said.

"You're strong. It will pass and you will get back to yourself."

"I should have stayed with you."

"Not really. You stopped loving me, you said that you weren't attracted to me, and that you were bored."

"I was stupid."

"You've got to get a hold of yourself, if not for your own sake than for Roi's," he said to her, looking her in the eye. "I'm not about to let him suffer for this. Do you want him to live with me until you feel better?"

"No, he's fine! If he moves in with you I'll die."

"Then get a hold of yourself. I'm flying back in two days, and I very much hope that I won't have to come back before I'm supposed to," he told her. Maybe threats will motivated her to get it together.

About a month later, Ludwig returned to Israel for a visit. From his conversations with Roi and his grandmother, he understood that his ex-wife's condition was starting to improve. The drugs had apparently balanced her out. He immediately went to Galia's house with a ring, proposed to her and received a resounding "I do," in response.

The next afternoon, he went to see Roi. They played soccer in the yard, and when they got tired, Roi went inside to bring them a cold drink. Ludwig lay back on the grass and closed his eyes, enjoying the quiet and the fresh air. After a few minutes, he opened his eyes in shock. Ariela caressed his face and placed her leg over his.

"What are you doing?"

"Don't get up, wait..." she tried to kiss him.

"Stop," he said and quickly got up.

"I want us to get back together," she said. "I made a mistake. I want us to get back together and be a family again."

"It's too late, Ariela. Too late. I'm marrying Galia."

She looked at him, got up, turned around, and went inside.

On his next visit to Israel, Ludwig and Galia were married at the rabbinical court. Only close family was invited. The office decided to locate her in Paris. They rented a small apartment in the center of the Latin Quarter, disconnected from the Israelis at the embassy. She enrolled in a French class and in the cooking school "Le Cordon Bleu" of Paris with the goal of becoming a pastry chef one day.

Once again, he wasn't alone every weekend. He was a happy man, efficient and friendly. Ludwig found his place in the system and was happy with his lot. He wasn't looking to move up in the system because he didn't like big changes.

Galia was the spice of the family they made together. When they returned to Israel, she opened her first pastry shop, which became a successful chain. Over time, they became the parents of Guy and Mika, who brought them joy and happiness. Roi visited frequently, and after his grandmother passed away, he preferred living with them.

Head of the Mossad

When the head of the Mossad resigned, a battle for his appointment ensued. The Mossad wanted somebody from the inside, while politicians preferred to bring in somebody with political connections and not necessarily professional credentials or proficiency. Politics won and a retired general, who was forced to learn everything from the ground up, was named as his replacement.

A few months after Noa's death, the former head of the Mossad and his wife went on a trip to New Zealand. Two adults with big backpacks and a guitar. When they landed in New Zealand, they rented a caravan and drove all over the country in a series of spontaneous trysts. They went on long hikes, sat in the evening with the guitar and sang songs. They went back to how they used to be: friends who loved each other in simplicity, no secrets, no inhibitions.

During their time abroad, the media made a lot of noise about the mistakes that were made and the need to form a new set of guidelines. They saw the headlines on the internet, and that was good enough.

After a few months, they returned to Israel and moved to a small but developing neighborhood in the south of the country. There they bought a piece of land with the hope that their boys would build their homes near theirs. However, a few months later, the former head of the Mossad received an enticing job offer from a huge company in Japan, and once again, he changed course to pursue new dreams. The new position was very lucrative.

His wife rented their homestead in the south to a young family and returned to the center of the country, to their old home, next to Noa. She felt a need to be close to her and visit her every day, talk to her and to bring flowers. She didn't return to her job at the bank, but painted and studied goldsmithing. She had almost completely forgotten about the vacation in New Zealand. He was an international manager, and she a homemaker waiting for him to come home. The boys understood that their father wasn't really capable of change.

Yaron
At the end of his service, Yaron came back to Israel and was promoted to head of the operational department within the division. He was an anemic commander with no charisma, and he spoke too much to the point of exhausting not only those under his command, but his commanding officers as well.

As soon as the right opportunity came up, they gently nudged him from his post. Since he was careful and calculating, he decided to wait it out in another position until he was able to quit and look for a new career.

Anton
Anton continued his work in the office, and after some personnel changes, an executive position opened up for him. He was the deputy chief of the instructional division. Many looked down on the position, but he saw the highest value in education. He'd had enough of traveling and operations, the loneliness, writing tedious reports and the debriefings, the need to make contact, to talk, to convince, to be manipulative and creative. He wanted quiet.

Udi
Udi's father passed away from a fatal illness about a year after the joint operation, and he decided to retire, taking over his father's world-wide businesses that needed to be attended to. As an only child, Udi had no choice and became a businessman. He bought a successful hotel in New York, invested in start-ups, one of which was acquired, and he did quite well. Udi chose to live with his family in his father's house in Savyon and found satisfaction in his accomplishments. His connections with the office remained, and he collaborated wherever he could.

Merlin
During the operation where Noa was killed, the system decided it needed to check itself. Merlin was asked to be the head of the commission that would conduct an investigation into controversial aspects of the Mossad's activities abroad.

For about two months, she and her team worked on the investigation and presented the summary of the commission and its recommendations to the divisional heads and the new head of the Mossad. Because she was not afraid to go after that which had always been seen as taboo, she achieved wide recognition.

After Udi's retirement, she took over his role. She was the correct choice and the one preferred by all. She had the ability to be a simple and natural leader. Merlin didn't look for a steady romantic relationship and dedicated days and nights, holidays and weekends to the job, which was everything to her. Her road to the top was paved.

Me
At the end of that year, Nathan and I, the girls and Louis, our French terrier puppy, came back to Israel. Nathan returned to his job, and the girls went back to school, where they had to learn to fit in all over again.

I went back to college, where I had taken a break, to decide how I wanted my life to look from here on out. I had a lot of questions: How do I win back the girls' trust? Do I want to keep advancing in the system, or have I weaned myself off of that? Do I continue on despite my criticism? Do I voice my criticisms, or is it better to just stay quiet? Can I reinvent myself and, if so, in what field?

Since I love change, it was no problem just picking up and leaving. I decided that the time had come to do something for my family and myself. My criticism, however constructive it may have been, was never going to make its way up the chain, because I knew nobody would listen. I found a way to get my girls back and to reinvent myself. I learned new skills and tried new things. I discovered that there are many trajectories life can take and there isn't just one right path. I am eternally grateful for the years that shaped my personality and made me who I am today. Today, I am mostly a wife and a mother. I'm proud to have served my country, happy with who I've become and, despite hoping for a better world, I'm not naïve.

Printed in Great Britain
by Amazon